Valentine IN A KILT

Other Books by Anna Durand

Dangerous in a Kilt (Hot Scots, Book One)
Wicked in a Kilt (Hot Scots, Book Two)
Scandalous in a Kilt (Hot Scots, Book Three)
The MacTaggart Brothers Trilogy (Hot Scots, Books 1-3)
Gift-Wrapped in a Kilt (Hot Scots, Book Four)
Notorious in a Kilt (Hot Scots, Book Five)
Insatiable in a Kilt (Hot Scots, Book Six)
Lethal in a Kilt (Hot Scots, Book Seven)
Irresistible in a Kilt (Hot Scots, Book Eight)
Devastating in a Kilt (Hot Scots, Book Nine)
Spellbound in a Kilt (Hot Scots, Book Ten)
Relentless in a Kilt (Hot Scots, Book Eleven)
Incendiary in a Kilt (Hot Scots, Book Twelve)
Wild in a Kilt (Hot Scots, Book Thirteen)
Unstoppable in a Kilt (Hot Scots, Book Fourteen)
Lachlan in a Kilt (The Ballachulish Trilogy, Book One)
Aidan in a Kilt (The Ballachulish Trilogy, Book Two)
Rory in a Kilt (The Ballachulish Trilogy, Book Three)
The American Wives Club (A Hot Brits/Hot Scots/Au Naturel Crossover Book)
Brit vs. Scot (A Hot Brits/Hot Scots/Au Naturel Crossover Book)
A Novel Secret (A Hot Brits/Hot Scots/Au Naturel Crossover, Book Three)
The Dixon Brothers Trilogy (Hot Brits, Books 1-3)
One Hot Escape (Hot Brits, Book Four)
One Hot Rumor (Hot Brits, Book Five)
One Hot Christmas (Hot Brits, Book Six)
One Hot Scandal (Hot Brits, Book Seven)
One Hot Deal (Hot Brits, Book Eight)
One Hot Favor (Hot Brits, Book Nine)
Natural Obsession (Au Naturel Nights, Book One)
Natural Deception (Au Naturel Nights, Book Two)
Natural Passion (Au Naturel Trilogy, Book One)
Natural Impulse (Au Naturel Trilogy, Book Two)
Natural Satisfaction (Au Naturel Trilogy, Book Three)
Fired Up (standalone romance)
Echo Power (Echo Power Trilogy, Book One)
Echo Dominion (Echo Power Trilogy, Book Two)
Echo Unbound (Echo Power Trilogy, Book Three)
The Janusite Trilogy (Undercover Elementals, Books 1-3)
Obsidian Hunger (Undercover Elementals, Book Four)
Unbidden Hunger (Undercover Elementals, Book Five)
The Thirteenth Fae (Undercover Elementals, Book Six)
Cyneric (Undercover Elementals, Book Seven)

Valentine IN A KILT

Hot Scots, Book Fifteen

ANNA DURAND

JACOBSVILLE BOOKS · MARIETTA, OHIO

VALENTINE IN A KILT

ISBN: 978-1-958144-35-0 (paperback)
ISBN: 978-1-958144-36-7 (ebook)
ISBN: 978-1-958144-37-4 (audiobook)

Manufactured in the United States.

Jacobsville Books
www.JacobsvilleBooks.com

Names: Durand, Anna, author.
Title: Valnetine in a kilt / Anna Durand.
Description: Marietta, OH : Jacobsville Books, 2024. | Series: Hot Scots, bk. 15.
Identifiers: ISBN 978-1-958144-35-0 (paperback) | ISBN 978-1-958144-36-7 (ebook) | ISBN 978-1-958144-37-4 (audiobook)
Subjects: LCSH: Highlands (Scotland)--Fiction. | Man-woman relationships--Fiction. | Scots--Fiction. | Whiskey--Fiction. | Romance fiction. | BISAC: FICTION / Romance / Contemporary. | FICTION / Romance / Romantic Comedy. | FICTION / Romance / Later in Life. | FICTION / Romance / Holiday. | GSAFD: Love stories.
Classification: LCC PS3604.U724 V35 2024 (print) | LCC PS3604.U724 (ebook) | DDC 813/.6--dc23.

Chapter One

Thane

I clamp my hands down on the walkway railing, gazing down at the odd shapes of the four copper stills on the floor below me. Why do whisky stills look like a bizarre version of a man's bollocks? There's something strangely erotic about the way the stills begin as fat ovals and stretch up into an almost dokey-like shape. Aye, now I'm thinking about my cock. The stills also resemble a woman's breasts. I'm not aroused, though, despite the imagery.

Why? Because I'm too bloody busy contemplating the fate of my wee distillery.

This is my company. I created it, I own it, and I am the man in charge. I'd always wanted to have my own business, and I love single-malt Scotch. So why not become a master distiller? But we need more stills if we're going to become competitive in the Highland whisky market.

A bonnie brown-haired lass walks up beside me, smiling down at the large stills. I smile at Fiona Sterling, but she's focused on the main floor below us. I sometimes forget that she's no longer Fiona MacTaggart, since she married Domhnall Sterling only a few months ago.

Fiona tips her head side to side as if she's studying the copper contraptions below us. "Have ye ever noticed that whisky stills look an awful lot like tits?"

"It would be sexist for me to admit that even if it's true."

"You are always cagey, Thane. Maybe that's why you've never had a long-term relationship."

"Did ye come up here to talk about my love life? Or are you actually doing your job?"

She shakes her head, giving me a long-suffering look. "Dinnae get grumpy with me."

"I have never been grumpy." But aye, I might be behaving in a less-than-serene manner right now. Fiona bloody well knows why. "You and the other lasses in our circle want to change me. I'm not interested in dating, for now. Saving my fledgling business is all I have time for."

Fiona smirks. "Are you regretting making me distillery manager? You probably thought I'd go easy on you because we dated briefly years ago and shagged a few times. But you put me in charge of the business. That means you have only yourself to blame if you're unhappy."

"Aye, I know that. You're doing an excellent job."

"Thank you." She sidles closer and hooks an arm around my bicep. "Now, tell me what's really fashing you today."

I take a deep breath and release it slowly, exhaling out all the tension in my body and mind. "Your mother and my mother have conspired to harass me about my single-man status."

"They want to help you, that's all."

"And I appreciate the thought. But I dinnae need help."

My thoughts rewind to several months ago and the thing Domhnall Sterling had told me at the engagement ceilidh for him and Fiona. "You'll be next, Thane Buchanan, mark my words."

"Next for what?" I had asked.

Domhnall's response had not placated me at all. "The meddling, of course. You can't escape the American Wives Club."

"I can, and I will."

Fiona kisses my cheek. "I know you won't be a grump about it when the meddling begins. You are the calmest, most rational man I've ever met."

I release a groaning sigh. "Not feeling particularly calm today. The business is swirling away down the drain."

The woman I have entrusted with my distillery steps away from me and studies the floor below us. "We need to expand, Thane."

"Aye. But I'm somewhat short on capital."

"Then ask your investors for help."

"But this was meant to be my distillery. I craft the whisky and keep this place running. I appreciate the money my mates have contributed, but I don't want to ask for more."

Fiona turns toward me and straps her arms over her chest. "I had a feeling you'd be less than cooperative. But you did put me in charge of the operation—"

"You already said that." I eye her sideways. "What are you plotting, Fiona?"

"I've hired a new employee, someone who knows how to pump up a business."

Not sure I want my distillery to be "pumped up." To be fair, though, I have no bloody idea what she means by that phrase. But it doesn't sound like anything I'd want to do.

Something to my left catches Fiona's attention. Her face lights up. When I try to glance in that direction, she lays a hand on my cheek to stop me. "Promise me you'll give this a real go. Please, Thane, I'm only doing my job." The lass pats my cheek. "And so is she."

"She?" A chill shimmies up my spine and the hairs at my nape stiffen. "Fiona, what have you done?"

The lass pats my cheek again, then walks past me.

I rotate toward the other end of the walkway. Fiona is talking to a woman, but I cannae see her face. Fiona's body blocks my view. When she sidles past the other woman, I finally get a good look at her.

Bod an Donais. That woman has the perfect body, with curves in all the right places and tits that could make a hundred-year-old man go hard in a heartbeat. Her reddish-brown hair hangs over her shoulders, and copper highlights shimmer in those locks. I experience a sudden, bizarre impulse to push her up against the railing and fuck her in full view of the distillery floor. Her skirt suit looks posh—possibly designer, as if I know anything about fashion. The suit hugs her figure without being unseemly.

The lass stops an arm's length from me. She has a leather portfolio tucked under one arm as she offers me her hand to shake. "Good day, Mr. Buchanan. I look forward to working with you."

"What?" I cannae understand what she said. My focus has narrowed to her bonnie honey-brown eyes and nothing else.

"Are you all right, Mr. Buchanan?"

I blink rapidly several times until I finally realize what she just said. "Who are you?"

"Rebecca Taylor."

"And why are you here?"

"Didn't Fiona tell you?"

I shake my head slowly, still confounded by my reaction to this woman. It's insane. But I suddenly realize I haven't let go of her hand, so I pull mine away.

Rebecca lifts her brows. "Is something wrong, Mr. Buchanan?"

"No. I apologize for my behavior. It's just that I'm bloody confused about who you are and why you're here in my distillery."

"Fiona hired me. I'm your new distillery marketing manager."

"My what? Dinnae recall hiring anyone."

Rebecca lifts her brows again. "Fiona told me that she has full authority to hire and fire employees."

"Oh, aye, of course she does." I feel my whole face cinching up into a tight expression. "I've never heard of a distillery marketing manager."

"Why don't we go into your office to discuss the matter? Then you can take me on a tour of the facility."

"Tour? Why?"

She peers past my shoulder. "Where is your office, Mr. Buchanan?"

The bloody woman won't give up, so I might as well find out what she means to do to my business. Fiona asked me to give this a real go, and I owe her at least that much. "All right. Follow me to the office."

I wave for her to do that while I stalk across the walkway, heading for the steps that will take us down to the distillery floor.

"Ouch! Gah!"

The feminine exclamation makes me stop and spin round.

Rebecca grips the rail with one hand while struggling to free her high-heeled shoe from the grate-like walkway.

"*Mhac na galla.*" I hurry back to her and try to carefully pull her heel free, but it's difficult. Her body is twisted slightly. "Put your arms round me, lass."

She does that without even asking why.

I have a wee bit of trouble concentrating with her body pressed to mine. She smells too good, and it's interfering with my thought processes. The second I free her heel, she jerks forward—and her tits are crushed to my chest. That's not the dangerous bit, though. No, I'm in danger of getting hard because she has her hand on my upper thigh, brushing against my cock.

Her eyes flare wide.

Aye, she must have realized where her hand is.

Rebecca freezes, her gaze nailed to mine. "Um, sorry about that."

"No worries, lass." But aye, I'm concerned that I might frighten her if I develop a raging erection. Then again, she doesn't seem like the sort who panics. I learned that in the thirty seconds I've known her. *Bloody eejit.* "Let me help you up."

"I'm kind of tangled up with you. Maybe I should disentangle first."

"Oh, no, I can take care of the situation."

Her brows lift as if she doesn't quite believe me. Well, we did meet a moment ago, so she has no reason to trust my claim.

I wrap my arms around her and jump to my feet, then march down the walkway steps until we reach solid ground. I set her down on her high-heeled feet. "There you are, lass."

She gawps at me even more now, as if I've sprouted large green boils on my body. "How did you—I mean, you just—" She shakes her head slowly, still gawping at me. "That was amazing."

"What was?"

"The way you picked me up and carried me down the steps. You did that starting from a prone position."

"Aye. What's odd about that?"

She roves her gaze over me from head to toe, and I doubt she realizes she's licking her lips. "I have never seen anyone do anything like what you just did. Thank you."

"Dinnae thank me. A man should always assist a woman in need."

Rebecca snorts. "Not the guys I've known."

"Have you met many Scotsmen?"

"No. This is my first time in Scotland."

"I see. Well, I'm glad my fellow countrymen are superior."

She straightens her suit jacket and smooths her hands over her hair, then straightens her posture too. "Let's go to your office, please."

"Aye. It's this way."

Rebecca glances at the stills as we cross the floor, heading for the hallway, but we don't actually walk through the main section of the distillery. I can give her the grand tour after I find out what Fiona thinks this woman can do for my business.

I push the door to my office open, gesturing for Rebecca to enter first. She sidles past me, careful not to brush against my body. After our wee problem a few minutes ago, I dinnae blame her for being skittish. I shut the door while she takes a seat in one of the two chairs that always sit in front of my desk. The lass watches me settle onto my leather executive chair. Fiona had insisted that, as the owner of the company, I should have a posh piece of furniture to rest my erse on.

At least it's comfortable. But I feel ridiculous whenever I sit on the thing.

Rebecca crosses her legs and lays her portfolio on her thigh. "Did Fiona tell you anything about what I do?"

"Only that you're supposed to be a marketing expert. I assume that's why you're called a marketing manager."

"And what does that term mean to you?"

"What term?"

"Marketing manager."

I drag my chair closer to the desk and rest my arms on it. "Why dinnae ye tell me what it means? That way, we won't need to spin in linguistic circles."

Rebecca's eyes widen even more than they had when we fell into a heap on the walkway. "Linguistic circles?"

"Aye."

"I didn't expect you to use a phrase like that."

"Why not?"

"Because—" She fidgets in her chair. "I guess I assumed you would, um…"

Oh, aye, I'm getting the picture now. "You assumed I must be a dolt because I make whisky. Or is it because I'm Scottish?"

"Neither one. I guess I made that assumption because your distillery is so small and…unassuming."

"Are you trying to say it's tiny and useless?"

She clears her throat and flips through pages in her portfolio. "I apologize if I've offended you. But honestly, it's my job to annoy people. Marketing isn't something most business owners want to do, and they certainly don't like having to hire someone else to manage such things."

Fiona must believe this woman can help my company. That means I should listen to Rebecca's ideas, even if they annoy me.

So, I lean back in my chair and wave a hand at her. "Go on, tell me your ideas."

"First of all, we need to discuss the name of your company."

"What's wrong with it?"

"Can anyone pronounce it?" She bites her lip as she squints at a page in her portfolio and struggles to pronounce my company's name. "Coll-aid…sig-yule…roo-in?"

"No, that is incorrect."

"It's Gaelic, right?" She pronounced the word as gay-lick.

"Gal-ick. Not gay-lick." I drum my fingers on my chair's arms. "And the name is pronounced 'collie scale rune.' *Collaidh Sgeul-Rùin* is a fine name, so I dinnae need to change it."

Rebecca pulls out a pen and begins to tap it on her portfolio. "What does the name mean?"

"Sensual secret."

"And that has…what to do with whisky?" When I open my mouth to speak, she holds up a hand. "Never mind. I'm about to give you the most important advice of your career as a master distiller."

"What is it?"

"Ditch the Gaelic name. Now."

Chapter Two

Rebecca

Thane Buchanan is not the kind of man I expected him to be. Fiona hadn't told me much about him, so my preconceptions had come from my own mind, I suppose. I thought a man who owns a whisky distillery would be more freewheeling and gregarious. Instead, Thane seems thoughtful and self-contained. I've known him for a few minutes, so I probably shouldn't judge his character based on our brief interaction.

I'm usually good at figuring people out quickly. My inability to do that right now makes me feel slightly off kilter. Having my hand on his groin bumped me off kilter even more.

He smells good. I know that much for sure. And those eyes… They're the most striking shade of blue I've ever seen, a sort of pale aqua color that's a bit darker closer to the iris. Dark rims encircle them. Maybe his eyes do enchant me, and maybe his face does too, but I never let an attraction to a client interfere with my work.

Is he a client? I'm now working for his company, so I guess that makes him my boss. But Fiona hired me. That makes the hierarchy more difficult to figure out.

"Why should I change the name of my company?"

Thane's question pulls me out of my thoughts. I straighten my spine, since I somehow managed to sink into a slight slouch. Then I look directly at him. "The name is unpronounceable, that's why. How many people still speak Gaelic? Not many, I'm sure. There are approximately two hundred thirty-five thousand people living in the Highlands."

"And roughly sixty thousand speak Scots Gaelic."

"So, that would be about one percent of the population."

He rests his elbow on his chair's arm and rubs his chin. "I reckon so."

"That's an incredibly small segment of the target demographic."

"Who do you believe is our target demographic? Not Gaelic speakers. You've made that clear."

"Please don't make assumptions about what I think. I'm trying to help you revitalize your business, Mr. Buchanan."

He gazes straight at me, those striking blue eyes staring into mine. His voice drops to a deeper, almost sensual tone. "If revitalizing my company means erasing a part of my heritage, then I dinnae want your help."

"I haven't suggested any such thing." I slide forward in my chair, leaning toward him. "Will you at least listen to my suggestions? If you hate them, you can feel free to fire me."

"No, I can't do that. Fiona is in charge of all our employees."

"All right. In that case, if you hate my ideas, I'll resign."

Thane rolls his chair forward until his abdomen is pressed against the edge of the desk. He slants his head toward me. "Why on earth would you give me an excuse to fire you? After you've come all this way to work at my company."

"I don't want to resign, especially since my—Well, let's just say that I have a concrete reason for wanting to stay. That means I will do whatever I need to do to keep this job."

"What concrete reason do you have?"

I shake my head. "Awfully nosy, aren't you? My reasons are personal. If you want to know more about me, first I need to know more about you. What makes Thane Buchanan tick, what matters to you, and how far you're willing to go to make this distillery a success."

Why did my voice turn huskier? No idea. I can't be attracted to Thane. I met him a matter of minutes ago, and I do not believe in lust at first sight, much less love at first sight.

Thane rises and marches around to my side of the desk. Then he rests his bottom on the edge. That places his dick less than a foot away from me. And for some crazy reason, I can't stop staring at it.

He hooks a finger under my chin and lifts until my gaze meets his. "Are you having inappropriate thoughts about me, *gràidh*? I'm having them about you, that's a dead certainty."

"What?"

I still can't focus on his words because his body has captured all my attention. My gaze has shifted up to his brawny chest. The tight shirt he wears accentuates every muscle. He must work out a lot. I mean, those biceps… I can picture myself lying on top of Thane while we're both naked and I'm straddling his hips just before I lower my body onto his cock.

Damn, it's been too long since I had sex.

Thane snaps his fingers.

I jerk and swerve my gaze to him.

He leans over until our eyes are only an inch or two apart. "I said, are you having inappropriate thoughts about me, *gràidh*?"

"Um… What did you just call me?"

"*Gràidh*. It's an endearment."

"We don't know each other. You shouldn't be calling me anything like that. It's unprofessional."

He leans in even more, and his nose brushes mine. "If ye want to understand what makes me tick, you need to understand that I cannae tell you everything. I have secrets, and I will never share them with you or anyone."

"Why?"

"Because."

This conversation is going nowhere. I need to get out of this office now, before I jump him. His voice is like whisky and chocolate, an addictive combination. I push my chair backward, which makes it scrape across the floor. "Give me the grand tour, please. I need to familiarize myself with the facility."

"If that's what you want."

"Yes, it is. Thank you."

I spring out of my chair, but my stupid high heels trip me up again, and I stumble into Thane for the second time in less than fifteen minutes. When he reaches for me, I stagger backward in an attempt to get some space. Instead, I bump into that damn chair.

And I flail, about to crash down to the floor.

Thane catches me, hugging my body to all his muscles. "Ye should be more careful, *gràidh*. Might crack that lovely head of yours."

He skims his gaze over me from head to toe, just like he'd done earlier. But this time, he does more than smirk. His lips curl into a suggestive smile while his eyes smolder with a heat that makes my breath catch.

Yeah, I'm beginning to realize why his whiskey is called "sensual secret."

I swallow hard. "Please let go of me."

"Are ye sure you can stay upright this time?"

"Positive. Please let go."

He peels his body away from mine so slowly that I'm sure he's doing it on purpose to tease me with his sexiness. How could I be attracted to a man I just met? It's crazy. But my body insists on cranking up the arousal meter higher and higher, just as gradually as Thane had released me.

The Scot finally steps backward, giving me some space but also a reprieve from the delicious scent of him. He must use cologne or aftershave. "Shall we begin the tour now?"

"Yes." I tug my jacket down and pick up my portfolio, which I apparently dropped when Thane pulled me close. "Let's go. I need to get up to speed on how this facility works."

He approaches the door and pulls it open, waving for me to exit first.

Well, at least he is a gentleman. Can't say I've met many of those. The guys I've worked with for most of my career didn't have complimentary things to say about me. I think I'm a nice person, but sometimes in business a woman has to put her foot down.

First, he leads me down the hall in the opposite direction from the distillery floor, walking rather swiftly. I should've worn sneakers.

"Can you slow down, please?" I ask. "These shoes aren't made for jogging."

Thane halts and half turns toward me. He scrutinizes my shoes and twists one side of his mouth upward at one corner. "Why would you wear something like that when you're working at a distillery? I reckon ye want to break your ankle, aye?"

"No, of course not."

"Then get rid of those shoes. I can find you a pair of wellies."

"You're talking about rubber boots, right? I don't need those. Unless we're going outside to trudge through muck."

He lifts his brows. "Dinnae like to accept advice, do ye? I'm trying to reduce the chances of you having another accident."

"And I appreciate that. But—"

"Toss your shoes into the rubbish bin. That's my advice."

"What?" I point at my feet. "These are Christian Louboutin, which means they're designer. I saved up for six months to buy these pumps. I will not toss them into a trash can."

He eyes my clothing. "Is your suit designer too? No one who works here dresses that way except on special occasions."

"To answer your question, yes, this is a designer suit."

"How long did you save to pay for that?"

I'm starting to get irritated, but I don't want to insult Thane. This is his company, and though I technically work for Fiona, I suppose he is the boss of the whole operation. That means I need to behave accordingly, which involves not annoying him too much. "Could we get the tour started, please? I'm anxious to learn about the distillery."

"Aye, but you really should change your shoes. Sure you dinnae want those wellies?"

"Okay, fine."

Thane sprints down the hall, disappearing into another room.

I wait here, tapping the toe of my ridiculously expensive pumps, and wait for the man in charge to return.

He emerges from that room and jogs up to me, offering me a pair of rubber boots. "Here you are. They should fit you, since they're Fiona's backup pair."

"She won't need them?"

"Not for a while, I'm sure." He holds out his free hand to me. "Best hold on to me while you take off your heels. It's the safest way."

"That's very kind of you." I accept his hand, then kick my pumps off and step into the wellies. I have to say I like that word. It's cute. Now that I'm properly attired, I pull my hand away. "Thank you, Mr. Buchanan."

"Please call me Thane. I've never cared for formality."

"That's fine."

"Do you go by Becky? Or Becca?"

"No."

"What about Becks?"

"No. Just Rebecca."

He sighs. "As you wish. Let's begin the tour."

Was that a disapproving sigh? Does he think I'm uptight? *Oh, please.* I'm too old to give a damn what a man, or anyone, thinks of me.

Thane leads me straight down the hall to another doorway. He pushes it open, and I see the outdoors beyond the threshold. "We should begin where whisky gets its start."

"And that would be where?"

"Outside. I'll explain once we get there. All right?"

"Sure. You're the boss."

He steps outside and holds the door until I'm through it. Then he leads me down a well-worn dirt path. It seems to wind through the forest, and I can't figure out what the woods have to do with whisky. Of course, I know nothing about this industry, so I'll just keep quiet and wait for him to explain. Since the path is narrow, I end up following him. That gives me a great view of his ass, thanks to the way his pants mold to his glutes.

Soon, I detect the faint sounds of burbling water.

I've been lagging behind him, so I can admire his ass. Now, I trot up beside him. "Are we going to a pond or something? Thought I heard water."

"Ye did. But it's not a pond."

"What is it, then?"

"Patience, *maise.*"

What did he just say? I have no idea what *maise* means, and I don't feel like asking him about that right now. Business first, conversation later.

"That means 'beauty,' in case you were wondering."

As we keep walking, the trail widens gradually. I can now see the water that I'd heard burbling.

Thane halts at the bank. "Here it is. All our whiskey begins with the water taken from this river."

"What is the river called?"

He shrugs. "It doesn't have a name."

"No one ever gave it one? That's odd."

"Aye, but Scots aren't known for adhering to conventions just for the sake of it. The river flows through the Dùndubhan estate, alongside the castle of Dùndubhan."

"What does that name mean?" No, I won't even try to pronounce it. I assume the word is Gaelic.

"Dùndubhan means fortress of the black water. The castle was built in medieval times, and the ancestors of the MacTaggart clan lived there."

"Are you at all related to the MacTaggarts?"

"No. I am a Buchanan." He smirks. "I wouldn't have dated Fiona Mac-Taggart—briefly, long ago—if we were in any way related."

I assume that means he slept with her, but I won't ask if that's true. None of my business. And it's bad form to ask the big boss about his sex life.

So, I change the subject. "I read that a lot of the distilleries in the High-lands were built by a man called Charles Doig. Was yours built by him too?"

"Not unless we could time travel back to the late eighteen hundreds. Doig was designing distilleries during that period. And I doubt he was im-mortal."

"I just thought your distillery might be that old."

"No, it's a new construction." He spins around, facing away from the water. "Let me tell you about this river and what it means to the distillery and the people who work here."

Chapter Three

Thane

Rebecca's gaze flicks to the river and then to me, not just once, but repeatedly. I reckon she's still confused by the fact the river has no name, but I don't see what's odd about that. But then, I understand the history of this region, having grown up here, while she is a newcomer. That's why I told the lass that I need to explain things to her.

I keep facing her, which means I'm facing away from the water. But I have always found that eye contact makes more of an impact on the listener. "This river has existed since the Highlands came into being, most likely. No one bothered to name it because such things were of little import in the distant past. And the region that encompasses Dùndubhan was never explored much because of the mythology surrounding its origins."

Rebecca's brows rise, and her eyes sparkle with excitement. "I love mythology."

I would never have guessed that she would get this excited about historical myths, but it's oddly endearing. "If you love legends, then you have come to the right place. The Highlands have some of the best myths and folk beliefs you'll find anywhere in the world. I might be slightly biased, though."

"Please tell me about the river and its mythology. You can't leave me hanging."

"I told you that the name Dùndubhan means fortress of the black water." I turn sideways to wave toward the river. «It's more than a description of the waters, though. For centuries, most of the people who have lived in this area have avoided the mountain on which Dùndubhan sits because witches once lived here."

"Wicked witches?"

"That's a complicated question. Ancestors of the MacTaggarts once lived in the castle—three witch sisters and their nephew, Kieran MacTaggart." I gaze down at the dark waters. "They were good witches, as the legend says, but most folk still feared their powers. These days, witchcraft is not feared in that way. Kirsty MacTaggart owns a metaphysical shop in Loch Fairbairn, and she and her two sisters are Wiccans."

Rebecca inches closer to the edge of the bank, peering down at the river. "The water really is black."

"No, it *appears* to be black. That's to do with the soil, and the things in it that make my whisky different. But the basic ingredients are the same for all Scotch whisky."

She leans forward a wee bit to squint at the water. "I don't see any magical ingredients floating in the river."

When she turns her head to smirk at me, I know the lass is having me on.

I cross my arms over my chest and shake my head. "You Americans are so easily duped."

Rebecca straightens, turning to face me. "You know I was joking. I'm not that stupid, and neither are you."

"I appreciate the compliment. And aye, I've already deduced that you are not an eejit or a heathen."

"Gee, thanks. You sure know how to make a girl feel special."

"Best move away from the bank. Might tumble in if you aren't careful."

Rebecca takes a few steps, then glances back at the river before turning her attention to me. "I'd like to know more about the river. If it has special things in it like you say, I could use that information in my marketing strategy. I am here to help you level up your business. Isn't that what you want?"

"Aye." For some reason, I find myself scratching my cheek. "But I dinnae want your marketing strategy to erase everything that's unique about *Collaidh Sgeul-Rùin.*"

"I don't want that either." She walks up to me, halting only inches from my body. Then she tips her head back, a necessity if she means to gaze into my eyes. The lass isn't short, but I'm several inches taller. "I have never created a generic marketing campaign. My work is always tailored to my client and the products they make."

"Glad to hear it. This distillery means a great deal to me."

She tips her head to the side. "Why is that?"

I want to refuse to answer, but I realize Rebecca is only doing her job. So, I sigh and tell her the truth. "My father always wanted to own a distillery and craft a unique brand of whisky. He never had the money to do that. Neither did he have wealthy friends who could offer financial assistance. He gave up on his dream."

"And now you have revived it."

"That's right. Da suffered a mini-stroke three years ago. Though he recovered from it very well, his body isn't as hardy as it used to be. He walks with a cane or a Zimmer frame sometimes."

"So, he isn't physically able to run a business."

Cannae help chuckling. "My father has barely lost a step since his recovery from that setback. He might need a wee bit of help now and then, but nothing can slow him down. He hasn't even retired yet."

"Then why didn't he want to run the distillery with you?"

"Because he lost interest. He prefers to play golf with Torcall Murdoch or spend time with family. Dreams can change, ye know."

Rebecca's smile turns a touch rueful. "Yeah, I know all about that phenomenon. I started out wanting to be an artist."

Her eyes flare wide briefly, as if she hadn't meant to tell me that. But she regains her composure swiftly. A lock of hair falls over her eye.

And I instinctively tuck it behind her ear.

She drags her tongue across her bottom lip while staring at my mouth.

Bod an Donais. I know I shouldn't kiss her, but the need swells inside me and forces me to summon all my willpower. A beautiful, sexy lass who's also clever and charming? No man could resist that.

Yet I have always kept my desires under control. That restraint saved my life more than once.

She leans in more and lays a hand on my chest. Her eyes have grown darker, making her irises become a deeper shade of whisky brown. I try not to notice how close her body is to mine, but it's bloody hard to ignore. She smells like bottled heaven and looks like sin in a skirt suit. Her eyes could intoxicate me with one kiss, I'm dead sure of that. Maybe that explains why my voice has grown deeper and huskier.

"Ah, lass, dinnae look at me that way. It's dangerous."

"You don't frighten me, Thane."

"But I should. You have no idea who I really am or what I've done."

She lays both hands on my chest now, and her body is pressed to mine. "I'll need to know everything about you, if I'm going to create a unique marketing campaign that accentuates the sensuality of your whisky."

Her voice has dropped to a sultrier register too. It makes my pulse beat faster and my skin grow sensitized to every sensation. I can hear the whispering of her breaths as they come faster and shorter. But when she takes one side of her bottom lip between her teeth and releases it ever so slowly…I lose my mind.

Aye, I lash my arms round her and kiss the lass.

For a few seconds, we gaze into each other's eyes with our mouths fused. Our breaths mingle and gust over each other, blustering out through our nostrils. I taste the barest flavor of her, but it's enough to push me over the edge. I grasp her erse with one hand, clasping it firmly while I shift the other hand up to the center of her back. Splaying my hand there, I clasp her to me even more firmly.

Then I thrust my tongue between her lips.

She moans. Her eyes roll upward briefly, then the lids flutter shut. And she thrusts her tongue into my mouth.

Rebecca kisses with so much passion that it takes my breath away, and I can't stop myself from roving my hands over every inch of her that I can reach. I fondle her erse and rock my hips into her body. She moans again. Never in my life have I shagged a lass I just met, but I cannae stop myself. I grasp her erse with both hands and stagger forward until we meet an obstacle. I crack one eye open just enough to see that I have her pinned to a tree.

I should stop this. I know that. But I can't do it.

Shoving one hand between her *cíoch*, I roughly massage it and scrape my thumb over the nipple, back and forth, until she lets out a cry that's muffled by our joined mouths. The scent of her arousal wafts around us. I groan so deeply that I can hardly believe I made that sound.

I tear my mouth away from hers. "We shouldn't—not here—but I—"

"Please fuck me, Thane. Right now."

"Dinnae have a condom."

"I had a hysterectomy four years ago, and I haven't dated much since then. I'm clean."

"So am I. Haven't dated much either. But…"

Rebecca rocks her hips into my cock. "Just do me already, for Pete's sake. Make me come, Thane."

For about three seconds, I fight the impulse. Then she takes my bottom lip between her teeth and sucks on it.

A guttural groan rumbles out of me. And I shove a hand under her skirt to push it up to her hips. I expect to meet the barrier of her knickers, but Rebecca is not wearing any. "*Mhac na galla.* Do you always do business with no knickers on?"

"I never wear panties, if that's what you mean."

"Aye, that's what I meant." Just knowing she had been touring the distillery while having no underwear on makes me so randy that I can barely breathe. I shove a hand between her thighs, feeling the heat and slickness of her cream on my fingers. "Bloody hell. There's no turning back now, lass. Ahm about to fuck ye."

"Yes, do it, hurry the hell up."

I fumble to undo the buckle on my belt and unzip my trousers. The second I've done that, Rebecca wraps her thighs round my hips. My dokey lies nestled between her folds. I gaze into her eyes while I pull my hips back and plunge my length into her sheath, groaning with a depth of relief that I've never experienced before. But I still need more of her.

Rebecca throws her head back and clutches my shoulders. Her eyes are closed again, and her breaths come swiftly and shallowly, as if she's almost panting in her desperation to have me fuck her. The lass's tits rise and fall with her every breath, and I can see the stiff peaks through the fabric of her blouse.

"Please don't stop," she whispers. "Please, Thane."

I love her voice, especially when she's in the throes of ecstasy and begging me to make her come. I slap my palms on the tree, at either side of her head, and begin to pump my hips in a fast and powerful rhythm. The sound of her cream sliding along my cock is almost drowned out by the scratching of her clothing rubbing on the tree trunk and the wee cries she unleashes. I grunt and groan and grasp her thighs to hold her as close to my body as possible.

The look on her face, a mixture of desperate need and pure pleasure, has me teetering on the edge of climax.

Not until she jumps off that cliff first.

I hoist her thighs higher. Then I pull out of her body to scrape my *slat* up and down her cleft with my crown nudging her clit with every lunge.

Her entire body goes rigid. She remains frozen with her mouth open and her eyes half closed and seems incapable of breathing.

I tease her with the head of my *slat*, swiping it up and down her cleft.

And she explodes. Her cries echo off the trees and nearly obliterate the gentle sounds of the river rushing past. While her climax winds down, I thrust my cock inside her body once more and pound into her three times until the glorious release rushes through me on a wave of rapid spasms. Then I rest my head on her shoulder, breathing too hard to speak. Rebecca seems to feel the same way.

Finally, I pull out of her luscious body and zip up my trousers.

She blinks rapidly for a moment before she tugs her skirt down and tries to brush off the bits of tree bark that became glued to her hair and clothing.

"Turn round," I tell her. "You'll never get that rubbish off your back without a wee bit of help."

"Oh. Right. I guess I could use some help." Her cheeks are still a rosy shade, and her pupils remain large, darkening her bonnie brown irises. She turns away from me. "Okay, go ahead and brush it off."

I flick the bits of tree bark off her suit, but then I need to fight the impulse to push her up against the tree again to fuck her from behind this time. It's not my fault. I can see her own juices dribbling down her inner thighs—and I can smell it too.

Mhac na galla. Why did I shag her? I've gone doolally, for sure.

Chapter Four

Rebecca

Thane studies me with a strange expression. It looks like a mish-mash of shock, lust, and concern. Well, I'm feeling a bit like that too. Sex with a man I met a few hours ago? Sex in the woods? With my boss? Holy shit, what is wrong with me? I'm getting fired, for sure. But Fiona is my direct superior, and she can't fire me for screwing Thane because I won't tell her about it, and I can't believe he would tell her either.

Well, at least now I know the rumors are true. Post-hysterectomy sex is amazing—with the right man.

Thane winces. "Ye must think I'm a predator. A *bod ceann* who uses and abuses women. How do ye feel, lass? I hope I didn't hurt you."

I can tell he honestly worries about that. So, I smile at him. "Relax, I'm fine. I feel incredible, actually. It's been a long time since I dated, much less had sex."

"Aye, it's been a long time for me too. I haven't really dated for several years, though I've had a few weekend flings. That sort of thing doesn't appeal to me anymore, though."

"I haven't been with anyone in four years." Not sure why we're exchanging this information. It's not like we're going steady. Does anyone use that term anymore? Probably not. My daughter would laugh at me for saying it.

Thane reaches for me.

And I shuffle sideways. "This was great, but we need to forget it ever happened. I mean, you are my boss, kind of."

"Kind of? It's my distillery."

"Don't get testy. I only meant that Fiona is my direct superior. She answers to you, right?"

"Aye. Sorry I snapped at you. It isn't like me at all."

I tug my jacket down, though I can't explain why. "Let's just erase this one crazy moment from our minds and go back to having a purely professional relationship. Two people who have essentially been celibate for years were bound to explode under the right circumstances. We're attracted to each other. That was the catalyst. But now we've gotten it out of our systems."

"Have we?" He takes one step, erasing the gap between us. "You and I have the sort of chemistry that could destroy the universe. It's more powerful than azidoazide azide."

"Az-uh what?"

He chuckles. "Azidoazide azide. It's the most explosive chemical on earth."

Yeah, I can't deny our chemistry is that explosive. I've never felt anything like it. But that doesn't erase the fact that he's my employer. I have no choice but to straighten my posture, lift my chin a touch, and pretend I don't give a damn that we just had the best sex in the history of the cosmos.

"We need to remain professional, Thane. What just happened, never happened. Got it?"

"If that's what you want."

"Thank you."

As I walk past him, he grabs my arm. "I haven't finished telling you how my whisky is made."

"I'll get Fiona to explain. Later. Right now, I need to find my office and start spitballing ideas for how to make everyone want your whisky."

"We had a poke, *gràidh*. Don't let that get in the way of business."

"Nothing distracts me from doing my job."

I shake his hand off my arm and march down the path to the main building. Just as the door shuts behind me, and I'm contemplating where the heck I'm supposed to go now, I hear the sound of shoes clapping on the hard floor. When I turn toward the sound, Fiona smiles and waves at me.

She halts beside me, and her smile fades. "What's fashing you, Rebecca?"

Based on the context, I assume she's asking what's bothering me. Learning the Scottish way of speaking will take some time. "I'm not sure where my office is."

"Let me show you."

I let Fiona lead me down the maze of corridors. Fortunately, we don't need to traipse across that metal walkway. I could break my ankle, just like

Thane warned me I might. *Damn.* Thinking about him gives me a flashback of our "poke" by the river. Did anyone hear us? I know I made a lot of noise. Couldn't help it. That man is an incredible lover.

Oh, please. We had a quickie. That doesn't automatically translate to "Thane Buchanan rocks the bedroom every time." He might be terrible if we made love the right way—on a bed with plenty of time to take it slow.

"Here's your office, Rebecca."

Fiona nearly shouted that statement.

I blink swiftly, trying to clear my head of thoughts of Thane Buchanan. "You didn't need to yell at me. I can read the words on the door. Rebecca Taylor, Chief of Marketing and Advertising."

"Aye, you heard me the fourth time I told you." Fiona smirks. "You were thinking about Thane, aye?"

"No. I was…thinking about lunch. I'm getting hungry, though it's still morning." Oh, hell, who am I kidding? Yes, of course I was thinking about that man. But I do not want to tell my boss that I'm fantasizing about the man who owns the company.

Fiona clearly understands the situation. She's tactful, though, and doesn't push me to talk about Thane. Instead, she explains the electronic door lock to me, though she also tells me that I probably don't need to lock the door. The workers here are like family. But Thane insisted on securing the premises. It's something to do with his former line of work, but Fiona doesn't feel comfortable revealing that information to me.

"If Thane wants to tell you, he will. That's all I can say."

"No problem. His backstory probably isn't relevant to my job, anyway."

Fiona winks at me. "I knew I'd hired the right woman for the job. Now, would you like me to help you get settled in? Or do you prefer to dive right in and work it all out on your own?"

"I'm the diving-in kind."

"All right, then. Ring me if you need anything."

"Thank you, Fiona."

While she trots down the hall, I step into my new digs. The door shuts behind me with a soft click. And I lean back against the door, sighing as my shoulders slump. I'm exhausted, and it's barely ten o'clock. I had flown to Scotland two days earlier, so I would have time to adjust to the time difference. After years of living and working in Boston, I realized it was time to make a change. Take a risk. Shake up my life. Can't get more shaken up than moving across an ocean to a country where the people speak with strange accents and use unusual phrases.

Scotland is gorgeous. But that's not the main reason I took a job here.

For an hour, I sort out my new office, getting everything the way I like it. My new digs don't resemble my old office in Boston. I wouldn't want a carbon copy of my former life. After forty-nine years on Planet Earth, I'm ready for an adventure.

Thane Buchanan has already given me that.

I push aside thoughts of him and continue setting up my office. That doesn't really take long. I have a desk with two file drawers and two tall file cabinets tucked into the corner of the room. Only after I've organized all of that do I amble over to the venetian blinds and roll them up to see what's beyond the windows.

Holy cow. I have a stunning view of the mountain Thane had mentioned. Does it have a name? The river doesn't, but I'll need to ask somebody about the mountain. A forest blankets the slope on this side, but I can't tell what the other face looks like. I can't see the river, most likely because of the forest. Despite the cloudy sky, the landscape leaves me in awe. Thane had also told me about a castle that sits somewhere on the mountain, but I don't remember the unpronounceable name of that structure.

As my gaze glides down the mountainside, I notice a large stone building that lies maybe fifty feet from the distillery itself. I wonder what that structure holds. It must have something to do with making whisky.

My cell phone rings.

I rush back to my desk, snatching up my phone. The caller ID shows me who it is. "Courtney, what's up?"

"Just checking on you. This is the first time you've ever left the United States, and you're in a country where the people use weird words."

"Are you talking about the UK? Or Scotland specifically?"

"Whichever." Courtney pauses—for dramatic effect, no doubt. "How's it going at your new job? Can't believe you wanted to work at a whisky company. You never drink anything harder than a glass of chardonnay."

"It's time for a change. Maybe I'll go wild and sample the company's whisky while I'm here."

She laughs. "Come on, Mom. You aren't the wild type."

My daughter has a point. I've always played it safe in my personal life, though I often took chances at work. Nothing that would qualify as wild. Professional chances aren't as intriguing as the personal variety.

I settle onto my cushy executive chair and kick off my wellies. Then I set my feet on the desk. That's a wild thing to do, right? "Aren't you supposed to be at work right now? Your father paid for your education, so we both expect you to sprint up the corporate ladder and become a billionaire by age thirty."

"Cool moms aren't supposed to tell their kids never to skip out on work."

"When did I become a cool mom?"

"Uh…not sure."

I cluck my tongue. "You naughty girl. You've been trying to butter me up, haven't you? Okay, it's time to tell me why you really called."

"Because I love you, Mom," Courtney says in a saccharine tone. Then she laughs. "Okay, fine. My friends want to go to a concert, but I don't have enough discretionary funds to pay for my ticket."

I'm so grateful that I have smart children who use words like "discretionary funds." Maybe I should cut her a little slack. "How much does a ticket cost?"

"You'll give me the money?" Her excited tone is cute and genuine.

"Maybe. But tell me how much it costs."

Courtney hums tunelessly for a moment. "One fifty."

"A hundred and fifty dollars? What, are you having tea with the royal family?"

"It's not a hundred and fifty dollars, Mom. It's a hundred and fifty pounds."

"Ohhh, well that makes all the difference." I slump in my chair and rub my forehead. "All right. I'll send you the money."

Courtney has a job—entry level, but that's how everyone starts—and she's a very responsible young woman. I know she won't be going to a kegger, or whatever British young people call a booze-a-thon.

I chat with my daughter for a few more minutes, but then it's time for her to get back to work. She'd been on a break during our phone call. As soon as we've said goodbye, someone knocks on my office door.

Without thinking, I shout, "Come in."

The door swings open, and Thane saunters into the room. He stops just behind the two chairs that face my desk. His gaze roves over me, from my bare feet to my slumped posture. "Settling in well, I see. Perhaps a little too well."

I jerk upright. "Sorry. I shouldn't slouch at the office."

"Dinnae mind if you do." He rakes his gaze over me one more time, then wipes a hand over his mouth before he finally looks me in the eye. "It's lunchtime. May I escort you to the cafeteria?"

Since I first met Thane earlier this morning, I've wondered if all Scotsmen talk the way he does. Probably not. He has a strange name to go with his unusual behavior. A strangely sexy name.

He lifts his brows. "Well, may I escort you?"

"What? Oh, sure." I hop out of my chair and slip my feet into my outrageously expensive shoes, the ones I'd been wearing before Thane gave me wellies. "Let's go. I'm starving."

Just as we exit my office, Fiona comes jogging down the hall. She halts when she sees Thane, and her brows wrinkle. "I thought we agreed I would show Rebecca the cafeteria."

"Aye, we did," Thane says. "But plans changed."

"Did they?" Fiona smirks at me, then at her boss. "Aye, you should escort her and have lunch with her."

"I only meant to take her there. She must want to socialize with the other employees."

When he spoke the phrase *take her there*, I flashed back to our interlude in the woods.

Thane touches my arm. "Are ye feeling all right, lass? Your cheeks are a bit pink."

"I'm fine, thanks."

Fiona is smirking again.

She can't know what I did with the big boss in the woods, can she? I pray no one could see us. But here on the top floor of the distillery, I have a spectacular view of the mountain. What if somebody in another office can see the river path?

"Are ye sure you aren't unwell?" Thane asks. He lays the back of his hand on my cheek. "You feel warm."

"Only on the right cheek. I'm fine, I swear." And I wish with every iota of my willpower that he would stop touching me. This man is my kryptonite, and I don't even like superhero movies. "You can, um, take back your hand. I'm not sick. But thank you for asking."

He steps back. "We're away to the cafeteria, then. Fiona, would you care to join us?"

"You should talk to Rebecca alone. No one understands this distillery better than you do, and our new marketing director needs all that knowledge."

Oh, yeah, she's playing matchmaker for sure.

Chapter Five

Thane

Does Fiona think I haven't noticed what's she's about? The *smuilceag* is trying to orchestrate a romance between me and Rebecca, though calling Fiona a chit hardly describes her attitude. She means to drag the American Wives Club into my life, but that's highly inappropriate and bloody annoying. Rebecca is my employee, not my girlfriend. I can't be angry with Fiona, though, since she's one of the kindest people I've ever met, and she has become my right-hand lass ever since she accepted my job offer.

Rebecca must wonder what sort of workplace she has joined. Fiona, who is her superior, shouldn't be pushing the lass to get involved with me. I have no time for dating, anyway. This company is my mistress.

How does fucking Rebecca in the forest fit into my work ethic? Not a sodding clue. I will never touch the lass again. Never.

I scratch my arm, then scratch my cheek, all while shifting my weight from one foot to the other three times. What a bloody stupid erse I am, seducing my new employee on her first day at work. Not that it would be acceptable for me to do that later on. *Mhac na galla.* What if I've ruined my business relationship with Rebecca?

The lass in question wrinkles her brows. "Are you okay, Thane?"

"Aye, fine." She must think I dinnae want to be alone with her, considering my uncomfortable demeanor. Rebecca probably worries that I'll drag her into the nearest janitorial closet and ravish her again. I would never do such a thing, but she hasn't known me long enough to realize that.

Fiona glances between me and Rebecca, her smile tightening the dimples in her cheeks. "You two don't need me anymore. Enjoy your lunch."

The *smuilceag* trots down the hall and glances back at us while grinning. Then she disappears down the hallway that leads to the cafeteria.

I have never been the violent sort or the type of man who swears at a woman, but Fiona's meddling makes me imagine all the ways I could murder her without anyone ever finding the remains. Aye, Fiona has driven me insane.

Rather than resorting to murder, I shove my hands into my trouser pockets and hunch my shoulders as I face Rebecca. "You shouldn't feel obligated to have lunch with me. That was Fiona's barmy idea. Ever since she married Domhnall Sterling and joined the American Wives Club, the lass has turned into a matchmaking machine."

"American Wives Club? What is that?"

I sigh and slump my shoulders. "It's complicated."

That is the understatement of the millennium.

Rebecca rolls her shoulders back. "Well, then, I guess you better take me to lunch in the cafeteria so you can explain what that club is about. Don't you think?"

"That does seem to be the best option."

"Good. Let's go."

She starts walking down the hall with her shoulders back and her head held high, as if she has a single sodding clue about where the cafeteria is located. When she reaches the next corridor, she stops and turns her head this way and that, clearly baffled about where to go. She chooses a direction seemingly at random and heads down the adjacent corridor.

I catch up to the lass and walk alongside her. "Have you visited the cafeteria yet?"

"Nope. I'm flying blind—unless you show me the way."

"Happy to assist you."

I continue walking beside her rather than moving ahead to lead the way, simply because my mother taught me that racing ahead of a woman is poor etiquette. Instead, I point to the corridor we need to go down and assure Rebecca that the cafeteria is just a wee ways off. She smiles brightly when I say that. What about that simple statement is entertaining? I reckon it's the fact that I used the word wee, but that doesn't seem amusing to me. It's a common word.

Once we reach the swinging doors on the left side of the hall, I hold one half open for the lass. She smiles brightly again. I fight the impulse to ask for an explanation of her behavior since it doesn't matter to me. I catch up to Rebecca as the door swings shut behind me and lead the way again since I know this cafeteria better than she does. A table in the far corner is empty, and it's away from most of the other gents and lasses who are enjoying their lunch.

A few people notice us, and they seem to be whispering to each other as if the fact I'm having lunch with our new marketing director is a noteworthy event. Based on their expressions, I have a feeling they're gossiping about us. No, I dinnae care about that, and I dinnae want to be alone with her. Well, aye, I do. But only so we can discuss business without anyone overhearing us. I have no plans to seduce her again.

Naturally, I pull her chair out for her.

She smiles at me again.

The lass is bonnie, and her smile only augments her natural beauty. But no, I will not shag her. My thoughts might be more convincing if I hadn't needed to clarify in my own mind that I will never touch the lass again.

Rebecca tips her head back to gaze up at me. "I think you might be the only true gentleman I've ever met. Unless you're overcompensating for the fact that you screwed me in the woods, but I don't think so. My intuition tells me you are a genuine gentleman."

"I appreciate the compliment." But I'm not used to being lavished with praise, and I'm not entirely sure how to respond. Changing the subject seems to be in order. So, I lean over her chair, which places my cheek inches away from hers. "Would ye like me to provide a curated meal for you? I know which cafeteria foods are the most edible."

"Sure, that would be great. You're a wonderful host."

Wonderful? Me? I think she must still be under the influence of the powerful orgasm she experienced earlier. Aye, she's still high on endorphins hours after we fucked.

I need to stop thinking about that. Right now.

When she moves to get up, I keep my hand firmly planted on the back of her chair to stop her. "I will gather the food. You should relax. Your first day at work must be stressful, especially since you're living in a new country too. Allow me to ease your burden a wee bit."

"That's very kind of you, Thane."

I nod, then stride off across the cafeteria. Within a matter of minutes, I've gathered a good meal for us, and now I'm carrying two trays of food back to our table. My path takes me past the table where Fiona and a few others have been enjoying the cafeteria food, and my right-hand lass winks at me. Then she tips her head toward the table where Rebecca waits for me—and she winks again, smirking too this time.

I ignore that and return to Rebecca. As I come up behind her, I cannae help noticing that she's busily texting with someone called Eric. Aye, I know I shouldn't spy on her, but I hadn't meant to do that.

Rebecca smiles as she types a response, and I find myself simply standing here behind her reading along.

How's the new job? Eric asks.

Rebecca types, *Fine so far, but it's only day one.*

Way to be positive, Mom.

Mom? I had no idea Rebecca had any children. Fiona had interviewed the lass, and I had virtually no part in the decision to hire her. That explains why I know almost nothing about Rebecca and her family. Does she have a husband too? No, I cannae believe she would be unfaithful.

Shouldn't you be at work? Rebecca types. *You won't discover a new type of igneous rock by chanting a spell.*

Eric sends her a single nonsensical series of letters: *LMAO.*

She shakes her head, and her lips curl up the slightest bit. *Is your phone malfunctioning, sweetie? That wasn't a word.*

The lad responds with a series of symbols. Emojis, the younger folk would call them. I have no idea what anyone is meant to glean from tiny cartoon images. Fortunately, a moment later, Eric explains. *That means I was laughing my ass off, Mom.*

You are a horrible child. Show some respect for your elders.

Love you too, Mom. A kiss emoji follows, and at least I understand that. Then the lad adds a winking symbol. I think that's what it represents.

Rebecca drops her mobile into her purse and glances about as if she's looking for me. Before I can move, and perhaps avoid her realizing I've spied, she twists her head around and sees me.

Her eyes flare wide. "Thane? What are you doing?"

"Well, I, ah…"

"It couldn't be the way it looks. My boss wouldn't spy on me during my lunch break."

Of course that's what I was doing. Inadvertently, but aye.

Like a numpty, I smack her tray down on the table and rush round to my side of the table. When I smack my own tray down, I nearly drop the ruddy thing. Fortunately, Rebecca catches the edge and steadies it for me. I mumble a thank-you and carefully settle onto my chair.

But I can't look her in the eye. Or anywhere in the vicinity of her eye.

She lays her palm over my hand. "Relax, I'm not angry. There won't be any lawsuit for workplace harassment."

"I wasn't worried about that." I stare down at my food to avoid looking at her. "But you must be angry. I read your text messages over your shoulder."

"Why did you do that?"

"Dinnae know. When I came up behind you, I saw those texts, and I was curious about who Eric might be."

She leans back in her chair and…smiles. "Eric is my son. He has a twin sister, Courtney. They're fraternal twins, not identical."

"I see. You didn't need to share that information with me. I'm an eavesdropping *cacan*, after all. That means I'm a wee shit."

Rebecca scans her gaze over me. "You aren't wee in any sense of the word."

"It's a colloquialism, that's all."

"Uh-huh." She studies her food, pushing it about as if she's not sure what sort of meal I've given her. "What is this? I've never seen anything like it."

"That's festy cock."

She clamps her lips between her teeth as her body quivers. Aye, the lass is struggling not to laugh at me.

I slouch back in my chair. "Go on, let out your laughter. That thing on your plate is a traditional Scottish food, an alternative to pancakes, that's made with oatmeal, water, and salt. Its shape is meant to resemble a rooster. Hence the name festy cock."

"Fiona warned me that Scots have strange customs and strange foods, but I had no idea you guys played with your food. I mean, it's shaped like a rooster."

"You don't have to eat it. I thought you might enjoy sampling some traditional dishes."

Rebecca gingerly peels a wee bit off the festy cock with her fork and sniffs it. She then makes a face that implies she thinks she might actually want to sample the Scottish pancake. After taking another sniff, she slides the bit of pancake into her mouth and begins chewing. Once she has swallowed that bite, she takes another. And another.

"Ye like it, then?" I say. "Festy cock hasn't offended your senses?"

"No, it's actually pretty good." She eyes the other items I had gathered for her. "Not sure about this big, round thing, though. It looks like an alien egg that might burst out of its shell to eat me."

"If that should happen, I will kill the beastie before it can touch you."

"That's very sweet, Thane. But you do need to explain these other foods to me, please."

I lean forward to rest my elbows on the table and point at the item in question. "Your alien egg is a clootie dumpling. That dish is a rich fruit pudding with ginger, cinnamon, and other spices. Normally, I would provide whisky to accompany your clootie dumping, but I don't recommend drinking in the workplace. I have given you clotted cream, however, and I think you'll enjoy that."

Rebecca samples the dumpling and smiles. "Tastes better than it looks. A lot better."

"Now try the mince and tatties. It's essentially a ground beef stew with carrots and celery. Tatties are potatoes that have been mashed with a bit of cream and butter."

"Now that sounds good."

"Try it, then."

She tastes the mince and tatties, then begins shoveling it into her mouth while trying to speak.

"What did you say, lass? I cannae understand the words when you've got food in your mouth."

Rebecca wipes her mouth with a napkin and gives me a sheepish wee smile. "Sorry. I don't usually devour food like a starved pig. But I didn't eat much breakfast. Too nervous about starting a new job."

"Nervous? You don't seem like the sort who would worry about that."

She shovels a large amount of clootie dumpling into her mouth and chews it while bits fall onto her napkin. Once she's done, she glances around furtively, then slants toward me to whisper, "I got fired from my last job."

No, I didn't expect to hear that confession.

Chapter Six

Rebecca

Oh no, why did I blurt that out? I know better than to tell my new boss that my previous boss gave me the ax. I'd been unemployed and living on my savings until I visited a jobs website and stumbled onto the distillery's listing for a marketing specialist. Now that I've spilled the beans all over my lap, I might as well confess everything to Thane.

"I should explain," I tell him. "First, you should know that, during my first interview, I told Fiona about what happened at my last job. She hired me anyway, though I'm not sure why."

"Fiona is a clever woman. She wouldn't have given you this job unless she was certain you could handle it."

He's being so nice about this. And that means I need to tell him the rest of the story.

I scarf down another mouthful of clootie dumpling first. Stress eating has always been a bad habit of mine. Then I straighten and face Thane. "At my old marketing firm, one of my coworkers was jealous of how successful my campaigns were. She made up lies about me and even faked documents that made it look like I was skimming from the company."

"She thought you were stealing money?"

"Yeah. My boss knew it was a bogus claim, but he had to fire me. That other employee was a founding partner in the company. Her family money had built the business."

Thane narrows his gaze, and I suddenly feel like I'm talking to a caged tiger that might burst out at any moment to kill my enemies. But that's crazy. Thane is easygoing. I've only known him for less than a day, so maybe I shouldn't assume I understand him.

He leans toward me, and his voice drops to a deeper, almost menacing, tone. "Never tell me that woman's name, or I'll be forced to hunt her down and mete out justice."

I wriggle in my chair. "Well, um, that's not really necessary. She was a rotten person, but I don't want her dead."

"Never said I'd kill her. I won't even come within ten miles of the woman."

"Uh-huh." What kind of beast have I unleashed by telling Thane about my former job? It's unsettling but also…a turn-on. Now I need to wonder what's been unleashed inside me. "Could we just forget about this conversation?"

"Aye." He relaxes and smiles. "Best eat your meal. I want to finish teaching you about whisky, so you'll understand how to market it."

"Oh, sure. That sounds great." As long as we stay away from the river. I think it has magical sex powers. Or maybe it's Thane who has that. "But won't Fiona wonder where I've gone? If her new employee disappears."

He plucks a cell phone out of his pants pocket and dials a number. "Would you come over here, please? Of course you know what I mean. You can see me over here sitting across from Rebecca. Good. No smirking, though."

Thane shoves the phone back into his pocket.

And Fiona jogs up to our table. "How may I serve you, my lord?"

She's talking to Thane, not me. He wears the pleasantly neutral expression that seems to be his normal resting face.

"Dinnae be cheeky," he says calmly. "I wanted to let you know that Rebecca will spend the afternoon with me—learning about whisky, not whatever else you're thinking right now."

"What would I possibly have to think about? You two are clearly having a business lunch. What else would our supreme leader be doing with an underling?"

Thane's lips twitch, almost forming a smile. "Go on, ye *smuilceag*. Leave my sight before I sic the hounds on you."

Fiona winks at me, then casually returns to the table in the far corner where she'd been hanging out with her work buddies. She and Thane have a very strange working relationship. I suppose that's because they dated for a while who knows how long ago. They probably had sex too. But that doesn't matter to me.

Thane carries our now-empty trays over to the cart where, apparently, everyone dumps their leftovers. He returns a moment later and politely asks me to go with him. I do that without questioning where we're going or why. He might be strange, but he's very polite. And that makes me trust him. Or maybe I'm willing to go wherever he wants because he's hot and I had sex with him a few hours ago.

I'm so glad my kids aren't here to witness my behavior.

Once we've walked out the cafeteria doors, I get nosy. "You know a lot about me, but I know almost nothing about you."

"Ask me whatever you like."

"That's a dangerously broad invitation."

He glances at me sideways. "I trust you not to take your inquiries too far."

"Okay. Then here's my first question. Have you ever been married?"

"No."

"Do you have any children?"

"No." He gently grasps my elbow to turn me down another corridor. "You have two children, but you haven't mentioned a husband."

"We divorced six years ago, once our kids were out of the house and on their way to starting their own lives." I want to ask an impertinent question, but I don't want to offend him. Thane doesn't seem like the kind of man who would get easily insulted. What the heck, might as well ask. "Why haven't you ever been married?"

"My previous career made it difficult to maintain a relationship."

"That's an intriguing statement. What was your previous career?"

He halts at a set of big metal doors, then swings one wide open. He nods for me to exit first. I let him get away with not answering my question—for now. As it turns out, though, I don't need to press him for a response. As we amble down a dirt path, in the opposite direction from the infamous location of our hot encounter earlier, Thane volunteers the information.

"After university, I was recruited by the Ministry of Defence. For years, I worked as a geospatial analyst." He lifts one brow. "What about you? Have you always been a marketing expert?"

"No, not always. I didn't go to college, so I learned everything I know about marketing from a mentor, Donna Wallace." I pause for a moment, just to watch a lovely little bird that flies by in front of us. Then I continue my story. "Donna gave me a job at her firm when I had zero qualifications, not even a degree. She did that because she believed I had the right skills and talent. She shared all her knowledge and experience from three decades in marketing and advertising."

"Was your mentor the one who sacked you?"

I stop walking, and Thane stops too. "No, Donna didn't fire me. She retired before that happened. It was her successor who gave me the heave-ho. She always hated me because I'd worked my way up."

Thane nods. "I can relate to your situation. When I was brought into the MOD, entry-level employees disliked me because I was given a higher-up job. But I had earned that right by working in a relevant industry while going to university."

I try not to gawk, but it's hard to restrain my surprise. The more I learn about Thane, the more I like him and respect him. We have quite a few things in common too. I wouldn't have expected that. Despite those commonalities, I'm sure we're still miles apart on many things. We come from different worlds, after all.

How long will it take for me to get used to living in Scotland?

That same lovely little bird, or one of its buddies, flies past us again. I halt to watch it swoop down, then soar up into the trees. "What kind of bird was that? I saw one like it earlier, but I have no idea what it was."

"A blue tit."

The critter's bright-yellow belly and bright blue-and-white accents are gorgeous. But when I glance at Thane, I realize one thing is more gorgeous than any bird—Thane Buchanan. His blue eyes and blond hair, combined with his muscles, ensure he owns the title of most beautiful creature on earth.

But I should not get involved with him. Workplace romance is a recipe for disaster.

Thane resumes walking but glances over his shoulder to make sure I'm not lagging too far behind. I catch up to him, and we continue down the path. Soon, I can hear the rushing of water that grows louder gradually as we draw closer to what I assume is the source of the river. Not sure why I believe that. I know nothing about this area or its landscape. Maybe what I'm hearing is a waterfall or a water wheel. Whatever the mystery source of the rushing water is, I still can't see it.

"You seem curious about something," Thane says. "If you tell me about it, I might be able to solve the mystery for you."

Can he read my mind? I sure hope not, otherwise he'll already know I've been fantasizing about him all day while I should be focused on work. "I was just wondering if that sound of water I can barely hear is a waterfall or a water wheel."

Thane's lips tighten into a closed-mouth smile. His eyes glint in a ray of sunlight that seems to spear down through the trees just to light his face.

Oh, jeez, I'm turning into a bad poet. I'm too old to be infatuated.

"You are very clever, Rebecca. Aye, we do have a water wheel here at the distillery. It's a vital part of crafting our whisky. It might be old-fashioned, but we believe tradition and technology both have a role to play."

"That's a great strategy. But have you leveraged that into a marketing strategy?"

"No. Isn't that why we hired you?"

"Yes, of course. But you've been crafting whisky for several years, right? And I would bet nobody realizes how much tradition and technology goes into what you do." I take a half step toward him. "We need to highlight everything that's unique or special about your distillery."

"Aye, go on and do that. Dinnae mind. It's your job, after all."

"But I need your cooperation. You are the face of the distillery, or you should be."

He winces. "You want me to put my face on the bottle."

"No. My ideas are more elegant." It's my turn to wince. "Though I don't have a fully-formed plan yet. It needs a lot more work."

"This is your first day on the job. Give yourself time to acclimate." He offers me his arm. "Shall we continue to the water wheel? It is the starting point for making whisky."

"Lead on. I'm interested in seeing that wheel, since I've never come across one before."

I accept Thane's arm, and we wander down the path together as if we were a couple. But I assume he's just being polite. The man has opened doors for me, and that's always a rarity these days, at least in America. Maybe Scots are always chivalrous.

After a few minutes, we step out of the woods and into a small clearing that surrounds the water wheel. The old wheel is attached to a small stone building that looks quite old too, though both are clearly in good repair.

Thane stretches an arm out toward the wheel and its house. "This is where a Victorian businessman from Edinburgh tried to make a go of distilling his own brand of whisky. He knew nothing about making whisky, so naturally, his attempt failed."

"How long have you owned this property?"

"I don't own the water wheel or its house. That belongs to a conservation trust that maintains the building for historic purposes." He shoves his hands into his pants pockets as he gazes at the big wheel. "But I thought you should see how whisky distilling used to be done. And I wanted to finish telling you about the importance of the river, which is still a vital element of crafting *Collaidh Sgeul-Rùin* Black Label."

"I'm ready to hear all about it."

"The soil here is black because of the peat layer that runs beneath this entire region. It's a vital element of Scotch whisky. But I need to explain the process in order, so you won't be confused."

I've been carrying my portfolio, so now I open it and pluck my pen out of its little holder. "I'm ready to take notes."

His lips curl up slightly. "You make taking notes seem almost erotic."

"Let's not go there again. Could you please just be my boss right now?"

"Aye." His lips curl up even more. "Afraid ye cannae keep your hands off me, eh?"

"You kissed me first."

"Then you begged me to shag you."

"Okay, we're even on the quickie-in-the-woods front. Let's move on." I tap my pen on the pad of paper in my portfolio. "Give me the step-by-step process of making Scotch whisky." I wag my pen at him. "No talking about kissing or sex, and no flirtation. Got it?"

"Aye." He winks. "I can do that. But can you?"

"Yes, of course I can."

I said that, but honestly…I have no idea if I can keep that promise.

Chapter Seven

Thane

The lass doesn't seem sure of her ability to resist me, and frankly, I'm not sure I can resist her either. This has never happened to me before. But I know how to control my passions, thanks to years of experience at the MOD. No, I will not explain to Rebecca that my job as a geospatial analyst often involved more than analyzing data. Most of what I did at the MOD is still classified, at any rate. I was never a spy, not precisely, and I certainly never did the things my mate Logan MacTaggart did during his time with MI6.

Right now, I need to focus on explaining the whisky distilling process to the beautiful, sensual, passionate woman who stands in front of me.

I probably shouldn't have thought the words passionate and sensual. That has nothing to do with my distillery.

Be professional, you eejit.

I roll my shoulders back and clear my throat. "The process of distilling whisky begins with water. That's why, in the olden days, every distillery would have a wheel like this one to transfer the water to the main building where all the magic happens."

Rebecca swiftly writes things down on her pad of paper. The pink tip of her tongue sticks out between her lips a wee bit. It's adorable. And it makes me want to kiss her. I want to smack my palm on my forehead to snap myself out of that idea, but Rebecca would think I'm a bampot if I did that. Many people think I'm strange, but so far, none have called me a raving lunatic. I'd like to keep that streak going.

Once she finishes taking notes, she raises her head to gaze at me steadily, waiting for more information.

I start walking up the trail again with Rebecca at my side, mostly so that I won't need to look at her. Aye, I'm a coward. Better that than being accused of sexual harassment. "We're heading toward the main building again, but we'll bypass the areas you've seen already. You're about to see where we begin the process of distilling whisky."

"Can't deny this is intriguing. I've never even thought about how liquor is made."

"Not just liquor. Single-malt Scotch whisky." As we approach a large set of doors, I pull them open and wave for the lass to go first. Every time I've done that, she has seemed a wee bit surprised. "Follow me. You're entering the bowels of the operation."

She smiles and bumps her shoulder into me. "You're enjoying the chance to turn this into a dramatic reveal, aren't you?"

"Aye. What's wrong with that?"

"Nothing. I like it."

She is an unusual lass, that's for dead certain.

I guide her down a corridor and stop at another large door, though this one is pulled open rather than swung open. It's more like a metal barn door than the interior sort. I drag it open.

Rebecca's eyes widen. "Wow, you're incredibly strong. That thing looks like it must weigh a ton."

"Not literally. But aye, it is quite heavy." I enter the room beyond first and keep a hand on her back as we cross the large, high empty space. I stop us in a spot where small cardboard boxes lie on the floor. And I pluck up a cloth mask. "Dinnae want to inhale barley dust. I recommend wearing a dust mask while you're in this room."

She grabs a mask too and doesn't even complain about it. I despise the ruddy things, but in this case, it's necessary. Inhaling barley dust can't be good for a body. I keep a hand on Rebecca's elbow as we walk around the room and I explain more about the malting process. I point out the sacks of barley, which was grown in the Highlands in an area further west of here. The grain has been soaked for three days in the fresh water from the river, so it's now ready for the next phase.

"For that," I tell Rebecca, "we need to move into another room where a few laddies will be working on the malting floor. That's where the grain is aerated and turned every so often to encourage the barley to germinate."

"Why does it need to germinate?"

"Because that process makes the barley ferment better. Then starch will be converted to sugar and, eventually, become alcohol."

"This is all so fascinating. I had no idea the process of making whisky was so complex and exacting."

I can't deny that I'm enjoying the chance to explain all of this to Rebecca. She genuinely wants to learn. I don't often get the chance to show off my knowledge and expertise. Even in the early days, when I'd been directly involved with every step of the process, I hadn't served as a tour guide the way I am now. It's invigorating.

As I'm leading her across the malting floor, I tell her more about how whisky is crafted. "Every step of the process must be handled with care to ensure every element of the whisky is in the right proportion. Too much or too little of anything might ruin the flavor. What you see here"—I wave toward the grain that's been laid out on the floor—"is perfectly malted. Not too much germination, but just enough."

"Who decides when it's just right?"

"The master maltster."

"And who is that? One of these guys in this room?"

A smoky chuckle draws Rebecca's attention to one of the gents manning the malting floor. Dougal Murray strokes his long gray beard, smiling with an impish gleam in his eyes. "No, lass, I am not the master maltster. Only one man is allowed to take on that sacred duty, and he is standing beside you."

Rebecca swivels her head toward me. "You are the master maltster?"

"Aye."

"Does that mean you visit the malting floor often?"

Dougal chuckles again. "Dinnae know Thane well, do ye? He's been known to sleep on the malting floor just so he won't miss the moment when the barley is perfectly germinated."

"Haud yer wheesht, Dougal. Ye know full well that I only did that back in the days when we didn't have many employees."

"That might be true. But you're still obsessed with finding the perfect moment to kiln the grain."

"No, I'm obsessed with crafting the perfect bottle of whisky." I steer Rebecca away from the malting floor and toward another doorway. "Get back to work, Dougal. Or are you planning to stare at Rebecca's erse instead?"

"Dinnae worry, Thane. The lass is yours."

"She doesn't belong to anyone."

But aye, I would love for her to be mine. I can't do that, though. We both have jobs to do, and romance plays no role in our work. Besides, I'm far too busy keeping tabs on the malting process to get involved with a woman.

As Rebecca and I exit the malting room, I gently steer her toward a doorway on the left side of the corridor. Naturally, I pull the door open for her. Every time I do that, she smiles. The door shuts behind us, and we halt so I can tell her about what's happening in this area.

"What you saw on the malting floor," I explain, "was the process that creates key enzymes that are essential for whisky. Now, the dried malt will be ground into a grist. Hot water is added, and the mixture will be gradually heated to release the sugars."

"I never knew that creating whisky required so many steps."

"Now, it's time to add yeast. Those wee beasties devour the sugar, transforming it into alcohol."

Her brows wrinkle. "Beasties?"

"Aye. Yeast is a living organism."

"Oh. Right. I do remember that now. What's next in the process?"

"Distillation. We distill our whisky twice to get rid of any solids that might still be in there."

She jots down more notes on her pad of paper while tapping her tongue on her bottom front teeth. Once she's done writing, she holds her portfolio to her chest and meets my gaze. "This is very fascinating and useful. But this all sounds like the usual method of doing things. You know, the way everyone crafts whisky. What I need to know now is if you have anything unusual that goes into the process. The more unique your whisky is, the more likely it is that I'll be able to create a memorable marketing campaign."

"I see." What can I tell her? Aye, we do have unusual methods here, but I would be revealing trade secrets. Well, she does work for me, indirectly. And employees are required to sign a nondisclosure agreement. Might as well let the lass do her job as thoroughly as possible. "Since you signed an NDA, I would like to take you into the building where the casks are stored to explain our secret methods."

"That sounds promising. And very intriguing."

"Follow me, then. We'll be leaving the main building to visit the dunnage warehouse."

"Okay. What is that, exactly?"

I give her what I hope looks like an enigmatic smile. I might be enjoying this a wee bit too much, letting Rebecca in on my whisky-making secrets. Dinnae care.

We cross through the malting floor again on our way out of the building, and Dougal winks at me while nodding toward Rebecca. The *cacan* is implying something that I do not appreciate. The lass would undoubtedly be furious if she noticed what Dougal did. I've known the man long enough to understand the meaning of his gestures. He was encouraging me to do something that I should not under any circumstances even contemplate doing.

No, I will not have a poke with Rebecca ever again.

I keep a hand on her back while we trudge down the path to the wood-and-brick structure set a wee ways from the main building. Pushing the door open, I wait for Rebecca to enter first. She seems to have stopped being surprised by the way I open doors for her, since she doesn't flash me a smile this time. Instead, she tiptoes into the darkened interior, glancing about as if she expects a monster to leap at her.

Once she has passed the threshold, I walk inside and flick on the light switch.

Rebecca winces, shielding her eyes with one hand. "Does whisky have to sleep in the dark? Or do you just like surprising women that way?"

"Why waste money by keeping the lights on all the time? Whisky isn't afraid of the dark." I raise my brows. "Are you?"

"Afraid of the dark? No, of course not." She hugs her portfolio to her chest while scanning the interior. "What did you say this building was called?"

"The dunnage warehouse. We store the casks here to let the whisky age and soak up the flavors of the wood."

She studies her surroundings, beginning with the concrete walkway that stretches from the doors straight down the center of the building. Then she swivels her head left and right to take in the sight of the whisky barrels that lie on their sides in rows three casks high.

Finally, she turns toward me. "Last year, I visited a Jack Daniels facility. But that was just for fun. My kids dragged me there."

"You let children visit a whisky distillery?"

"They were twenty-one at the time, so of legal age. The tour was mostly a historical thing about the history of Jack Daniels himself and how the distillery evolved."

"Didn't you learn about the distilling process? I assumed a famous outfit like Jack Daniels would include such things on their tours."

She shrugs. "My mind wandered during that part. It wasn't as intriguing as getting a personal tour from the master distiller of a Highland whisky brand."

"Ah, well, I'm glad to know Scots do that better too."

"What do you mean 'too'?"

"Scots do everything better than anyone else on earth does. Didn't anyone tell you that?" I tap her nose with one finger. "We are the best at everything, *gràidh*." I lean forward to gaze directly into her eyes. "And I do mean *everything*."

"Uh-huh. Arrogance isn't sexy."

"Of course it is—when it's done the Scottish way."

Rebecca flips her portfolio open and pulls out her pen. "Tell me what these wooden barrels are for."

"They are not simply wooden barrels." I spread my arms to encompass the entire contents of the building. "These are casks that hold the precious amber liquid until it's ready to be bottled. Once the whisky is distilled, it comes here to the dunnage warehouse where it will sleep until it has reached its premium age."

She's been scribbling furiously on her pad of paper, so focused on the task that she can't tear her focus away from the pages.

"Are you ready to digest more information?" I ask. "Or should I sit down and wait until you're done in an hour or so?"

The lass lifts her head to squint at me. The slant of her lips tells me she isn't annoyed. Rebecca is teasing me. "I need every sliver of information—about the whisky and about you."

She points her pen at me.

Cannae help chuckling. "I am not the focus of this operation. The whisky is."

"But Fiona told me you're a man of mystery. Even though she dated you for a while, she still doesn't understand you." Rebecca moves even closer to me, so close in fact that I can smell her natural scent wafting around me. "I need to do a deep dive on this facility—and you, Mr. Buchanan."

"Ahmno as intriguing as you think. Best focus on the whisky."

"Nope. Can't do that." She moves closer still, and her tits brush against my chest. "I will be interrogating you, Thane. Get ready for it."

Interrogate me? She has no idea what sort of man I am. No one gets information out of me unless I allow them to do it. But I can't deny I might enjoy letting her try. It could be quite…erotic.

I doubt that's what she has in mind, though.

Maybe I can change her mind.

Chapter Eight

Rebecca

I follow Thane down the strip of concrete that runs the length of the dunnage warehouse. I had already known that making whisky requires oak barrels, but I have a feeling Thane doesn't stick to the usual methods of doing anything, so I'm not at all surprised that he has a "secret" method. He promised to tell me all about the process, from start to finish, and I believe he will stick to that vow.

We pass by row after row of casks that look the same. I assume they're all made from the same type of oak. They must also hold the same flavor of whisky, or whatever they call the variations. As far as I know, Thane only makes one kind, the version he labels with that unpronounceable Gaelic phrase. It means "sensual secret," but I have no idea what goes into the distilling process.

I stop and wait a couple of seconds for Thane to realize I'm not walking right beside him.

He spins around and scrunches his brows. "What are ye doing, lass?"

"Tell me about these barrels. What's in them, how they're constructed, how the flavors of the wood affect the whisky."

He sighs. "I did promise to explain. All right. Let's walk over here to this cask." He lays an arm across the round top of the barrel. "This is *Collaidh Sgeul-Rùin*, our first generation of whisky. This vintage has been aged for seven years. Would ye like to taste it?"

"Yes, I would love to."

He crooks a finger at me. "Then come over here."

I approach the cask but halt on the opposite side from where Thane stands. He tells me to wait, then jogs off down the concrete aisle. I twist my head around to watch him, but I can't figure out what he's doing. He disappears down the first row of casks, reappearing a moment later—now carrying something in his hand.

Thane stops beside me and holds up what looks like a spigot. He uses a pocket knife to pull a round piece out of the cask's top, inserting the spigot into the hole. Then he rolls the barrel gently until the spigot is on the bottom. Finally, he pulls a shot glass out of his pocket and pours a measure of whisky for me.

"Here you are," he says as he hands me the glass. "Your first taste of the most sensual and unusual whisky in the world."

I accept the glass and take a delicate sip. Since I'm not a whisky drinker, I have no idea what to expect. My first sip is tantalizing, but I can't decipher the elements of the flavor. Sweet, for sure, though it's not overwhelming. I lick my lips before I take another sip and let it sit on my tongue for a moment.

Then I hum with pleasure. "This is delicious and not what I expected. It tastes sweet but also fruity and smoky, with hints of nutmeg and vanilla." I try one more sip. "Mm, do I detect heather and honey? The whisky has nice body with an earthy but sweet finish."

His brows shoot up. "Thought you weren't a whisky drinker, but you described my single malt perfectly."

"I like to take part in the occasional wine tasting."

"Ah, that does explain it." He smiles and winks. "You will certainly appreciate my new whisky varieties, then."

"Tell me all about them." I throw back the last bit of whisky and let out a satisfied sigh. "With this variety alone, I could come up with a marketing campaign that would skyrocket your sales."

"You're that confident?"

"Absolutely. This whisky is incredible. And with you as the face of the company—"

"No. I do not want my face on the bottle or in adverts."

"Come on, Thane. This is your whisky. Why are you so camera shy?"

He pours himself a shot of the good stuff and knocks it back. "Dinnae want my face to be shown in public, that's all. End of story. Work around that limitation."

"But you swore you'd share all your secrets with me."

He scrunches his lips, twisting them side to side. Then he blows out a breath, and his shoulders wilt. "I did make that vow, and I never renege on a promise. But let me show you the newer versions before you interrogate me."

"I would love to taste all of them."

Thane chuckles softly. "Take it easy, lass. Dinnae want to get drunk on your first day at work."

"Oh, please. I never get drunk. Rarely drink at all, except for the occasional glass of wine—and that's only at tasting parties."

"Your unfamiliarity with whisky makes you vulnerable to overdoing it. Take my advice and only have one sip of each variety I'm about to show you."

I salute. "Yes, sir."

"Are you sure you aren't already tipsy?"

"My salute was sarcasm. I'm not drunk. Your whisky is amazing, but it's not strong enough to get me tipsy after a few baby sips."

He shepherds me further down the aisle to a row of casks that have multicolored wood. Then he pats the barrel. "This vintage was our first experiment with making casks that have three types of wood in them—sessile oak, hazel, and wild cherry."

"What do you call the whisky that was aged in these barrels?"

"The one you tasted was *Collaidh Sgeul-Rùin* Black Label. It's a single malt. This newer version is also single malt, but it has a richer flavor profile thanks to the three woods in the casks. So, we call it *Collaidh Sgeul-Rùin* Triple Threat."

"Are you serious?" I shake my head at him. "You gave your whisky a threatening name. That's bad marketing, Thane. Have you actually sold any of this type of whisky?"

He winces and scratches his cheek. "Not as yet."

"Probably because of the name." I nod toward the cask. "May I taste it?"

"Aye, of course." He brings out his spigot to pour a small amount of whisky into the shot glass, then offers it to me. "Sip it slowly and carefully. You aren't used to Scotch yet, and I dinnae want you to be shocked or to vomit all over the casks."

"I'll try not to soil your barrels. But I'm not as wimpy as you seem to think."

"Never meant to imply you are 'wimpy.' But Fiona thinks it's quite a bit stronger than the Black Label, which is itself stronger than average."

"Okay. I'll take it nice and slow." I accept the shot glass and take a dainty sip. "This is interesting, bolder and yet sweeter too. I can taste flavors that I can't quite place yet. Do you want to tell me? Or should I keep sipping?"

"I will share my secrets with you, if only to spare you from getting tipsy. You have tasted quite a bit of whisky in the last few minutes."

"Well, go on and tell me. Please."

He sets a hand on the cask and taps one finger while he shares his secrets with me. "Sweet cicely, wild damson, wild garlic, and elderflower—for a start. Then there's a touch of elderberry and rose hips, not to mention meadowsweet."

"You crammed all that into one type of whisky? No wonder it tastes like nothing I've ever drunk before."

"My newest variation has a few of the elements in Triple Threat. But it also offers one final, top-secret ingredient." He raises his hand when I'm about to remind him of his promise. "I know, I know. You wanted to learn about everything, and I will tell you my secret ingredient. But I think I should show it to you rather than describing it."

"I'm fine with that."

He leads me down to the last row of casks, then gives me a small amount of whisky to drink. This must be his new ultra-secret variation. Thane asks me to close my eyes while I taste it so I can "let the flavors and aromas take hold." I see no reason not to follow his suggestion, so I do it.

My first sip makes my eyes fly open. "Wow. That's…unusual."

"Do you like it?"

I take another sip and shiver a little. "Holy cow, this is amazing. It makes me feel… Oh, never mind."

"You can tell me, lass. Nothing shocks me."

"Let me try one more sip first." When I do that, I shiver again. And I experience the same bizarrely good sensation. "The first time was not a fluke. I actually do feel…um…"

"Aroused?"

"Yeah."

"In what way?" He touches my arm. "Relax, *gràidh*. I'm only interested in whether you like the whisky. This isn't an attempt to seduce you."

"Uh-huh." But something about this variation is arousing me in more ways than I would have expected. And I suddenly find myself confessing all of that to a man I met this morning. "It arouses my taste buds for sure, with many of the same flavors as the previous version but with hints of other things too. It's almost spicy and also not. It's almost sweet yet also not. It feels like my nerves have been sensitized in the best way, and I feel turned on by the complex array of flavors."

"You have described it perfectly. Rebecca, you might be a whisky savant."

I laugh, but it comes out as a snort. "Please don't go overboard on praising my taste buds. I'm no savant. But I am wondering what your secret ingredient is."

"Time to show you."

We exit the dunnage warehouse at the opposite end from where we started, then make our way down the trail into the woods. I can hear the river, but we're clearly heading upstream and away from the main complex. Thane turns down a narrower trail, taking us away from the river. Within a minute at most, we've reached a small hothouse.

Thane opens the door for me. "Lasses first."

I have never met a man like him before. He's polite and deferential toward women but also strong and virile too. Now, I'm also realizing he's creative and determined to make his company a success. Those are all traits that make him very attractive—as a business owner and a lover. Not that I ever plan to have sex with him again.

But I accept his chivalry and enter the hothouse first.

He shuts the door behind us. "Take a look around, Rebecca. Tell me what you think my secret ingredient is."

"I see plants. They seem to be growing some type of crop." I inch down the center aisle, studying the plants, but I still can't figure out what exactly they are. "I would guess these are some kind of peppers or chilies."

He grins. "You have a brilliant mind. Aye, you are correct. But these aren't simply 'some type of peppers or chilies.' They are a unique hybrid created by me after years of trial and error."

"What species went into this mix?"

"Cayenne Buist, a milder yellow pepper. Aji Dulce, another milder one that's somewhat sweet. It's a Caribbean variety. And finally, African Bird's Eye which is moderately high on the heat scale."

"I'm not normally a fan of hot peppers, but the way those flavors mix with the other ingredients really turns me on."

Why do I keep using words like "turns me on" and "aroused"? It's inappropriate at work, but then, I'm only describing the chilies.

Thane gives me a sneaky smile. "Want to taste the peppers? Then you'll have the most information possible about my newest whisky."

"No thanks. I ate a teeny tiny piece of a ghost pepper once, and I was coughing for ten minutes after that." I open up my portfolio again and jot down some notes. "Sipping that whisky gave me all the heat I want. It is delicious, though, and like no other Scotch I've ever tasted. I can't wait to get started on a new marketing campaign."

He watches me with his lips curling into a cute little smile. Thane clearly enjoyed showing me all his secrets, and I can't deny I enjoyed learning all about the distillery and his new variations. But I still don't know enough about the man himself.

"I haven't given you a proper look at the most important room," Thane says. "We should end your tour where the stills are."

Though I had gotten a glimpse of those weirdly shaped stills, I accept his invitation. Once he has told me about that room, I will know everything about this operation.

Once we're inside the main building again, he shepherds me down the long hallway that ends at the room where the whisky is distilled. Fortunately, he doesn't take me up onto the metal walkway. I have no desire to repeat the calamity that happened this morning. At least I learned an important lesson.

Never wear high heels in a distillery.

As we stroll among the stills, I can't help noticing their strange shape. "Why are the stills shaped like giant onions?"

"I think they look more like a man's *bagais*, or perhaps a woman's *cíoch*."

"Uh, what strange Gaelic words did you just spout?"

He slants his head down to murmur into my ear, "I said the stills look more like a man's bollocks or a woman's tits."

"Oh, I get it. 'Bollocks' means balls, right?"

"Aye." He straightens and eyes me with appreciation. "How did you know what 'bollocks' means? You're American, and I was under the impression you had never visited the UK before."

"I haven't. But my son and daughter live in England."

"Do they? Why haven't you visited them?"

"Well, um, I..." Don't want to answer his question, obviously. It's humiliating. But I like Thane, and he's been very helpful in getting me up to speed on the distillery, so maybe I do owe him a little bit of truth. "I couldn't afford to travel that far. I've been unemployed for long enough that my savings had nearly run dry."

Chapter Nine

Thane

The more I learn about this woman, the more I admire and respect her. She worked hard to become a successful marketing executive, only to be sacked for no good reason. Then she struggled to find work. And I'm dead sure that during all that time, she never complained once about her lot in life. She clearly loves being a marketing guru. Most importantly, though, she's willing to take risks. And I dinnae mean only that she took a chance on coming to work here. She also risked her taste buds by sampling my unusual whisky concoctions.

Yet I have one question about what she just told me. "You were skint? But you wear designer clothes."

"I bought this suit for a job interview—the one with Fiona."

"Ah, yes, she did fly to America for that." I touch her arm. "I'm sorry you've had such a hard time lately."

She shrugs. "That's life. Sometimes it's amazing, and sometimes it sucks. But just so you know, I'm not struggling financially anymore. My signing bonus for this job put me in good financial shape. I'm grateful to you and Fiona for being so generous with my salary too."

"That was all Fiona's doing." I twist one side of my mouth into a rueful expression. "And most of what you see here at the distillery was made possible by the generous donations of my friends and family. They invested in the company."

"What's wrong with having investors? You clearly don't like the idea, but it's how virtually every company gets a leg up."

"Aye, but most companies aren't funded by the owner's mates and family members."

She hugs her portfolio to her chest, as she has often done today. "Do your 'mates' and relatives feel like you're freeloading?"

"Of course not. They're kind, generous blokes and lasses."

"Would you mind if I talked to some of your investors? Strictly to understand their roles in the organization and what goals they have in mind for the company."

I groan. "You can try that, but it won't give you anything useful. My mates and family have no expectations for monetary compensation or the like. They all told me to 'do what you like, laddie' and also suggested that the only dividend they want is first dibs on a bottle of each new vintage."

"You have amazing people on your side. They must really believe in your vision for the distillery."

"Well, ah, I reckon they must. I only hope I won't disappoint them."

Rebecca's lips curve into a sweet, closed-mouth smile. "I'm positive that no one will ever be disappointed by you. The more I've learned about this company, the more certain I am that you've really got something special here."

I check the time on my mobile. "It's getting late, already well past your normal work hours. You should go home and get some rest."

"Can't believe it's that late. Time flies, huh?"

"Aye, it does." I lean forward a wee bit, then abruptly stop and pull back. I'd been about to kiss her goodbye. What the bloody hell is wrong with me? Instead, I shake her hand. "Ah, good night, Rebecca. I look forward to seeing what sort of marketing campaign you dream up."

"Thank you. And good night, Thane. I appreciate you taking so much time out of your day to show me around."

And then she walks away.

I remain rooted to this spot while I watch her figure recede in the waning sunlight. She doesn't glance back, not that I expected she might. I like Rebecca Taylor. I like her very much. The lass is not only bonnie but also clever and a delightful woman. We shagged this morning. I still can't wrap my mind around that fact. It feels like a strange, intense dream. But it actually happened.

Have I ever believed in love at first sight? No, of course not. It's a barmy, romantic idea. I still can't believe I seduced her in the forest. And yet, somehow, we managed to behave like mature adults and put that incident aside to conduct our business. Now, I need to go on behaving in a professional manner and forget about what we did by the river earlier.

I am not the sort of man any woman should want to date.

As I turn away from the car park, I shove my hands into my trouser pockets and hunch my shoulders. I'm halfway to the doors of the main building when a strange noise catches my attention. Is it an animal? No, it sounds electronic. I spin round to search for the source, hurrying toward the car park.

Then I notice Rebecca's car is still there, though it seems to be running. That means her car isn't broken. The sound of muffled rock music emanates from the vehicle. The engine is running, and the headlights are on, so I can see her inside the car singing along with the music. Singing rather boisterously. She claps her hands too and bobs her head in time with the beats. She also shimmies her hips, which I can tell based on the movements of her upper body. But when the lass begins to play air guitar, I cannae stop myself from grinning and chuckling.

Her enthusiasm for the music is adorable. I wonder what artist she's listening to, but I won't interrupt to ask her.

Rebecca glances my way, and she freezes. Her eyes fly wide. Her mouth falls open. She frantically moves the dials on the radio, accidentally raising the volume even more before she finally turns it off. Then she rolls down the passenger window.

I bend over and peer inside the car. "Having a cracking time, eh? I love music too, but I never play it that loud."

"Sorry. I just needed a little pick-me-up before I drive back to my apartment." Her eyes go even wider. "Oh, shit. I didn't mean that working here is an ordeal or depressing or—"

"Hush, *gràidh*. You have no need to explain anything. But you've had a long and eventful first day, so you should get some rest."

"You are such a nice man. I promise not to blare music in my office."

I rest my arm on the car door, leaning in a wee bit. "Dinnae worry. You can always wear headphones if you need a pick-me-up at work. I sometimes listen to bagpipe bands if I feel tired on the job."

"Think I'll stick to Duran Duran."

"You like them? So do I."

"Really?" Her face lights up. "You aren't just saying that to make me feel better?"

"No. I honestly enjoy their music."

She unhooks her seatbelt and slants toward me. "Have you heard their Halloween album? It's amazing."

"Can't say I have heard it." I reach out to tap the tip of her nose. "Best get home. You have a lot of work ahead of you here."

I back away from the car.

She rolls up the window and fastens her seatbelt, then waves at me as she drives away. I wave back.

That woman is wonderful. I could fall for her.

No, I cannot ever do that. For her sake, I must maintain a distance between us from now on.

Aye, because I've had such great luck staying away from her so far.

Once I verify that all my employees have gone home, including Fiona, I finally leave the distillery and head back to my house. It's small but comfortable, and I live on the outskirts of Loch Fairbairn with no close neighbors. Maybe I do cherish privacy more than most people. I have my reasons for that, reasons I will never share with anyone.

In the morning, I arrive at the distillery well before anyone else does. At least, that's what I assume. But as I stride down the hall, heading for my office, I notice that the door to Rebecca's office is partway open. Did she forget to close it last night? She can lock her office, though no one else here bothers to do that. As I reach the door, I can hear her humming.

I push the door open. "Rebecca? What are you doing here so early?"

She's bobbing her head rhythmically while humming.

The lass must be listening to music. I can't see headphones, but she might have worn earbuds. So, I march up behind her and rip one of those wee things out of her ear.

She shrieks and jumps. Her chair slides backward, and she's about to hit the floor on her erse.

I catch her from behind. Now the backside of her body is molded to my front. "Take it easy, lass. You could've cracked your skull on this hard floor."

She spins round and stumbles backward. "What were you doing? I nearly had a heart attack."

"At least it was only a near catastrophe, then." I right her chair and pat the seat. "Rest your lovely erse, Rebecca. I apologize for frightening you, but you aren't meant to be here this early."

"Fiona told me I have a master key, which means I can get into the building anytime I want." She hesitantly sits down on the chair. "I wanted to get an early start. I've got a ton of work to do."

I set my erse on the corner of her desk. "What's the rush? The distillery won't vanish tomorrow."

"Maybe not. But last night, I had a vision of the perfect marketing strategy."

"Still not seeing what the rush is."

Rebecca wriggles to get fully seated on her chair, then rolls it forward so she can rest her arms on the desktop. "Valentine's Day is in five weeks."

"Aye."

"Don't you see?" She taps her finger on her desktop calendar. "Valentine's Day. It's the perfect way to promote the distillery."

"You're wanting everyone to get drunk and have inappropriate sex, and somehow that will sell more whisky."

She rolls her eyes. "Obviously not. But your whisky is sensual, delicious, and irresistible. Valentine's is the perfect tool for promoting it."

"Dinnae understand. Valentine's Day is about sappy cards and boxes of chocolate, not single-malt Scotch."

Rebecca crosses her legs and sets her hands on the arms of her chair. "Do you trust me to create a fantastic marketing campaign for your business? Or would you rather fire me?"

"I do not want to sack you. But I've never advertised my distillery before, and it feels a bit, ah…"

"Sleazy?"

"Aye. But that's my preconception, and I'm sure other people wouldn't feel the same way. So, the answer to your question is yes, I trust you to find the best ways to promote the company."

"Should I keep you in the loop about everything related to the marketing? Or would you rather be in the dark until I'm done?"

"I reckon it'll be best if you don't give me a daily update."

She clasps her hands over her lap. "I'm happy to hear you say that. Delegating authority can be stressful, but you'll be glad you handed the reins over to me, I promise."

A bizarre image appears in my mind—Rebecca on all fours with a bridle strapped to her forehead while I stand behind her gently slapping the reins on her erse. We're both naked in my fantasy. Then I hand the reins to Rebecca, and she begins to slap my erse.

Bod an Donais. I'm getting aroused, and that is not a good thing at work.

"Thane, are you okay?"

"What? Oh, aye, I'm fine." I rise and straighten my posture. "I'll leave you to your work. I'm sure Fiona will be happy to help you in any way she can."

"She already made that offer yesterday."

"Good. Will I see you at lunch?"

The lass shrugs. "Not sure. I might grab something from the cafeteria and bring it back to my office."

"But you need to take a break at least once during the day."

She smiles, and her cheeks dimple. "Thank you for worrying about me, but I've been taking care of myself since I was eighteen."

"Aye, of course you have. Well, then, I'll say goodbye."

While I stride toward the door, I glance back to see Rebecca already hunched over her desk thumbing through papers. The lass does seem to have a workaholic streak, but that's not a healthy attitude. I've just shut her office door behind me when I make an abrupt decision.

I will do whatever I can to ensure she doesn't burn herself out by working too bloody hard. Do I have a plan for how to accomplish that feat? Not at the moment. But I will come up with one.

By the time I reach my office, I've cemented my resolve to keep that lass from burning herself out. Five weeks to boost sales doesn't sound like a great deal of time, especially considering that virtually no one knows about my company except friends and family. Aye, Rebecca will most likely work longer hours than she should.

I sit down at my desk. The chair looks and feels like new because I rarely sit on it. My work is on the malting floor, in the dunnage warehouse, in the hothouse, in the room where the distilling actually happens. That means everywhere except in an office.

Why am I sitting here staring down at my own feet?

I lift my head to gaze out the window, where I can see the huge stills and all the equipment required to keep them running smoothly. Despite the view, I can think of nothing but Rebecca Taylor. Maybe I should take a page from her book and make notes. That might inspire ideas about how to save Rebecca from overwork. So, I hunt about in my desk until I find a small pad of paper, and I begin jotting things down.

Why I care so much about her work habits is…something I'll consider later.

Chapter Ten

Rebecca

All morning, I've done nothing but pour over the copious notes I took yesterday when Thane showed me around the distillery and gave me a crash course on how to make single-malt Scotch. The Black Label version, which was Thane's first successful attempt, tastes delicious. The Triple Threat variety offers more exotic flavors, and I love the way it tastes and the way it feels on my tongue, not to mention the way it slides down my throat on a stream of warmth.

But his newest creation blew me away.

If I can't concoct a phenomenal marketing plan for that whisky and make it a worldwide hit, then I'd better just run away to Antarctica. I won't deserve to call myself a marketing expert anymore. I've created some great campaigns that I'm very proud of, but I have never helped to rocket a brand up into the stratosphere. Yet the moment I tasted Thane's whisky, I got a shivery feeling of excitement, as if this might be my big moment—and Thane's too. Together, we can make everyone crave Thane Buchanan's creations.

But my first task is to rename the company and the whiskies.

Thane and Fiona have both left me in charge of the marketing. But I will, of course, share my ideas with them before I make drastic changes.

I skim through my notes, drumming my pen on the desk. I can't even pronounce the company's name—*Collaidh Sgeul-Rùin*—not even in my head. I love what the words mean. "Sensual secret" is an apt description for Thane's whisky. But how can we convince people to buy it when they can't pronounce the name? I need to come up with alternatives that he will approve of, a task that will take considerable time.

For the entire morning, I struggle to come up with ideas. I pace the entire width of my office, over and over, while listening to my favorite pop band. I have my earbuds plugged into my phone, and I hold it in one hand while making vague gestures with my other hand. Maybe I am a little strange, but I don't care. A woman approaching fifty isn't supposed to love eighties pop, right? Oh, who cares. I love this music, and it activates all my brain cells.

I drop onto my chair every so often, but then return to pacing. No ideas yet. When my absolute favorite song comes on, I can't stop myself from singing along with "Hungry Like the Wolf." Who wouldn't start singing along to that song? It's an eighties classic.

Soon, I'm dancing too. With my eyes closed. Probably not the smartest idea.

I whirl around, opening my eyes. And I jump.

Thane is standing just inside the doorway smiling at me. His blue eyes seem to glitter in the light steaming in from outside the window. That smile broadens into a grin.

I rip the earbuds out. "Thane? Why didn't you knock?"

He chuckles. "I did. Three times."

"Really? I'm so sorry." I toss my phone and the earbuds onto my desk. "That was highly unprofessional behavior. I shouldn't dance and sing at work."

"Why not? This isn't the international headquarters of a soulless megacorporation. We're a family here."

"You don't think I'm slightly insane? Or at least very immature?"

He leans against the doorjamb with one hip cocked and one hand stuffed into his pants pocket. "Everyone thinks my bum's oot the windae. That means I'm off my rocker. So no, I would never criticize your behavior."

"You really are an unusual man. But I like that."

He lifts one brow. "You've known me for a day and a half. Best wait until you've gotten to know me better before you decide to like me."

Sometimes he says the strangest things. And since I've developed an insatiable curiosity about him, I can't stop myself. I clear my throat and lift my chin. "It's time to interrogate you."

"It's lunchtime. We should eat first."

"But then you will answer my questions. Right?"

He pushes away from the jamb and steps out into the hall. "Hurry, lass, or we'll be enjoying the leftovers from lunch instead of an actual meal."

I know he's delaying on purpose, and for now, I'll allow him to do that. Maybe after a week or so he'll feel more comfortable talking to me about his secrets, whatever those might be.

Fiona joins us for lunch, and Thane sits beside her while I'm alone on the other side of the table. He mostly sits there silently eating while we ladies have a chat. When she brings up the subject of dating, and the fact that neither Thane nor I have a significant other, he's clearly uncomfortable with the topic. I manage to steer the conversation away from dating, thankfully. But Thane still doesn't say much. He eats and avoids looking at me. That's pretty much it.

As we're leaving the cafeteria, Fiona catches Thane by the arm and pulls him aside, far enough away that I can't hear what they're saying. Based on her facial expressions, it looks like she's teasing him about something. He clearly does not appreciate whatever she said.

Thane marches down the hall and out of sight.

Fiona walks with me back to my office.

"Lunch was fun," I tell her. "We should do that every day."

"Aye, we should." She eyes me with curiosity. "Are you eating alone every night in your apartment?"

Not sure if that's a proper work-related question, but I won't complain. I like Fiona, and I'm sure she's just being friendly. "Yes, I am dining solo."

"That must be lonely. Tonight, you must come to dinner at my house. Domhnall would love to meet you."

Well, since I haven't met that many people since I moved to Scotland, I can't deny her invitation appeals to me. "I would love to have dinner with you guys. What time should I be there?"

"Domhnall will pick us up in the car park after work."

"But I'll need my car to get home."

"Tosh." She waves a hand dismissively. "I will give you a ride back to your apartment."

"Um, I still won't have any way to get to the distillery in the morning."

Her smile turns mischievous. "Dinnae worry about that."

I should probably worry about what that cryptic statement means, but I like Fiona and trust her. Why not go with her mysterious plans? I'd wanted to shake up my life, so I might as well take that vow as far as possible.

Fiona heads back to her office or wherever it is she goes all day. After spending the whole morning in my office, I need to get some fresh air. Luckily, my job gives me a great excuse to do that, since I need to tour the facilities again to really get the lay of the land. I meant that literally. The land is a key component of what makes the distillery special. Yesterday, Thane had shown me all the buildings. But now, I need to get to know the land and the river too, almost as well as the Scots do.

I suppose I could get that information faster if I invited Thane to be my guide. That sounds like a dangerous proposition, though. The only other time we went to the river together, we wound up having sex. Of course, yesterday was an unusually warm day, with temperatures in the low fifties. A front rolled through last evening, and it's a bit chilly out this afternoon. So, I won't be tempted to get it on with my boss outdoors. The weather isn't conducive to that.

Still, the safest bet is to explore on my own. I shouldn't have even considered bringing Thane with me. He's a busy man, tinkering with new variations of whisky.

I'm pathetic, aren't I? Yeah, definitely. I can't stop thinking about *him*.

At least I dressed appropriately today. No designer skirt suit. No designer skyscraper heels. I chose wool slacks, a sweater, and a sturdy-but-stylish pair of waterproof boots. I feel much more at ease today, like I've settled into my job.

I catch Fiona in the hallway and tell her I'll be outside getting the lay of the land. She agrees that's a good idea, and she would love to come with me. But she has other business to take care of. When I tell her I can get all the information I need on my own, she offers a suggestion.

"You should ask Thane to go with you."

"Uh, no, I don't think he'd want to do that. He's busy. Honestly, I can find my way on my own. Thane showed me all the buildings and the river yesterday. I just want to get another look, that's all. Please don't bother Thane."

"If you change your mind, just ring the boss and he will come running. We have surprisingly good cellular service out here."

By "the boss," she means Thane, of course.

Fiona and I go our separate ways. I head outdoors. As I exit the main building, a stiff breeze slaps me in the face. Holy cow, that's cold. Fortunately, I have a soft, warm scarf in my car. I jog out to the car park, which is what everyone here calls a parking lot, and retrieve my scarf. I've just shut the car door when I notice a familiar figure at the other end of the parking area. Thane is talking to Dougal, the older man I'd met yesterday on the malting floor.

I take the coward's way and rush across the car park while the man I'm trying to avoid is still busy chatting with Dougal. By the time I duck around the main building and start down the river path, my pulse has calmed down. It had accelerated only because I was sprinting. Seeing a certain Scotsman again had nothing to do with it.

Yeah, I'm overcompensating again.

The sun is out this afternoon, so the cold doesn't feel quite as wintry as it would otherwise. The further I go down the trail, the less I feel the wind too. Well, this isn't so bad. My wool coat starts to feel a bit too warm, and I take it off, opting to drape it over my arm. I reach the river quickly, though I hear its burbling water before I can see it.

When I reach the riverbank, I stop and hang my coat on a tree branch. Thane had told me the river is black because of the peaty soil, and that the water is very clean and crisp. The bank descends toward the water at a rather steep incline, and I don't want to fall in. To prevent that, I sit down and let my legs dangle over the edge while I study the water. I'm not sure what I hope to achieve here. Water is water. It's not like a fairy will surface from the depths to share all the magical secrets of the river with me.

I set my hands on the ground behind me and lean back. The relaxing sound of the river lulls me. I close my eyes and let the gentle burbling wash over me.

A sigh spills from my lips.

"May I join you, Rebecca? Or is this a solo contemplation?"

Oh, damn, it's *him*. Without opening my eyes, I say, "Wanted a little time alone to drink in the atmosphere. It will help me do my job better."

"I'll go if you like. But I might be able to help you with drinking in all that atmosphere."

"Okay, fine, you can join me."

Some strong woman I am. A few words from Thane, and I cave. I open my eyes and roll my head sideways to watch him settling that muscular body onto the ground beside me. His legs hang over the edge too, but his feet nearly reach the level of the water, unlike mine.

"I told you the reason why the water is black," he says. "But I haven't shared the mystical aspects of the river."

Can he read my mind? I've wondered that more than once because he always seems to bring up questions I've only asked in my head. "If there are myths associated with this river, I might be able to use that in the marketing campaign. So please, tell me all about it."

"I really should take you to the Dùndubhan Museum to give you the complete picture. But we can start with the river."

"What does the museum have to do with it?"

"The castle was erected on Beann Dealgach for a reason. That's the name of the mountain we're sitting on. The ancient Scots revered Beann Dealgach, and their medieval descendants built a castle there for that reason."

I sit up straighter and wriggle around to face him.

He waves a hand toward the river. "It's said that the water here is cleaner and sweeter than anywhere else in the world. There's also a legend that couples who bathe in the waters together will become with child."

"Didn't think anyone actually said 'with child' anymore."

"I thought it sounded more intriguing than saying couples pop out bairns."

"You have a point there."

He sits up and leans forward, gazing into the dark waters. "There's also a legend about the *Daoine Sith* and the river. Would ye like to hear it?"

Chapter Eleven

Thane

I can tell Rebecca wants to hear all about Scottish folklore, but she seems hesitant to admit to her interest in it. Why? I can't say, but I wonder if it has anything to do with her ex-husband. She hasn't mentioned him but once or twice, and then only in vague terms. I know she and her husband have been divorced for several years. I also know her two adult children live in the UK. But I haven't a clue how to coalesce those facts into a meaningful insight into her past or present.

Not that her past matters to me. It's curiosity only.

She pulls her knees up to her chest and wriggles about to turn halfway toward me. "Since I have no clue what that phrase you just said meant, I can't say for sure if I want to hear about the legend."

"That's understandable." I bend one knee, resting my arm on it, and rotate my torso toward her. "The *Daoine Sith* are known as the good folk or wee folk, and also sometimes as the 'people of peace.' They are essentially the fairies."

"Oh. In that case, yes, I do want to hear the legend. I've always loved mythology, the older the better."

"Some of the *sith* are friendly, others are decidedly not. But the Scots in times past believed that by giving the fairies titles that sound sweet or at least pleasant, they could remain on the good side of the *sith*."

"I guess that makes sense. Were the fairies thought to be dangerous?"

"Some were, yes, but not all. The *sith* who were friendly belonged to the Seelie Court, while the most dangerous ones were found in the Unseelie

Court. Most people feared the Unseelie, since they were known to assault humans without warning and for no reason." I have never discussed Scottish fairy lore at length with anyone, not until today. Yet I can't deny I'm enjoying the chance to share the folklore with Rebecca. She watches me with rapt interest as I continue. "The legends include the tale of the Dame of the Fine Green Kirtle, who is friendly to humans."

Rebecca shimmies closer, and her eyes are alight with interest. "What about the myth that involved the river? I'd love to hear about that."

"I was about to tell you." I wave toward the dark waters. "Last year, the MacTaggarts uncovered a manuscript at Dùndubhan that had lain in a hidden passage for hundreds of years, apparently abandoned there. Only recently have they mapped all the hidden passages. The manuscript was in the last one they discovered."

Falling silent, I gaze down at the river. I wonder how long it will take the lass to grow agitated because I've stopped talking.

Not long at all, as it turns out.

Thirty seconds after I fell silent, Rebecca folds her arms over her chest and gives me a stern look. "You can't stop without finishing the story."

I can tell she's teasing me with that sharp look, and I like that. She's a mature woman, aye, but she also has an impish side. And she loves British pop music. I never would have guessed that. "Calm down, *gràidh*. I was about to elaborate."

She hugs her knees to her chest. "Well, hurry up, then."

A soft chuckle rumbles out of me. "As you wish, my lady. I am your faithful servant."

"Just get on with the story, please."

"The manuscript was written by an ancestor of the MacTaggarts who lived long before Kieran MacTaggart and his three aunts moved to Dùndubhan. It's a mystery how the manuscript came to be at the castle." I place two fingers on her lips when I can tell she's about to speak. "Let me finish."

Rebecca clamps her teeth down on her lips and nods.

"The mysterious manuscript was written by someone called Ciannait, but no surname is given," I explain. "Ciannait is a female first name. The text she wrote discusses the *Daoine Sìth* at length and a previously unknown Highland myth about this river. It's said that the black waters are the purest on earth, and that when a woman or a man bathes in the river or drinks from it, that person will meet their true love within a fortnight."

"Have you drunk from the river?"

"No. And I dinnae believe in magic or the *Daoine Sìth*."

She tips her head to the side and studies me. "But you seem like the kind of man who would love mythology."

"Why would you say that?"

"Your whisky proves it."

I feel my brows shoot up. "My whisky? Dinnae follow your logic."

"There's something rather mythical and almost epic about the flavors." She kneels beside me, so close now that I could kiss her with only a small movement of my head. "You call your first vintage 'sensual secret.' And your new varieties embody that sensuality too, in their unusual mix of flavors and the way they slide down your throat and make your whole body feel warm and liquid."

My whisky doesn't do that. Does it? "I think you drank too much Triple Threat yesterday. Best stay away from it for a while."

"You don't want to admit that you make erotic Scotch. But that's what we need to show the public—how sensual and unusual your product is."

I can do nothing but gawp at her. I called my whisky "sensual secret" because it sounded intriguing, not because I want customers to feel randy while they drink it. But perhaps she has a point. Sex sells, isn't that how the saying goes? "You honestly feel that my whisky is…erotic?"

"Oh, yes, absolutely." She lays her fingers lightly over her mouth and drags them down her chin, along the column of her throat, straight to her breastbone. Her hand lies between those mounds. "I swear I could almost orgasm just from drinking your whisky."

Bloody hell. If she goes on speaking in that husky voice, I might fuck her again, right here on the same spot where we shagged yesterday. Rebecca Taylor is the bonniest, sexiest, cleverest, and most sensual woman I've ever met. Even her penchant for dancing about while singing along to Duran Duran songs makes me want to have a poke with her.

I clear my throat. "We should return to the main building. You must have work to do, and I need to check on the newest batch of barley to make sure the malting process is up to my high standards."

"You're right. But I was hoping to gain insights into your whisky by learning more about the river and the areas around it."

Mhac na galla. I need to get away from this woman, so we won't wind up fucking on the riverbank. I would love to do that, but not now, not here. I should never do it again, anyway. But I must help Rebecca get whatever information she feels she might glean from learning about the area.

I stand up and offer her my hands to help her up too. "What is it you'd like to see? The castle? The mountain? The river?"

"Any location that's involved in the process of making the whisky."

"That's a very broad subject area, but I will do my best." I tip my head back and point upward. "It all begins in the sky. The Western Highlands receive abundant rainfall that provides many elements that improve the soil—mainly potassium, nitrogen, phosphorus, calcium, magnesium, sodium. But other compounds can also find their way into the water, such as iron, ammonia, manganese, and nitrate. All of these elements have played a role in creating the perfect peaty soil for making whisky."

Rebecca gazes up at the sky briefly, then stares into the dark waters that churn below us. "All the water for the whisky comes from the river. That's what you said before. And the castle is upstream, isn't it? But does the entire length of the river belong to Rory MacTaggart?"

"Aye. Rory owns Beann Dealgach itself and some of the surrounding area. The headwaters lie at the top of the mountain and snake down the south side, bypassing the castle on their way down the western slope."

"Where is the mouth of the river?"

Ah, she is a clever lass. Not many people would refer to the river's end as the mouth or know what the headwaters are. "The mouth lies about five miles downriver, where the waters flow into Loch Linnhe."

Rebecca shuffles closer to the bank's edge and clutches her portfolio while she gazes down into the water. Little by little, she begins to slant forward ever so slowly.

"Watch yourself, *gràidh*. Ye might fall in."

She continues gazing deeply into the dark river, seemingly entranced by the flowing water. The lass shuffles forward a wee bit, leaning far too close to the edge.

I reach out to grasp her elbow.

But a chunk of earth breaks away beneath her shoe, making her teeter.

The instant that happens, I rush forward to sling an arm around her waist and hoist the lass off her feet. Then I back away from the bank with her in my arms. Though I set her down, I cannae make myself release my hold on her body.

"You can let me go now, Thane."

Her words barely penetrate my mind. The warmth and softness of her body has eradicated all other thoughts. She feels good. She smells good. And I want to kiss her more than I've ever wanted that before.

"I'm fine, Thane, honestly. Thank you for rescuing me from falling into the river, but I swear I can stand on my own now."

My cock has begun to thicken. She must feel that, yet she doesn't shout at me to let her go. She doesn't even kick my shin.

But I finally manage to reassemble my wits and release her. "I apologize, Rebecca. That was inappropriate."

The lass turns round to face me. "I enjoy having you hold me in your arms, but you're right. It's inappropriate."

She enjoys it? I fucking loved holding her.

As I avert my gaze, I cough into my fist. "We should both get back to work."

"Yeah, you're right."

"I need to return to the malting room. Have a good afternoon."

Then I whirl round and march off down the trail.

For the rest of the afternoon, I need to rally all my willpower, repeatedly, to stop myself from hunting down the bonnie American lass I want to kiss with a fervor I've never experienced in my entire life. Just feeling her body pressed to mine cranked up my lust.

At the end of the day, I switch the lights off in my office and shut the door, heading down the hall.

Fiona catches up to me from behind. "You're coming to dinner at my house tonight, Thane. Dinnae argue. Domhnall will be sorely disappointed if you refuse our offer."

"You said 'my house' instead of 'our house.' That sounds like poor Domhnall has no say in the matter."

"Of course he does, you cheeky sod." She pokes me in the ribs. "You are coming to *our* house. If you try to wriggle out of it, Domhnall will steal Callum's Harley and hunt you down."

"Your cousin Callum is a bampot, and Domhnall is not terrifying to me. You'll need to come up with a better inducement."

Fiona grips my arm, and I let her pull me to a halt. "Please, Thane, come to dinner at our house. You spend too much time alone."

She might have a point. But I won't tell her so.

Instead, I sigh as if I'm only agreeing because she pestered me. "What time should I be there?"

"You can come home with me."

"No. I will drive myself there. What time, Fiona?"

The lass shakes her head. "I'm always amazed by how politely obstinate you can be. Ye never snarl or gripe."

"Fiona, when—"

"Right now."

It's my turn to shake my head. "No, Fiona. I need to check on the hothouse before I leave. I will meet you at your home in thirty minutes."

The lass clearly wants to argue with me, but she knows full well that when I set my mind to something, I do not give up. So, Fiona trots out of the building. I emerge a moment later, just in time to see Domhnall's car pulling out of the car park. I think I see a third figure in the vehicle, but I don't get a good enough look to know for sure.

After checking the hothouse, and finding all the plants doing well, I climb into my pickup truck and drive to Domhnall and Fiona's home in Loch Fairbairn. When I knock on the door, Domhnall swings it open.

"Thane, *feasgar math*," he says in his usual gruff tone. "Fiona and I have arranged a surprise for you."

Bod an Donais. That's the last thing I need tonight. "Good evening to you too, Domhnall."

He steps aside to let me enter the house. "The surprise is waiting in the dining room." He shuts the door and shouts over his shoulder, "Fiona! Our second victim is here."

Aye, "victim" is the word every dinner guest wants to hear when they enter a mate's home. But with the MacTaggarts, it's par for the course.

I let Domhnall lead me into the dining room, where he takes a seat at the head of the table with Fiona at his right. And on his left...

Mhac na galla. They've roped Rebecca into this nonsense.

Her eyes widen as she furtively glances at Fiona, who simply smiles with too much sweetness.

"Have a seat," Domhnall tells me. "Right beside Rebecca. We've been having a fine chat while we waited for you to arrive."

Outwardly, I appear calm and unaffected. I know this because I've cultivated that attitude for the better part of my adult life. On the inside, however, I'm plotting ways to get my revenge on the meddling couple who lured me here on false pretenses.

Chapter Twelve

Rebecca

Fiona orchestrated this blind date, and while Domhnall seems to be on board with her plan, I get the feeling he's only humoring his wife. Fiona is a wonderful woman—great at her job, friendly to everyone, willing to take risks. I'm the beneficiary of her risk-taking. She gave me a job when no one else would and gave me free rein to do that job in whatever way I see fit. But I don't appreciate being tricked into a blind date.

Thane seems calm and unperturbed as usual.

Is that an act? I know he hides an explosive amount of passion underneath his placid exterior. I'm itching to know more about him, but not in front of Domhnall and Fiona.

Fiona aims a sharp look at Thane. "Well, go on. Say hello to Rebecca. You're being very rude, and it's not like you at all."

Thane's expression tightens the tiniest bit, almost as if he's annoyed. But that look vanishes quickly. He sits up straighter and turns to me. "Good evening, Rebecca. It's lovely to see you again." He aims a teasing half smirk at Fiona. "Even if this was a bloody annoying engineered reunion."

"You'll thank us later. Won't he, Domhnall?"

Her husband sighs and aims a tolerant smile at his wife. "Eventually, he will be grateful. But I'm waiting for Thane to blow his top at last and show us the avenging warrior that's buried inside his Buddha-like exterior. That's when the fun will begin."

Thane sinks back in his chair. "I am no Buddha. That title belongs to Iain MacTaggart."

I really can't keep track of all the Scots I've met and the ones I've heard about. MacTaggarts apparently swarm the Western Highlands, like a benevolent plague of locusts. But that thought triggers a question.

And I look at Thane. "I've gotten the impression that there are a lot of MacTaggarts around these parts. Are there just as many Buchanans?"

"Oh, no, we are not as prolific as Fiona's clan. I believe the Sterlings aren't that prolific either. Are they, Domhnall?"

"No. Only the MacTaggarts breed like rabbits."

Fiona jabs her elbow into Domhnall's ribs. "Careful, *mo chridhe*. You are insulting a feisty clan with those words."

Whatever "*mo chridhe*" means, I suspect it's probably an endearment based on Fiona's tone of voice.

He clutches his chest. "Och, my heart breaks at the thought that I might have insulted the MacTaggarts accidentally."

I could listen to these people trade jibes all evening. They're wonderful people, and I haven't had this much fun in a long time. Maybe I should be more annoyed than I am about the blind-date nonsense, but I can't stay mad at Fiona or Domhnall. I believe they honestly want to help me settle in here in Scotland, and I'm positive they believe a surprise date with Thane will help me do that.

But for most of the evening, no one mentions dating. We have normal, fun conversations. Domhnall tells hilarious tales about how the MacTaggarts meddled in his life, twice, to bring about his happy ending with Fiona. And I learn that Domhnall and Fiona met at her sister Catriona's wedding—at a nudist resort in Oregon.

Would I ever go to a nudist resort? Uh, no. Not my style.

"You never know," Fiona says. "I never would have imagined I'd go nude in public either, but I changed my mind. Domhnall even did a nude headstand."

"Are you kidding? You must be."

Domhnall chuckles. "No, lass, it's not a joke. I was showing off to impress Jessica O'Connor, my former girlfriend. She was underwhelmed."

As much as I would love to hear more about what Domhnall did at that wedding, I can no longer hold back my curiosity about another Scot. "How long have you two known Thane? Fiona, I remember you mentioned dating him."

"Oh, aye. But I've known Thane most of my life. The Buchanans and the MacTaggarts have a long-standing tradition of playing shinty together. That's a Scottish sport. It's sort of a fusion of field hockey and lacrosse."

"I've heard of the Highland games, but not shinty."

"You'll learn about it soon enough. The more time you spend with Thane, the more likely it is you'll find yourself sitting on the sidelines cheering him on during a shinty match."

Thane manages to seem annoyed even while maintaining his placid expression. It's something about the way the faint wrinkles around his eyes tighten the tiniest bit. "Rebecca and I are not dating. She works for me, so it would be highly inappropriate for me to have a relationship with her."

"Oh, tosh. The distillery has a sexual harassment policy, but that doesn't forbid employees from fraternizing outside of work." She folds her elbows on the table and stares directly into his eyes. "I should know because I wrote the policy."

Domhnall clears his throat. "Thane, why dinnae ye entertain Rebecca in the sitting room while Fiona and I clear out the dishes?"

Thane squints the tiniest bit. "I will do that, but only to be polite."

Fiona is grinning.

Domhnall shakes his head, but it's an affectionate expression. Then he and Fiona clear the table, and soon, I can hear water running in the kitchen.

Thane pulls my chair out for me and guides me into the sitting room. It has a big picture window, but the drapes are closed right now. I bet this house has fantastic views. It's perfectly situated for that.

While Thane drops onto an armchair, I settle down on the sofa.

"I apologize for this blind-date nonsense," he tells me. "I had no part in plotting that scheme."

"Relax, I'm not annoyed. And I never believed you were a co-conspirator." I tuck my legs under me while I contemplate whether I should pester him for information right now. My curiosity makes the decision for me. "Could I ask you a few personal questions?"

"Go on."

"What exactly did you do at the Ministry of Defence? You said you were a geospatial analyst, but I don't understand what that means."

He slouches down in his chair and stares at the fireplace, where no fire is lit. "Geospatial analysis is bloody boring, for the most part. I found it fascinating because it's like a giant puzzle. I spent most of my time studying imagery from satellites, aerial photography, and ground-based imaging systems to hunt for signs of unusual activity. My job was focused on intelligence gathering."

"You were a spy?"

"I was never labeled as such."

Not exactly an answer, but I understand that he probably can't talk about the secret things he did as part of his job. So, I take a slightly different tack. "I've never heard of geospatial analysis. If you're comfortable talking about the basics of it, rather than your specific job, I'd be interested in listening."

Thane wriggles in his seat until he's sitting upright. Then he rests his arms on the chair and sets one knee atop the other. "During my final year at the University of Edinburgh, I was contacted by an official from the MOD who encouraged me to join the army's geospatial science program. I had been studying computer science at university. The recruiter had taken notice of my excellent scores on various tests throughout my academic career before and during my university studies."

"Wow. You must have had impressive scores to draw that kind of attention."

He shrugs. "I've always been good at crossword puzzles and similar sorts of things. And I did do very well with computers. Never imagined I'd wind up in a job that required a top-secret clearance. That's all I can tell you about my specific duties."

"Can you tell me more in general terms?"

"Aye." He gazes out the window while he talks. "I joined the army after graduation. Then I went through the standard program, which meant twenty-three weeks of basic training at Harrogate, a military facility in England. After that came even more training, first at the Royal School of Military Engineering in Surrey for twelve weeks and then a stint at the Defence School of Transport in Leconfield. And finally, I was sent to the Royal School of Military Survey in Berkshire, where I studied every aspect of geospatial science."

"That's a lot of hoops to jump through before you actually got the job."

"Didn't matter to me. I did what was required. Would've gone through even more training, if necessary, because I wanted the job that much."

I suddenly realize I've scooted forward on the sofa and set my feet on the carpeted floor. I'm leaning forward too. Yeah, hearing about Thane's past has me on the edge of my seat, for sure. "Did you stay in England after all that training?"

"Aye. I was sent to the DIO—the Defence Infrastructure Organisation. That's where I served for most of my career."

He can't tell me more. Of that I'm positive. I understand the limitations. Classified jobs come with all sorts of restrictions, but I can't deny I wish he could tell me everything. His former career sounds fascinating. But more than that, *he* fascinates me. I've never been so enthralled by any other man. Maybe enthralled isn't the right word, since that makes me sound like a brainwashed groupie. It's more that he intrigues me.

I realize, though, that I haven't asked Thane about another enigma concerning him. Several enigmas, actually. He's a mysterious man. "What did you do when you left the army? Did you go straight to opening a distillery?"

"No. I needed time to readjust to civilian life, so I spent several years taking whatever work I could get." He finally turns his gaze to me. "For a while, I did odd jobs for whoever needed my help. I took on tasks from cabinetry to mucking out barns to tailoring and even getting the messages for elderly people."

"You handled their mail?"

"No," he says with a slight laugh. "In Scotland, 'messages' are groceries."

"Oh, I see. The word messages doesn't sound like Gaelic, so I'm guessing I need to learn both Gaelic and regular Scottish slang."

"Gaelic isn't prominent in Scotland, though it's a wee bit more popular in the Western Highlands." He stretches his legs out, crossing his ankles in a posture that implies he's very relaxed. I doubt that's an act. When his lips curl into a soft smile, my point is proved. "Tell me, *gràidh*, how did you come to be a marketing expert?"

"I told you that already. I skipped college and went straight to work. Donna Wallace was my mentor."

"Aye, ye told me that. But you have created complex campaigns for various types of businesses, and those campaigns nearly always were successful. I reckon what I'm asking is how does that brain of yours work?"

"Just like everyone else's."

He shakes his head. "No, you are not like everyone else."

"I suppose that's true for everyone. We are all unique individuals."

"Some people are dead boring and not unique at all."

Well, he's got me on that point. But I stand by my belief that most people are unique and talented in some aspect of their lives. "I guess I'm the hopelessly optimistic type. Human beings can surprise you in amazing ways once in a while."

"True. But I would love to pick your brain to solve the mystery of Rebecca Taylor."

"Mystery?" I say with a tiny, hiccupping laugh. "I'm not that fascinating."

He stares at me with an intensity that makes every hair on my body stiffen and tingle, though not in a bad way. The sensation is…sensual. "Never downplay your intelligence, determination, and creativity. You are the most intriguing woman I've ever met. Maybe one day I'll plumb your depths and at last strip away your businesswoman exterior to reveal the passionate lass underneath. I caught a glimpse of that yesterday, but I'd love to see more."

That sensual tingle rushes over my skin again, awakening parts of my body that I would rather stayed asleep. Even from across the room, Thane can turn me on and make me feel like I'm the only woman in the world.

Someone knocks on the sitting room door. "Is it safe to come in yet?"

Domhnall's words propel Thane to leap out of his chair and stalk over to the door, yanking it open. But as always, his tone remains calm. "We were having a chat, nothing more, so dig your thoughts out of the gutter, please."

"You assume I'm implying something filthy. I only meant that we didn't want to interrupt your conversation."

Domhnall's innocent expression is pure sarcasm. Even I can tell that, and I met the man a couple of hours ago. Past his shoulder, I can see the top of Fiona's head.

"It's getting late," Thane announces. "Rebecca will be wanting to go home."

Fiona sidles around her husband. "Aye, it is late. You should drive Rebecca back to her apartment. She must be jeeked."

"Aye, I'm sure she is tired. But she'll be wanting to drive herself home, so she'll have her car there in the morning. How else will she get to work? She'll need a vehicle."

"Wrong, Thane. I drove her here, so she has no way to get home unless someone offers her a ride."

Thane glances at me sideways, and his Adam's apple jumps a teeny bit. "Domhnall can give her a ride, then."

Jeez, Thane really does not want to be alone with me in a car. Does he think I'll tear his clothes off? Or that he won't be able to resist seducing me? Maybe if I tell him that I promise not to do anything of the sort, he'll feel more comfortable giving me a ride.

No, I can't say that. It would sound stupid.

Fiona saves me, unwittingly. "Domhnall would need to drive all the way to Rebecca's apartment in Fort William, then drive home after that. He'd be jeeked in the morning. But Rebecca's apartment is on the way to Thane's house. He could easily give the lass a ride."

Domhnall smirks.

Fiona smiles a bit too cheerfully.

Thane sighs. "All right. I will drive the lass to her apartment."

A few minutes later, I'm sitting in the passenger seat of Thane's car while he starts up the engine. And we are alone.

Chapter Thirteen

Thane

I am trapped in a car with the only woman who has ever inflamed my lust to wildfire levels. This does not seem like the wisest decision, not that Fiona left me with any other options. Of course, I couldn't insist that Domhnall should go out of his way to give the American lass a ride when I'll be going in the same direction. Now, as we start down the street, I realize just how far Fiona will go to engineer a relationship between me and Rebecca.

She probably conspired with her mates in the American Wives Club to make it happen. That doesn't mean I'm required to fall for Rebecca. Lust is not always the same as romance.

"Are you okay?" the lass asks. "You seem very tense."

"I am never tense."

"Uh-huh, sure. You're gripping the steering wheel like you're worried it might pop out and crash through the windshield."

Bloody hell. She's right about that.

I take a breath and exhale it gradually until my fingers loosen their grip on the wheel. "Dinnae like driving at night, that's all."

"The former secret agent is afraid of being out at night? Oh, come on. I'm not that gullible."

"I was never a spy.'"

Not technically. I won't even try to explain that to Rebecca since I'm still bound by the Official Secrets Act. To avoid responding to her statement, I switch on the radio and let the music drown out any further questions she might have. No, I am not a coward who refuses to admit he wants the beautiful woman who sits beside him. I'm simply behaving like a gentleman. Aye, that's it.

Mhac na galla.

"What does that mean? Is it Gaelic?"

Had I spoken those words aloud? I'd meant to say it in my mind only. This woman drives me off my head. "Aye, it's Gaelic. The phrase means 'son of a bitch.' "

"Are you cursing at me? Or the road?"

"Neither."

I'd been cursing at myself, but I won't admit to that. So, I crank the volume up on the radio.

Ten minutes later, we pull into the garage of Rebecca's apartment. The bottom level is strictly for parking, while the upper floors are filled up with living quarters. I have never before visited this luxury apartment complex, and I have no idea how luxurious it might actually be. Adverts I've seen depicted it as the height of luxury, but advertisers often lie to make people want what they're offering.

Rebecca would never do that.

When I've pulled into a parking space for guests, I leave the engine running. "Well, good night, Rebecca."

She glances round the gloomy garage. "Would you mind, um, walking with me? The guest parking spots are pretty far away from the elevator."

I cannae say no. Dinnae blame her for being wary of who might lurk in the shadows, though I doubt it's dangerous here. Still, I shut off the engine. "Aye, lass, I'd be happy to accompany you."

Her grateful smile gives me a brief pang in my chest. "Thank you, Thane."

"It's no trouble at all. Stay where you are. I'll come round to your side."

"Sorry Fiona pushed you into giving me a ride."

"Dinnae fash." I suddenly realize she won't know what I said. "That means don't worry."

I unlock the doors and jog around to her side, pulling the door open for her. She gives me that grateful smile again. As we walk side-by-side down the aisle, I click the button on my key fob to lock the car again. Then I place a hand lightly on her lower back. She seems to relax when I do that. By the time we step into the lift, she doesn't seem anxious at all anymore.

She reaches into her purse, bringing out a set of keys. One of the purse's straps falls off her shoulder. In her attempt to return it to its rightful place, she instead accidentally lowers her shoulder, which causes the purse to drop onto the floor. As Rebecca leans over to retrieve the bag, her cheek brushes against my groin. Seemingly oblivious of that fact, she bends over even more, tightening her trousers so that her erse is on full display.

My cock twitches.

The contents of her purse have spilled over the floor. She struggles to gather them up again, but her fingers keep slipping. I suspect she's nervous because we're alone in the lift.

Maybe I should help her. Aye, that seems like a reasonable response.

I kneel beside her—and abruptly realize I've made a terrible mistake. Her blouse has fallen open enough that I can see nearly all of the slopes of her bonnie tits. Her bra only covers one-third of them. I might be known for never revealing my passions, but this woman is testing my willpower. I have only one option to end this torment.

I scoop up all of her belongings and dump them into her purse. Then I rise, offering her the bag.

She stands up and brushes off her trousers. As she accepts the purse, she smiles. "Thank you for the help."

"Your womanly things in there are most likely out of place now."

"That's okay. I'm not very tidy with the stuff in my purse, anyway."

Fortunately, the lift stops, and the doors glide open. We walk out of the lift, brushing past the lasses and gents who were waiting to step inside. I manage to keep an arm's length between myself and Rebecca as we stroll down the hallway to her apartment door.

She unlocks it, then leans against the jamb. "Thank you again for giving me a lift."

"I haven't presented you with your very own lift. Everyone uses it."

Her brows crinkle in the sweetest expression of confusion. "I don't think we're talking about the same thing. I meant 'a lift' as in 'a ride.' What were you talking about?"

"The lift." I wave toward the far end of the hall, where the contraption in question is. "It's the thing that ferried us up to this floor."

"Oh, you mean it lifts the car to a higher floor."

"Aye. That's what I said."

Her smile becomes a grin. "In America, we call those things elevators."

"Oh, aye, of course. I knew that, but I forgot momentarily."

She swings the door open further. "Want to come in for a drink?"

"I should be away. We both need rest after this evening's get-together."

"But Fiona gave me a bottle of your best single-malt Scotch." Rebecca sashays across the threshold, then half turns to look at me. The lass licks her lips and rubs them together. "I can still taste the whiskies I tried yesterday. Please won't you share one drink with me?"

Though I know I shouldn't do it, my mouth has a mind of its own. "Aye, lass, I would love to have a dram with you."

Her entire demeanor lights up like fireworks in the night sky. When I shut the door behind me, she kicks off her shoes and ambles over to the island that fronts the open kitchen. As I follow her over there, I can't help glancing out the huge picture windows in the living area. This is indeed luxury living, though not quite as posh as the apartment Evan MacTaggart owns in Inverness. He's a billionaire tech mogul, though. Rebecca is not, and neither am I.

The lass tosses her suit jacket over one of the four stools at the island on her way to the drinks cabinet in the corner. "Sit down. I'm just getting the whisky."

I park my erse on a stool and continue with my visual inspection of the apartment. Despite the darkness outside, I know this building sits near the water. I also notice that where the picture windows end, a glass door leads out onto a patio. That might be a nice place to enjoy our whisky if it weren't so bloody cold out there tonight. To my left, I can see a bedroom through its half-open doorway. The living room offers a sofa and two armchairs as well, not to mention a coffee table.

Rebecca comes around the island to hand me a whisky glass that's one-third full. She hops onto the stool beside mine. "This is your black label whisky, the one that has an unpronounceable Gaelic name."

"*Collaidh Sgeul-Rùin*. It's not as difficult to pronounce as you think. I'd be happy to teach you."

"Maybe another time. I'm wiped out after two days of work, which doesn't bode well for my stamina in this job."

"You shouldn't think that way. After all, you've moved to another country thousands of miles from your home and started a new job in an industry you've never worked in before." I pat her hand. "Give yourself a chance to settle in. Then I'm sure you'll fall in love with the Highlands."

"Think I already have." She takes a wee sip, then closes her eyes and sighs with deep contentment. "You really do know how to make whisky."

Her sultry tone does nothing to alleviate my growing state of arousal. I don't have an erection yet, but I will do soon. Very soon. Unless I walk out the door and drive home. But I cannae do that. Rebecca has cast a sensual spell around me without even trying.

She takes a larger taste of the whisky and moans. "I've never been big on drinking alcohol, but your stuff could make me a convert. It tastes so deliciously, erotically spicy, and it feels warm and silky going down my throat."

Walk out the door, man. Do it now.

I start to back away from the island, but then Rebecca takes another sip and drags her fingers down her chest while moaning even more deeply. My cock is beginning to stiffen. I cannae tear my gaze away from the lass. Her soft, sexy smile makes my dokey jerk. But when she slides her tongue across her bottom lip while petting her throat, I lose the last vestiges of my self-control.

She opens her eyes, gazing at me with sleepy-sexy desire.

And I rush up to her, seize her about the waist, and drag her into my body.

Her eyes flare wide for a moment, then she blinks rapidly. "Thane?"

I snatch the glass from her fingers and down the rest of the whisky in one gulp. Rebecca is right. The black label single-malt does taste erotically spicy and silky. I never thought of it that way until tonight. "Ah, lass, no more whisky for you. I need you sober if I'm going to make love to you tonight."

She freezes, not even blinking her eyes. Then her entire body relaxes.

I can feel the hard peaks of her nipples through our clothes, and that makes me hunger for her even more. Should I be seducing my employee? No. But we are both consenting adults. "Dinnae want you to feel pressured. I want you, but only if it's what you want too."

She slips her arms around my neck. "Oh, Thane, I want you too. But this has to stay between us. Nobody at work needs to know."

"Aye. It will be a secret affair."

"Yes." She virtually whispered that single word. "Make love to me, please. Don't rush this time."

"Willnae do that. Ye have my word." I skim my palms up and down her back, gently, deliberately, arousing her little by little. She exhales a long, soft sigh as she sags into me. I brush her hair away from her face with one hand, then go on skating my palms over her back. "This will be slow, tender, and intensely pleasurable. I promise ye that, *m'eudail*. Ye willnae regret this."

"Oh, God. That sounds wonderful." She rises onto her toes, rubbing her cheek against mine, as she murmurs into my ear, "And then you'll go home, and this will be just one night of forbidden pleasure. That's all."

What? I never said that. I need more than one night with this woman. She might have said that only because she believes it's what I want. I need to make certain, though. "If you think I'm looking for a fling, that's not my intent. Dinnae believe that's what you really want either."

She pulls her head back and squints at me. "But that was the whole point of this. One night, no strings."

"I never said that."

"But we had a quickie by the river. Naturally, I assumed that you wanted another quickie tonight, just to let off some steam."

Now it's my turn to pull my head back. "What happened yesterday was a fluke. A confluence of events that led us both to do a barmy thing."

Rebecca wriggles out of my embrace and jumps onto a stool. "I'm confused. What do you think is going to happen if we have sex? If it's a regular thing? You're my boss."

"We agreed that we're adults and we can keep our personal and professional lives separate."

"Yeah, but—" She grabs the whisky bottle and swigs a mouthful. "This is getting way too serious for me. I need time to think about whether this is a good idea."

"I didn't mean to upset you, *gràidh*, and I apologize. " But I clearly have upset her, and I need to rectify the situation. "I won't suggest anything like this again. Not unless you make it clear you're ready. You are adjusting to many new things right now—a new country, a new job, new people. I should leave you be and remain only your superior at work. Good night, Rebecca."

She watches me walk out of the apartment, her eyes large and her hand still on the whisky glass.

By the time I reach my home, I want to do nothing more than sleep and try to forget about the mistake I made this evening with Rebecca. I hope one day she will help me understand why my offer upset her, but I need to wait until she decides she's ready.

All night, I dream of Rebecca.

Chapter Fourteen

Rebecca

For the next three days, I stick to doing my job without any trips to the river. Every time I'd gone there, Thane had turned up to offer me his expertise on how whisky is made or to share lovely little legends about the river. I enjoyed those times with him. But the other night… Ugh, I acted like an idiot. I'm a middle-aged woman, not a sorority girl. The strangest part of our encounter in my apartment is that he made me feel safe and cherished even while I was essentially telling him to go to hell.

All right, maybe I wasn't that harsh. But he wanted to make love to me, and I shoved him away like he had leprosy.

Maybe Thane was right. Maybe I have had too many changes too quickly, and I just need more time to settle into my new life.

So, I do what screwed-up people everywhere do. I pretend that night never happened. Whenever I bump into Thane in the hall, we nod to each other and offer tight smiles. This is not the dynamic I want to have with the big boss. What if all the other employees start to resent me because I seem to be shunning the man in charge? They all adore Thane. That much is obvious. Strangely, I adore him too. But I need to sort myself out before I can even start to find a way to apologize to him.

On Wednesday and Thursday, I eat lunch alone in my office. Fiona knocks on the door to invite me to join her in the cafeteria, but I make excuses for why I can't do that. On Friday, I finally get so disgusted with my behavior that I realize I need to either quit my job or suck it up and behave like a mature woman. Yes, I had sex with Thane on my first day at work. Yes, I desperately wanted him to make love to me the other night. But I've done some soul searching over the past two days, and I finally figured out what my problem is.

It's time to tell Thane.

Though I did try to find Thane so we could have a private discussion, Fiona tells me that the big man on campus has gone to town to run errands. So, I accept Fiona's offer to have lunch with her in the cafeteria. We sit across the table from each other, eating while we talk. Not at the same time, of course. We aren't barbarians.

"Have you and Thane had an argument?" Fiona asks. "You've been ignoring each other for days."

"There was no argument. We're both busy, that's all." I'm sure Fiona will buy that flimsy excuse. If she suffered a brain injury this morning.

Fiona puckers her lips as if she's trying not to smile. "You don't need to be coy with me. I won't tell anyone if you and Thane had a row."

"Honestly, there was no argument. I don't feel comfortable discussing what did happen."

"So, there was something." Fiona raises her hands. "But I won't bother you about it. I only hope you two can patch things up. We've all noticed the tension between you and Thane, and it's spreading into the rest of the employees."

Oh, fantastic. My hang-ups are affecting everyone. "I need to talk to Thane about this. Then, I'm sure everything will get back to normal."

"Aye, I'm sure too. But if you need someone to talk to, about anything, you come find me."

"Thank you, Fiona. You're a great boss and a great friend." I wince. "Though I shouldn't assume we are friends."

"Of course we are." She pats my hand. "Once you've gotten used to your new life, you'll feel much more at ease. Dinnae fash."

After lunch, I'm sitting in my office working on various ideas for marketing the distillery when a knock at the door rouses me from my intense focus. "Come on in."

I hear the door open and close, but I'm still focused on my task.

Thane's head appears beside mine. "What are you about now, eh? I didn't think anyone still used index cards. That sort of thing is done on computers now."

"Yes, but I prefer to do things the old-fashioned way."

"So do I, though I never use index cards."

His proximity and the scent of his aftershave are making me antsy. He smells too damn good, and every time he speaks, his warm breath teases my cheek. I banish those thoughts as best I can and stand up to face him.

Thane straightens and gives me his patented casual smile.

I try to tug my suit jacket down, out of habit, but suddenly remember I'm not wearing a jacket today. "Did you need something?"

"Aye. I needed to check on you."

"Oh. Well, I'm fine." *Suck it up, woman, and tell him the truth.* "I'm sorry for the way I've been acting lately. It's just that I, um, still feel kind of out of place here. I'm the only American, and I had never been to Scotland before. Everyone is so kind to me. My hang-ups are the problem, not anything that anyone here has done."

"I can understand that. But I'm sure what I did the other night made you feel uncomfortable too."

"Not uncomfortable." I take a breath and just say it. "I want more than sex with you. I haven't wanted to get involved with anyone, not seriously, ever since my divorce. But I would love to date you, Thane."

He gazes at me yet again with that casual smile and inscrutable expression.

I begin to feel itchy all over, though I fight the urge to scratch.

At last, Thane strides up to me and clasps my hands. His casual smile has turned into a sweet one. "I would love that too."

"Do you think everyone else at the distillery will be okay with that?"

"Oh, aye. They've been telling me to patch things up with you." He pulls me close and kisses my forehead. "They'll probably throw a big ceilidh to celebrate."

"A ceilidh is a dance party, right?"

"Have you been studying Scottish traditions?"

I hunch my shoulders. "Maybe a little."

Thane grins. "You'll be a true Scot soon enough."

"No offense, but I'd rather stay American—and still fit in with Scots."

"Understandable. I was having you on, anyway."

I know that, and I love that he feels comfortable teasing me. I also know that he doesn't mind if I tease him right back. I can't believe I basically told him to go away the other night. The way he's smiling now gives me a wonderfully warm sensation in my chest. Maybe I can make it up to him.

Since he's still holding my hands, I give them a squeeze. "Would you like to have dinner at my place?"

"When?"

"Tomorrow night. I need time to buy groceries." I bite my lip. "Could you tell me where the nearest store is?"

"No need for that. I can bring the ingredients, then you can cook everything."

"Perfect." I suddenly realize there's one problem. "But if you buy Scottish foods, I won't know how to cook them."

"Never mind that. I won't buy anything you won't recognize."

"Whew. That's a relief."

For a moment, we just stand here holding hands, looking into each other's eyes. I've never experienced this before, feeling so close to someone yet not speaking a word, just enjoying the way it makes me feel. I barely know Thane, but I want to change that this weekend. My kids have been pestering me to start dating again, despite my lackluster track record with romance. Now, they'll get what they've wanted.

I'm dating a Scotsman. A smart, charming, damn sexy Scotsman.

"For the sake of full disclosure," I tell him, "I haven't dated in a long time. My last date was awkward, to say the least."

He dips his head to brush his nose against mine. Then he touches his forehead to mine too and winks. "Dinnae worry, *gràidh*. We can take this as slowly as you want."

"You are so sweet and understanding."

He touches his lips to mine, rubbing them gently. "If you aren't ready for sex yet, just let me know. I can wait as long as you need."

"I'm so sorry I freaked out the other night."

"Forget about all that. Let's just enjoy our first official date and see what happens next."

Thane kisses my cheek, then walks out the door.

And I drop my ass onto the desk and sigh. Everything inside me feels warm and liquid, and I know one thing for certain. I'm completely smitten with that man. I'd say it's like a teenage crush, but I never felt this way about any of the boys I dated in school. No one in my past could hold a candle to Thane.

Could I fall in love with him? It's much too soon to even entertain that idea. But I can't deny that I want to find out how this little romance will play out. And if one day he does pop that question...

Well, one thing is for sure. I won't panic.

After finishing my first week at the distillery, I head home in the evening feeling better than ever. I have a date. My kids will be thrilled, but I think I'll hold off on telling them until after my date night with Thane. Don't want to jinx it. Not that I believe in silly things like that. It just seems prudent to keep my plans to myself until I see how dinner goes.

The next day, I have nothing to do. Thane will bring the raw ingredients, and we agreed via text message that he should arrive at six o'clock, so I'll have time to cook everything. We forgot to discuss an arrival time yesterday.

At three o'clock, I start unpacking all my clothes. I'd only taken out the items I would need for work plus a couple of casual outfits. Now, I need to find my dressier stuff. I'd been wearing a pantsuit on that ill-fated night when Thane confessed that he wanted to make love to me. For our first date, I want to look hot.

Really hot.

But I don't want to go overboard, in case he shows up in jeans and a T-shirt. So, I lay out all my nicer clothes on the bed, and some of it on the dresser, to get a look at my options. As I study the garments, I tap my finger on my chin while humming tunelessly. It's a quirky habit of mine. I'm glad Thane isn't here to witness my behavior. I'm debating whether to wear slacks to be more casual or a dress that will make it easier for him to strip me.

Yes, I'm already hoping for sex tonight.

But I don't want to choose a fuck-me outfit. I'd rather let him see the real me before I go all-out on the seduction. Besides, I'd love to let him do the seducing.

Finally, I make a decision. Now that I'm dressed, I fix my hair and makeup before slipping into my shoes. Thane will love my outfit, I'm sure of that. I suspect that if I wore camo fatigues, he'd love that too. A burlap sack would probably also work. He's not the fussy type.

I still have an hour to go.

To pass the time, I watch TV until that gets boring. Honestly, it only takes me ten minutes to get sick of that. Then I pace the width of the picture windows.

The doorbell rings.

And I sprint for the door, yanking it wide open. "Thane, you're here."

He chuckles. "Aye, lass, I'm here. Am I late?"

"No. I was just excited to see you, that's all."

"I'm excited too. Haven't had a date in a very long time." He steps across the threshold and slides an arm around my waist. "I could hardly wait to see you tonight. Arrived half an hour early and just sat in my car listening to music until it was time. Being early might seem rude."

"You have my permission to arrive early anytime you're coming to my place." I move backward while Thane moves with me, keeping his arm around me. Then he kicks the door shut, and I wrap my arms around his neck. "Were you blasting bagpipe music in the parking garage?"

"No, it was, ah…something else."

I tickle his lips with my fingertip. "Come on, you can tell me your dirty little secret. Was it polka music?"

He shakes his head and winces. "I was listening to Duran Duran's greatest hits. I, ah, downloaded the album."

I can't stop myself from grinning like an idiot. "You listened to my favorite band. That's the sweetest thing any man has done for me." It's my turn to grimace. "Though I shouldn't assume that's why you did it."

"Of course it's why. I wanted to get caught up on your favorite music. I listened to *Danse Macabre* last night."

"The whole album?"

"Aye." He brushes his fingertips through my hair, then glides them down my cheek. "I want to know everything about you, *gràidh*."

"I want to know you inside out too, but I get why you can't tell me everything. There's a law about it, right?"

"The Official Secrets Act, aye."

"My dad worked in the defense industry in the US, so I understand there are things that sometimes can't be discussed with anyone."

Thane kisses the tip of my nose. "I'd like to hear more about your family, but not yet. This is our first date, after all. We should concentrate on each other."

"I agree. But I need to get a good look at your outfit. Step away, please."

He takes three strides backward and tosses his winter jacket across the living area where it lands on the sofa's back. Then he spreads his arms. "Look all ye like."

Though I'd noticed his clothing when I opened the door, I'd been so thrilled to see him that I paid little attention to anything but his beautiful face. Now, I take a good long look. The most obvious part of his ensemble is the kilt. The plaid design features shades of green, blue, and red as well as wide yellow lines that serve as the focal point. He wears a golden-brown shirt that complements his dirty-blond hair and also spiffy reddish-brown shoes. Gray plaid knee-high socks finish off the ensemble. The overall effect is classy, casual, and sexy as hell.

Oh, yeah, I need to get naked with this man tonight.

Chapter Fifteen

Thane

"Wow, Thane, you look incredible," Rebecca says while she walks around me in a circle to admire my clothing. Women are usually very interested in kilts, but I've never before had a lass inspect me in this manner. It's making me randy. Thankfully, she stops in front of me and raises her gaze to mine. "Never wear anything but a kilt ever again."

"You like the Buchanan clan tartan?"

"No. Well, yes, but it's not the design that makes me horny. You turn that kilt into something smokin' hot."

"I've never had a lass react this way to my kilt. Best not lick your lips anymore until after dinner, or I'll lose control and fuck you up against the door."

She clasps my hands and shuffles backward, leading me toward the island.

I stop us halfway there, then back away a few paces. "It's my turn to admire your clothing."

"My outfit isn't as sexy as yours. If I'd known you would wear a kilt, I would've picked something sexier to wear."

"No, *gràidh*, what you're wearing is perfect. It's dead sexy."

I allow myself to enjoy a slow appraisal of every inch of her body, beginning with her casual, sunny-yellow dress. Slender straps, tied atop her shoulders, hold the frock up, and the flowing skirt portion stops just above her knees. Sandals with low heels show off her bonnie wee toes and sexy ankles. She painted her toenails a muted shade of pink.

Bod an Donais. I want to devour those wee toes and lick my way up her legs until I reach her mound.

"Spin round for me once, love. Let me see all of you."

Rebecca twirls once, then curtsies.

My cock jerks. I cough into my fist and try not to think about her toes anymore. So, I change the topic of conversation. "Ready for dinner?"

"Yes, I'm starving. But we have a small problem." She points a finger at me. "You were supposed to bring the food."

"Oh, aye, that's right. And I did bring it." I trot to the door and swing it open just enough that I can pick up the paper sack I'd left in the hall. As I kick the door shut and return to Rebecca, I hold up the sack. "Everything we need is in here. I brought the ingredients. Now the cooking is up to you, though I'm happy to be your assistant."

"Thank you. I would love to have a gorgeous man in a kilt do my bidding."

"I'll do your bidding anytime, anywhere."

Rebecca gives me a sly smile, then hurries to the other side of the island. I follow the lass and set the bag of groceries on the counter. She immediately begins to remove the items and sort them, studying each one. I watch with fascination as she sets the items out in some sort of order, though I can't deduce her reasoning. Dinnae give a toss about reason. This woman has turned my world upside down in all the best ways, and I would let her do anything she wants as long as she doesn't tell me to bugger off.

She handles most of the cooking and issues orders for me. Neither of us knows where anything should go in this kitchen. She's only lived here for a week. The apartment was meant to come with kitchen utensils, fortunately, so I need only hunt about until I find the right ones. We get into a rhythm as we collaborate on the meal, and we tease each other often, making us both laugh. I haven't had this much fun in the kitchen since I was a wee laddie serving as my ma's helper.

I won't tell Rebecca that, not just yet. We need to get to know each other better before I start regaling the lass with tales of my family.

Rebecca is clearly impressed when I offer to set the table. I find a half-empty box of candles under the kitchen sink as well as holders for them, so I set those up on the table too. Rebecca has just finished the final touches for the meal, and she smiles appreciatively at what I've done.

Aye, I also moved the table closer to the windows. We will have a grand view of Loch Linnhe and the mountains. Rebecca insists that I must sit down and wait for her to bring the food. I cannae deny the lass anything she wants. When she finally takes her seat across the table from me, I pour wine for us both.

Our date has officially begun.

We might have enjoyed a swiftly rising physical attraction on the day we met, but that doesn't translate to an immediate conversational attraction. No, we struggle with awkwardness and discuss the merits of the food and the wine rather than talking about each other. Why have we suddenly become uncomfortable? It must be nerves, though I have never suffered from that problem. I'm feeling it now, though. Maybe we're struggling because of the simple fact that we had a poke on the day we met, and it was bloody incredible. The pressure to reinvigorate our attraction is palpable.

And it's killing the romance of this evening.

Rebecca picks at her food while staring down at her plate. When she takes a sip of wine, she still keeps her head down.

I know how to seduce a woman, for pity's sake. But it's been a very long time since I did that. *Dinnae fuck this up, man. She was putty in your hands a few nights ago.*

Aye, I can do this. And I'll start by relocating.

That means I drag my chair around to the side of the table, close to where Rebecca sits.

Her head jerks up. Her eyes go wide.

I clasp her hand. "Dinnae need to be so far apart, do we? This is meant to be a romantic dinner. We have candlelight, but no conversation and no music. Let me rectify the situation."

"Thane—"

I seal two fingers over her lips. "Hush, lass. We need to deepen the mood with sensual music and sensual conversation. Stay right where you are."

The moment I pull my fingers away, her lips fall open a wee bit. She watches me as I wander over to the island, where I had seen her leave her mobile. When I caught her singing along with the music coming through her earbuds, I'd noticed she was listening via her mobile phone. But when I'd been in her apartment a few nights ago, she had a small stereo system. Now, I realize it has Bluetooth capability. That must be how she listens when she's at home. I use her mobile to connect to the stereo and start up the music.

I sit down beside her again as the first song begins to play.

The hard-driving beat at first seems incongruous with romance, but I soon realize it's precisely what we need.

Rebecca rocks her hips in time with the music. She casts sidelong glances toward me. "Do you like this song?"

"Aye. Let's get up and dance."

"What?"

"You heard me." I stand up and hold out my hand. "Dance with me, love. Right now."

She bites the corner of her lip. "This isn't a slow song."

"I know. But I want to dance with you anyway."

When she still doesn't move, I pluck her off the chair and only set her down once we've moved into the open area between the table and the sofa. Then I splay a hand over her lower back to pull her close. We move together while the driving beat pulses inside us.

Rebecca swallows hard enough the movement is visible. "This song is called 'Mr. Mysterious.' Seems appropriate. You are a man of mystery."

"Am I? Not intentionally."

I guide her across the floor in circles while the song changes to one of her favorites—"I Don't Want Your Love" by Duran Duran. Ah, but I do want her love. First, I'll take her body. The rest will come in time. I twirl the lass so her back lies flush with my front and hold her right hand while lashing my other palm to her belly.

She sucks in a breath.

We shuffle across the floor with our bodies melded, and I roll my hips into her over and over in sync with the song, until it ends. Another one takes its place, a softer, far more sensual number.

I press my lips to her throat and inhale deeply. "Ye smell so good, I'd love to devour every inch of your flesh starting here"—I sweep my hand down to cup her mound through her yellow dress—"and after that, I'll fill you up with my cock. You'll be drenched with your lust for me."

"No whisky until after. I want to be wide awake when we make love."

"Aye, we'll save the whisky for after."

I grasp one of the ties on her dress and undo it with my teeth. Rebecca gasps just as I let the strap fall off her shoulder. "Thank you for wearing this frock, *gràidh*."

Her chest heaves, and her cheeks have turned faintly pink.

Using my teeth once again, I undo the other strap. Only her folded arms prevent the dress from tumbling to the floor. I move in front of her, kneeling at her feet. "Lower your arms, Rebecca."

"Oh, God, Thane. When you say my name, I almost come."

"Good, Rebecca. I want you to come for me over and over."

She lowers her arms. The dress falls down to her waist but gets stuck there thanks to the waistband. I grasp the dress and yank. The fabric falls into a puddle at her feet.

Cannae resist chuckling. "No knickers or bra? My, you are a naughty lass, aren't you?"

"Wanted to make it as easy as possible for you to undress me."

"How did you know I wouldn't want you to strip for me?"

She kicks her shoes off. "I might not know everything about you, but I figured out on day one that you're the kind of man who wants to undress a woman."

"I didn't strip you on that day. We kept our clothes on, mostly."

"Still, I had your number." She pushes her dress and shoes away using one foot. Then she kneels before me. "My turn to strip you, Mr. Buchanan."

"Anything you want, Rebecca."

She shivers faintly. "You're going to kill me with your sensual skills, aren't you?"

"Only in the metaphorical sense."

The lass waves her hands. "Get up, please."

I obey her, naturally.

She takes hold of my kilt's waist and tugs on it experimentally. "Elastic? Oh, I'm so glad you wore your casual kilt. I guess the formal one isn't as easy to remove."

"It is a touch more difficult. There's no elastic, and the kilt is one long length of plaid."

"Hmm, it might be fun to try stripping that off your body sometime."

She drags the kilt down over my hips, and I kick it away the second it hits the floor. The lass keeps her head down as she rolls her eyes upward. "Gee, I'm not the only one who went commando tonight."

"Knew I'd need to pounce on you the moment our meal was over."

"Pounce?" she says with a laugh. "You know what? I might actually do that to you."

"Feel free, lass, feel free."

She rises gradually with her hips undulating and grasps the top button on my shirt. Just as she begins to undo that button, she stops and aims a sexy smirk at me. "No, that isn't the way I want to do this. How attached are you to this shirt?"

"Not at all. It's only a piece of fabric." My chest is rising and falling more heavily. I cannae take my eyes off the naked woman who has her body pressed to mine. The scent of her lust is driving me half mad.

She grasps the button with her teeth and yanks. It goes flying and clacks down on the floor several yards away. Rebecca repeats the process with every button until my shirt hangs open. Then she steps behind me, grasps the halves, and rips the fabric off me from behind. A second later, my shirt flies past me to land on the sofa.

The music has changed to another of her favorite songs—"Hungry Like the Wolf." Bloody hell, I'm as ravenous as a wolf, and it's all because of the woman who just literally tore my clothes off.

I kick my shoes off and strip the socks away too. Then I turn round to face Rebecca. For a moment, we stare at each other while struggling to catch our breath. Lust is a powerful thing, and I mean to show her precisely how much like a wolf I am.

"Run, Rebecca, run for the bedroom now. I'm hunting you."

She grins, plants a hard kiss on my mouth, and races for the bedroom.

Whatever madness has come over me, I dinnae give a fuck. This is the most fun I've ever had in my entire life. I gave the lass a head start, but when I finally gallop into the bedroom, I dinnae see her anywhere. "Are ye hiding, Rebecca? The wolf always gets his prey."

I growl and sniff the air.

Her scent permeates the room.

Dropping to my knees, I peer under the bed. Nothing there except for dust bunnies. I want to devour a lass, not a bunny. That won't satisfy my hunger.

Next, I search the closet with no better luck. The bathroom is empty too.

Then I catch sight of a shadow that stretches out from behind the door. I pretend I'm going back into the living room, but then slam the door shut instead.

Rebecca stands there wedged into the corner with her palms on the wall. "You caught me. Now come and get me."

I reach for her.

The clever lass ducks around me and leaps onto the bed. Her tits bounce. When she spreads her legs, I dinnae need any more of an invitation. I race toward the bed and leap onto it to land straddling her body. I'm breathing just as hard as she is.

"Clever lass," I murmur as I nuzzle her throat. "You've awakened the beast in me, and now you're about to learn how much like an animal I am." I shove a knee between her legs, pushing her thighs apart. "Prepare yourself, Rebecca. I'm going feral tonight."

Chapter Sixteen

Rebecca

He must be joking, right? Thane the ever calm wouldn't go wild in the bedroom. Of course, I've always heard that it's low-key men who turn out to be animals in bed. I've never experienced that myself, so I can't confirm or deny the adage. But damn, I want him to fuck me like a wild beast.

Right now, he's hovering above me, not moving a muscle, with his gaze nailed to mine.

"Please, Thane, do something. I can't stand the suspense anymore."

He lowers his body inch by inch, descending so slowly that my pulse revs up from the anticipation of what he plans to do to me. He maintains his unreadable expression as he bends his elbows to lower himself even more, but then he freezes. His biceps bulge, and his lips tighten. He's trying to stay in this position, but I can't figure out why. His face hovers directly above me. And when he bows his head, his mouth is millimeters from mine.

"When I tell you to," he says, his voice rough, "wrap your ankles around my calves. But not until I say so."

"Okay." I have no clue what he wants to do, but I don't care. A drop of moisture falls from the tip of his erection, dripping onto my skin. "I'll do whatever you want. Just please, keep going."

He growls, like the wolf he claimed to be, and my clit pulses. "Spread your legs a wee bit more, love."

I obey without reservation. The sensation of his cock brushing over my skin makes me so aroused that I can barely catch my breath.

He pulls his hips back, still hovering slightly above me, and slides his length inside me just as deliberately as he'd lowered his body. The sensation of him inside me feels even better than the first time we'd had sex. I love experiencing every inch of him filling me up, and it makes my heart race even faster.

"Now, lass. Hook your ankles round my calves."

I follow his command mindlessly, too turned on to think.

At last, he settles all of his weight on me. I lay my hands on his lower back while he begins to pump his hips at a maddeningly slow pace. His face remains directly above mine with only a few millimeters of separation. The heat of his breaths teases my lips as they fall open, our breaths mingling, while he groans and I release desperate little sounds. I've never needed a man inside me as much as I need Thane to fill me up and never stop.

With every thrust, his chest rubs against my breasts, getting me even more aroused. I've become so wet that I feel my cream dribbling down my inner thighs. Hushed pleas of "yes, yes, please, don't stop" are all I can manage to say. The pressure to come builds inside me, at first like a gentle swell on the ocean, then becoming a tidal wave of need that spurs me to dig my nails into his back and wriggle in a desperate attempt to encourage him to go faster.

Thane ignores my pleas. He keeps thrusting at a measured pace.

I throw my head back, mashing it into the pillow as my mouth falls open.

He licks a path up my throat even while he groans and shoves his hands under my head, forcing my neck to arch even more. He holds my head delicately while he keeps on licking his way up to the shell of my ear. But when he suckles my lobe, I scrape my nails up his back.

Thane winces the tiniest bit, though only for a second.

I shove my fingers into his hair, trying to pull his head down a few millimeters more. I need to feel his lips on mine, need it so badly.

His nostrils flare. He flattens his lips. Sucks in a breath. Blows it out so forcefully that my hair flutters.

Then he crushes his mouth to mine.

I wrap my arms and legs around him while we both plunge our tongues into each other's mouths, tangling, thrusting, so hungry to taste each other that we can't hold back even if we wanted to.

And all the while, he pumps his cock into me faster and harder.

When he nips my tongue gently, I go off. My every muscle freezes, I can't breathe, and the orgasm barreling through my body makes my legs curl up and my head snap forward on a strangled scream.

Thane pounds into me a few more times, hoisting himself up on his straight arms to go even deeper. I swear I can feel it when he comes while buried inside me to the hilt. For a moment after it's all over, he remains propped up on his arms, gasping for breath.

I fall into a human puddle on the bed, wiped out in the most incredible way. "Holy shit, Thane. You really know how to unleash your wild side."

He drops onto the mattress beside me, on his back. "I've never done anything like that before. You bring out desires I never realized I had inside me."

"Same for me."

He rolls onto his side, facing me, and props his head up with one hand. "Should we have dessert now? Or would ye rather fuck again?"

"After a drink of water, I'll be ready for more sex." I fan myself with my hand. "Whew. Good thing I work out regularly. Getting dirty with you requires plenty of stamina."

He kisses me sweetly. "Aye, making love to you is a workout. I'll get you a glass of water. I could use some too."

"There's a glass in the bathroom."

Thane pats my hip, then vaults off the bed to trot into the bathroom. Oh, yes, that means I get a clear view of his taut ass. I could do nothing but admire his body all night long, he's that hot. Thane Buchanan is an amazing lover, but more than that, he's an incredible person. Why he hides all that passion from the rest of the world, I can't fathom. But I want to find out.

Just not tonight. I need more orgasms delivered by Thane.

He saunters out of the bathroom carrying two items—a glass of water, and my vibrator. He waves the device at me. "I thought we could play with this together."

"That's a fantastic idea."

He sets his fine ass on the bed near my hip and hands me the water glass. "Drink, *gràidh*. You need to rehydrate."

I down half the contents of the glass, then offer it to him. "You need to rehydrate too."

"Aye, I do." He swallows the rest of the water in two gulps and sets the glass on the nightstand. "Feeling ready to go again? Or do ye need more of a break?"

"Oh, no, I'm raring to go right now."

Thane slides closer to me, resting one hand on the mattress on the opposite side of my body. He leans over to gaze into my eyes. "Afraid I cannae get hard again immediately. While we wait for my cock to recover, we can enjoy sex play without penetration—for me. I have many ideas for fucking you inside and out."

I wouldn't care if he vowed to screw me in a mud-wrestling ring. The thought of playing with him gets me hot and bothered all over again. I love seeing the playful side of him, but more than that, I love being the only one who knows about this aspect of his personality. Being with him has revealed elements of my own psyche that I had no idea were hidden inside me.

"May I play with you first?" I ask. "Or would you rather be the one to get things going?"

"Go on, lass, have your way with me." He lies down beside me on his back. "I'm yours tonight." He winks. "And every night, every day, every moment in between."

I snatch the vibrator from his grip. "I'll be needing this."

He clasps his hands beneath his head on the pillow.

As I switch the vibrator on, I study his body and start thinking about how I want to use this on him. Maybe I should start with something simple.

So, I straddle his thighs and sit back on my heels. When I touch the vibrator to his skin with the barest contact, he sucks in a sharp breath. But when I begin to drag the vibrator over his chest in slow circles, his chest rises and falls more heavily. I love teasing him this way, so I slide the device down to his groin and lightly touch it to his dick. He jerks.

I raise the vibrator. "Is this okay? Don't want to hurt you."

"Dinnae worry about that. I'm not in pain. It feels bloody good, but I'm not used to this kind of sensation."

"Want me to keep going?"

"Aye. Do what you want with me. I'll speak up if necessary."

I'm certain he would tell me if he didn't like something I do, and he wouldn't lie to spare my feelings. Neither would he be rude about it. I was married for a long time, but my husband would have been embarrassed if I tried to talk to him about what he likes or dislikes during sex—and especially about my own likes and dislikes. I've finally met a man who is mature in age, yes, but also mature in his attitudes and behavior. It's refreshing.

As I drag the vibrator down his inner thigh, he groans deeply. His eyes have drifted half closed. Thane definitely likes this.

I tease him for another few minutes, then shut off the vibrator and offer it to him. "Your turn. Drive me wild, please."

"My pleasure." He sits up and takes the vibrator from me. "What I should have said was you gave me pleasure and it's my turn to reciprocate."

We switch places, with me now lying on my stomach and Thane crouching over my thighs. He begins by using his hands to massage me from head to toe, lighting that fire once again until I'm breathing more heavily and biting my lip so hard it almost hurts. The roughness of his hands turns me on, but it's the Gaelic words he whispers that ramp up my desire so much that I start wriggling.

He gives my ass a light slap. "Try not to squirm, *gràidh*. Cannae have you coming before I'm ready."

"I'll try. No promises."

"Dinnae fash. I will never be annoyed with you."

And I know that's true. I met him six days ago, yet I believe what he says.

Thane slides a long, cylindrical object under my hips and pushes it up until the top rests just below my belly button. Then he turns the vibrator on.

I gasp and writhe.

He rests his arms on my thighs to keep me from wriggling too much. While he cranks the vibrator up to its highest speed, I fist my hands in the pillow. But instead of burying my face in the pillow, I twist my head sideways so I can keep watching Thane. He lowers his head, peeks up at me over my own ass, and finally thrusts his tongue out to lap at my clit.

My whole body jerks. A sharp cry erupts out of me.

He licks and suckles and nips my nub, over and over, until I lose control. Cries burst from my lips, and I thrash so wildly that if Thane weren't holding me down, I'd probably tumble off the bed.

Then he stops.

"Please, Thane, please keep going."

"Dinnae fash, love."

He slides the vibrator out from under my body and pushes it inside me with all the speed of a sloth. Inch by decadent inch, he penetrates me with the device while it keeps humming away. Once its length is seated fully inside me, he shuts off the vibrator.

I make a frustrated noise that's somewhere between a grunt and a whimper.

Thane chuckles and pulls the vibrator out, only to slide it inside me again slightly faster than before—and then pulls it out again. Another desperate, annoyed sound emerges from me. Thane kisses my ass, literally, then thrusts the device into me and switches it on again as he initiates a slow and steady rhythm of fucking me with the vibrator. I'm so slick with my own cream that the device makes a sucking sound with every thrust.

He massages my bottom with one hand, sensually, lovingly.

I'm on the verge of orgasm, so close I can almost taste it.

Naturally, that's when he shuts off the vibrator but leaves it nestled inside me. "How do you feel, love? Need to come now? Or can ye handle a wee bit more?"

"I want as much as you can give me. Take me to the edge and tease me." Can't believe I just said that. But it's true.

"All right, then. Shut your eyes and let the sensations take over."

Of course I follow his command. I love the way he takes control of me.

Thane revs up the vibrator again. But this time, instead of pumping it inside me, he just holds it there on its highest setting.

And he licks my folds roughly.

"Oh, God!" I shout as my body convulses and pleasure burns me up from the inside out while Thane keeps licking me. I thrash and cry out, pounding my fists on the pillow. Just as the sweet bliss winds down, I collapse. "Thane, I… That was…"

"Hush, *gràidh*. Give yourself a few minutes to come down from that high."

Thane removes the vibrator and disappears into the bathroom, emerging a moment later. He's holding a damp towel. "Let me soothe you with a warm cloth."

I'm incapable of moving or speaking right now, so I simply nod. My lips have curled into a small smile that must seem blissful. I lie still and allow him to soothe me as he said he'd do, gently running that warm towel over my skin.

When I've recovered enough to sit up, I grasp his face and kiss him. "You are amazing. I need to give you something incredible in return."

"That's not necessary."

"But I insist." I wag a finger at him. "Don't say no. I won't allow it."

"I have no choice, aye? Do you want me lying down?"

"No. I have a different idea." I hop off the bed and walk around to the foot. "Sit here, please."

"I want to ask why, but I'd rather wait to see what you're about."

He crawls up to me and swings his legs off the bed, now sitting in front of me.

And I kneel between his thighs.

Chapter Seventeen

Thane

I understand what the lass is about, and I seem incapable of denying her anything she wants. That's why I did as she asked. Now, I must disappoint her. So, I crook a finger under her chin and slant forward until our noses almost touch. "I want to have another go, but ahmno as young as I used to be. Despite having the stamina of a young laddie, I can't change the fact that I'll need a wee bit more time before I can take your body again."

She turns her face into my palm and kisses it. "I understand. My ex-husband is a few years younger than you, but even five years ago he couldn't do it again so soon after sex. I got a little overexcited and forgot the laws of nature for a minute."

"No worries. Why don't we enjoy the dessert you made for us? I'm sure after that, I'll be ready again. Doesn't usually take more than thirty or forty minutes."

Her brows hike up. "Only forty minutes? My ex always needed at least two hours."

"Every bloke is different." I wrap my arms around her waist and hoist us both onto our feet. "Besides, I once spent a weekend with a lovely woman who taught me all about meditation and tantric sex. That's how I learned to make love to a woman slowly, sometimes for hours."

"But you didn't go that slowly with me."

I chuckle softly, and affectionately, as I brush my fingers over her cheek. "Rebecca, you are the only woman who has ever aroused me so intensely that I forget about all my own rules."

"You mean your rules of sex."

"No. I mean all my rules." I draw her into my arms, tucking her head under my chin. "Believe me, *gràidh*. I wish I could tell you everything about myself, but I cannae do that."

"I know, and I understand why you can't share more with me."

Rebecca is the most unusual woman I've ever met. She doesn't get angry when I can't tell her my secrets but simply accepts my limitations. Is she the perfect woman for me? I believe she might be. But I have no idea whether she can accept my secrets for the long term. That might be too much to ask of the lass.

We amble out into the living area and spend a few moments admiring the view and the starry sky. Then she jogs over to the kitchen to retrieve our dessert. I sit down at the table and enjoy the view of her erse until she moves behind the island. That lass has the bonniest cheeks I've ever seen, and I'm not referring to her face.

She jogs back to me, giving me the chance to admire her bouncing tits.

Rebecca holds one plate in her hand. It contains a single slice of some sort of pie. She settles her bonnie erse down on the chair beside mine, then sets the plate on the table along with a dessert fork. "I made this yesterday, since it wouldn't have been done in time for us to eat it this evening if I'd tried to make it today."

"Dinnae care when you baked our dessert. It looks lovely and delicious, just like the lass who cooked it."

She kisses me firmly on the lips. "You're the best date any woman could hope for."

"Are ye going to tell me what you've whipped up for our dessert?"

"Oh, yes, of course." She pushes the plate toward me, so it's now squarely between us. "I found a recipe online and modified it a bit. It was originally bourbon peach streusel cheesecake, but I realized that for you, I needed to switch up some of the ingredients."

"Whatever you've done, it looks like something you'd find in a posh restaurant. If the pie itself is as good as the presentation, I'll be eating more than one slice."

She smiles, and her cheeks dimple. Then she focuses on the pie, pointing at each element in turn. "It starts with a graham cracker crust for a simple cheesecake that's laced with thick, dark caramel. Instead of peaches, I used strawberries, both in the cheesecake and on top of it as part of the brown sugar streusel topping." She aims a teasing look at me. "Can you guess what the secret ingredient is?"

"Hmm." I pretend to think deeply about the answer to her question. "If it's not bourbon, then it must be beer."

She laughs but tries to suppress it, resulting in a snort. "I know you don't really think I'd put beer in a beautiful cheesecake."

"Go on and tell me about your secret ingredient."

The lass leans in to whisper into my ear, "It's your whisky, Thane."

"Ahhh, I see. Dinnae think anyone has ever used my whisky in this way. You are a clever lass."

"Wanna taste my dessert?"

"Dinnae need to ask. I'm waiting with bated breath to experience your culinary masterpiece."

She pats my cheek. "Don't go overboard with the phony praise."

"It's not phony. I am very impressed by your prowess in the kitchen."

Rebecca hands me the fork. "I want you to try it first."

"Haven't you tasted it already?"

She shakes her head. "I wanted us to enjoy it together. And I really hope it doesn't taste like sewer sludge."

"Nothing crafted with your lovely hands could ever be sludge." I hold up a hand when she seems about to dispute my claim. "Dinnae try to tell me I should temper my expectations."

I pick up the fork. Then I decide to have a wee bit of fun with Rebecca. I'm going to narrate my first taste of her concoction. "My fork penetrates the delicate flesh of the cheesecake so smoothly, sinking down into the caramel, straight through the pliant crust."

Out of the corner of my eye, I can see the lass rubbing her teeth over her bottom lip with her gaze fastened to my mouth.

She clearly likes my barmy narration, so I continue—and lift my forkful of cheesecake. "Watch the caramel stretching sinuously from the creamy flesh while I close my lips around the fork and devour the sweetness."

The lass stares at my mouth.

I pull the fork free while keeping my lips sealed. Then I begin to chew, slowly, sensually, while I watch her expression. Dinnae think she's licking her lips again because she desperately wants cheesecake. "Mm, the flavors combine in the most sensual way, and the sweet-yet-spicy taste of the whisky enhances the pleasure."

By the time I've swallowed the bite of cheesecake, Rebecca's pupils have dilated, darkening her honey-brown eyes.

She drags her tongue across her lips, and her eyes drift shut. "Wow, this tastes even better than I hoped. Makes me feel warm and soft. It's so…delectable."

"It's not the dessert that makes you feel that way."

"That's for sure." Her lids flutter open, and she aims those sultry eyes at me. "It's you, Thane. You and your whisky. But those two things are inseparable because you *are* the whisky. Its flavor and body come from you and you alone."

"No one has ever suggested that before. But it's exactly how I feel about my whisky, and it's why I'm protective of the single malts I create."

"I figured that out on the day we met. Maybe that's why I've had trouble coming up with an appropriate marketing campaign. I've tried to ignore the huge elephant in the room—your innate connection to the Scotch you create."

She thrusts another forkful of pie into her mouth and consumes it with all the sultry yet casual hunger that only a mature woman could embody. Once she's done, she spears another forkful, raising it to my lips. "You need to have more of this. It's luscious."

"Not as luscious as you." I let her feed me another mouthful. "Mm, this is *drùis-mhiannach*. I swear I can taste you in this dessert."

"What does that Gaelic phrase mean?"

"I said the cheesecake is erotic."

Rebecca leans in to swipe her tongue across my bottom lip, licking up a spot of the cheesecake's flesh. Then she glances down at my groin. "Guess dessert did the trick."

"Aye, I'm getting hard. You did this to me, so it's up to you to relieve the pressure."

"Not just yet."

She spears a bite of the cheesecake and slides it into her mouth, moaning as she gradually pulls the fork free. Then she pushes one finger between my lips. I realize what she wants and open my mouth for her. She seals her lips to mine and opens her mouth too, thrusting her tongue deep to spread the melting confection. It tastes like whisky and caramel, naturally, but also of her. I pull her onto my lap, lashing my arms around her.

And we devour each other with abandon.

I grasp fistfuls of her hair, tugging her even closer, while our tongues tangle and my cock grows stiffer by the second. She rocks her hips into me as if she's trying to ride my *slat* but cannae quite get it inside her. I keep kissing her with a passion no other woman could inspire in me, even while I struggle to rise and set her erse on the table. Blindly, I flail one arm to clear the tabletop.

The plate of cheesecake and the fork clatter to the floor.

Rebecca rips her mouth away from mine. "Take me the wolf way. Please, Thane."

I've lost all capacity for coherent speech, so I simply nod and grunt. I set the lass on her feet, and we both need a moment to catch our breath. Rebecca rests her erse on the table's edge. I simply stand here with my dokey as stiff as a board, struggling to recover my voice. At last, I succeed.

"Ye want me to take ye the wolf way, aye? Then get on your hands and knees on the floor."

She hurries to obey my command and wriggles her erse while glancing over her shoulder at me.

I drop to my knees and grasp her hips, thrusting into her in one swift movement. Cannae restrain my lust for her, though. I maintain a firm hold on her hips as I pump into her faster and harder, grunting with every thrust. Her hair flies around her face while she cries out over and over, calling out my name in between those shouts.

Her sheath convulses around my cock. The lass unleashes even wilder cries and barely coherent shouts for me never to stop fucking her. The way her body milks my cock, I cannae hold out any longer. Throwing my head back, I shout and pound into her once more as I spill everything I have inside her body.

Then I slump to my knees on the floor.

Rebecca collapses onto her belly.

After a moment, I crawl over to her and pull the lass onto my lap. She rests her head on my shoulder. I pepper kisses over her forehead and down her nose to the tip. Her eyes have fluttered shut.

"Ready for bed?" I ask. "I'm jeeked for sure."

"Mm, yeah. Sleep sounds good."

I carry her into the bedroom and gently lay her down on the mattress. By the time I've laid down beside her, she has already fallen asleep. I cradle her to me, and soon, I slip into slumber too.

What do I dream of? Rebecca, of course. No other woman has ever invaded my dreams in this way, and I dinnae mind at all.

I spend the rest of the weekend with her. But on Sunday night, after making love to Rebecca for an hour, I need to drive home and change clothes for work. I kiss her goodbye at the door. When I try to walk away, the magnetic pull of her presence draws me back, and I need to kiss her again. And again. And again. Finally, I force myself to leave the building.

As I'm walking to my truck in the garage, the slithering shape of a shadow catches my eye peripherally.

I halt and pretend to be fiddling with my keys.

The shadow slithers closer, coming up behind me.

One more step and then...

I whirl around and seize the man's shirt, hauling him closer. Shock immobilizes me for a split second, but then I regain my composure. Despite that, I can't erase the snarl in my voice when I speak to him. "What are you doing here? How did you escape from prison?"

"Didn't need to escape," the British scunner says. "I was released three weeks ago. Paid my debt to society."

"Just released? And the first thing you did was track me down. I'm flattered that you care so much."

The scunner huffs. "I'm not here to beg you to be my mate."

"Must be on holiday, then. Why dinnae ye go search for the Loch Ness Monster? Nessie must be hungry, and you look like a perfect snack."

"Shut your bloody mouth." He shakes my hands off and backs away a few paces. "This is your warning. When you see me again, I'll tell you what your punishment will be."

"My punishment? You were the traitor, not me."

He stabs a finger in the air toward me. "You are going to pay, Thane. Ratting on me is not something I can ever forgive." He peers around me to stare at my truck. "You've parked in a visitor slot. Who were you here to see? A woman? Ah, yes, I'm sure that's it. You always thought you were God's gift to women."

I scoff. "If you think you can goad me into confirming your assumption, then you don't know me as well as you believe. Go home, wherever that is, and forget about your pathetic wee vendetta. Walk away now. This is your last chance before I batter you to a bloody pulp."

He shuffles past me, keeping a wide gap between us. "I'll go, for now. But I will be back. Mark my words."

The scunner sprints out of the garage, disappearing down the sidewalk.

I pull out my mobile and dial a number I swore I would never call again.

"Hello, Thane, darling. What calamity has befallen you? It must be something truly cataclysmic if you're ringing me."

The lass's British accent prickles my nerves, but not because I dislike her. No, it's because that part of my life ended long ago—or so I believed. "Aye, I have a problem. Holden De Boer just accosted me in a parking garage in Fort William."

"Oh, that is unfortunate. But alas, we can no longer offer you assistance in such matters. I suggest you ring the police."

She hangs up on me.

Aye, Holden De Boer is my problem. The ghosts of my past have come back to haunt me at last.

Chapter Eighteen

Rebecca

I sit in my office chair with my legs tucked under me, spinning my chair round and round and round. The fantastic sounds of Duran Duran dazzle my senses through my earbuds. I can't stop myself from humming along. And then singing along. And finally, jumping out of my chair to dance along with "Black Moonlight."

My weekend with Thane energized me more than anything else could. We had fun. We had hot sex. We fed each other and made out and finished off that bottle of *Collaidh Sgeul-Rùin* Black Label. No, I have not mastered the pronunciation of that phrase yet. I'd love for Thane to teach me that Gaelic phrase and more, especially the dirty ones.

I might stink at pronouncing Gaelic, but I have mastered every way to get Thane so turned on that he'll growl and fuck me on every surface in my apartment. Next time, we'll do that in his house. Thane suggested it. He told me he has a large bed and several bottles of his whisky on hand, not to mention a box of candy he'd ordered from his British friend, Hugh Parrish, who owns a company called Sommerleigh Sweets.

As I flop back down on my chair, I nab a candy from that box. Turns out Thane had bought two boxes of Hugh's candies, and he gave one to me. Now, I stuff a chocolate pecan truffle into my mouth. Mm, this is the best chocolate I've ever eaten.

Three crisp knocks resound from my office door.

"Come in," I call out. My words are slightly muffled thanks to the candy I'm still devouring.

As the door swings open, I whirl my chair around.

Thane shuts the door and halts halfway to me. He shoves a hand into his pants pocket, cocking his hip. "Ready for lunch, *gràidh*? Or are you so engrossed in your music that you don't care about food?" He peers around me. "Then again, maybe you're too full of sweets."

"I'm having an appetizer."

He cups a hand over his ear. "What did you say? I can't hear it through the sound of you gnawing on that chocolate."

I swallow the last of the truffle and lick my lips clean. "Sorry. I got hungry, so I decided to eat a couple of Hugh's candies to tide me over."

Thane strides up to me, grasps my chair's arms, and crushes his mouth to mine. I can't help it. I slump in my chair and moan while he thrusts his tongue between my lips and consumes me. By the time he pulls away, I feel like I've just taken a Valium pill. Somehow, Thane can make me feel relaxed and aroused at the same time.

He straightens. "I'd like to take you out to lunch today. There's a café in Loch Fairbairn that›s quite good."

"Isn't Loch Fairbairn half an hour away? It would take our whole lunch break just to go there and back."

"One of the benefits of dating your boss is that you can take extra time off and no one will dare complain."

I wag a finger at him. "We agreed that you wouldn't treat me differently at work. If everyone else only gets an hour for lunch, that's what I should get too."

Thane smirks. "I was having you on, Rebecca. You will not receive special treatment. I've told everyone to take two hours for lunch today because they work so bloody hard and deserve the extra hour."

"Oh. Well, that's okay, then."

He offers me his hand. "Shall we go?"

Only now have I noticed that he's wearing a wool coat. My brain doesn't run on all cylinders when I'm in the vicinity of Thane Buchanan. I accept his hand, and he helps me get my own wool coat on. During my first week at work here, I realized I needed to dress for the Scottish weather instead of dressing like I work at a big corporation. Today, I chose a nice-looking pair of jeans that have a flannel lining, along with warm winter boots that Thane helped me pick out during our weekend together. He also insisted I should buy thicker socks and some sweaters too.

He sweeps his gaze over me. "You make winter clothing look sexy."

"So do you. Are those your flannel-lined pants?"

"Aye. They're a necessity in the Highlands this time of year."

"That's for sure. I've learned a lot about winter clothing since I moved to Scotland. Can't believe I showed up on my first day dressed like a CEO, with high heels and everything."

He clasps my hand as we walk out of my office. "Dinnae feel bad, lass. I suffered from the same problem when I was in Egypt. Had no idea how to dress my first time there."

We've gone halfway down the long hallway, heading toward the exit, but I suddenly stop dead, unable to move a single muscle except to veer my gaze to him. "You've been to Egypt? I've always wanted to go there."

He freezes. His expression goes blank, though only for a couple of seconds. Then he scrunches up his face and hisses, *"Mhac na galla."*

Thane is cursing—at himself, clearly. But why?

He groans and shoves a hand through his hair. "I shouldn't have mentioned that. Cannae tell you why. I'm sorry."

"I understand. You warned me from the start there would be things you couldn't tell me."

He gives me a grateful, if small, smile. "You are very understanding. I appreciate that."

"Let's forget about all of that and go to lunch."

As we walk out of the building, Thane suggests that we should take his pickup truck because my car is "designed for munchkins, not full-grown Scots." When I tease him about being a fan of *The Wizard of Oz*, he doesn't mind at all. I suspect that nothing I could razz him about would faze him, though I haven't tested that theory by teasing him about sex. Men can be prickly about that. Thane might be the most unusual man I've ever met, but I wouldn't be surprised if he suffers from the same sexual insecurities that most guys have. He might just hide it better.

My car is not tiny, but Thane is rather large.

He opens the passenger door for me and even gives me a boost to get into the truck. It's bigger than two cars like mine stacked on top of each other, not including the tires. Naturally, he cups my bottom to give me the push I need to hop inside the vehicle.

While he hustles around to the driver's side, I admire the upholstery. Trucks usually aren't this plush. He must've bought the luxury version. I run my hands over the velvety seat but lament, in my mind, the fact that he has the center section of the seat down, so it serves as an armrest. I'd much rather cuddle up to Thane. Can't do that now.

He climbs in and whumps down on the driver's seat, making the truck wobble a smidgen. As he starts up the engine, he waves toward me. "Buckle up."

"Oh, sorry. I forgot. I was too busy admiring your spiffy truck." I start to buckle up, then stop. "Would you mind raising the middle of the seat so I can cuddle up to you during the drive? I might get cold if I don't have your hot body nestled against me."

He chuckles. "How can I say no to that request? I would love to have your lush, warm body pressed against me." He raises the center of the seat and pats the bench. "Slide on over, *gràidh*."

I do exactly that and buckle my seatbelt, then snuggle up to Thane as much as is reasonably safe to do.

He kisses me sweetly, then revs up the engine. Seconds later, we're rolling out of the parking lot and heading down the road. Since I'm not driving, I have the luxury of soaking up the scenery, from the dusting of snow on the ground and on the trees to the starkly beautiful mountains and the deep, dark lochs. Thane had assured me that the majority of the Highlands doesn't usually get tons of snow during the winter. It also doesn't stay icy cold for the duration of winter either.

"Today it's cold and snowy," he tells me. "But tomorrow, you might not need a coat at all. That's Scotland."

I take advantage of having Thane trapped in a vehicle with me to talk business with him. He prefers to tinker with his whiskies and leave the business stuff to Fiona and me. But I can't let him get away with that anymore. So, I snuggle up to him even more, resting my chin on his shoulder. "We need to talk about the Valentine's campaign."

"You're at war with a holiday?"

I nudge him in the side. "Don't get cute with me. I've let you scurry away to your office every time I mentioned the new marketing campaign, but I need your input. Don't tell me to ask Fiona instead. You are your whisky, which means you must be involved in the marketing of it."

He groans. "Could we please enjoy lunch first?"

"Nope. I'm not falling for your excuses anymore." I settle my hand on his thigh. "You will cooperate, Thane. And after our weekend together, I know every way to make you do what I want."

Thane switches the radio on, and the CD player starts churning out Duran Duran songs. I can't help smiling. He's become a convert. And I can't pass up the chance to tease him about that.

I place my lips millimeters from his ear. "Welcome to the cult."

"What cult?"

"You're a Duranie now."

"I reckon I am, thanks to you." He peels my hand off his thigh. "Best keep your soft wee hands to yourself while I'm driving."

"Have you ever had sex in a car while driving down the road?"

Thane clears his throat and focuses on the road ahead. "Behave yourself, Rebecca."

I shake my head as I lay my hand on his leg again and slide it down his inner thigh. "I'm done with behaving myself, and it's your fault. So tell me, have you ever screwed in a car while driving?"

"If I told you the answer to that question, I'd have to kill you."

My nosiness meter just shot up to the top. I give his thigh a light squeeze, making him cough into his fist. "How can the answer to my question be top secret? Just nod your head once if you've done what I suggested."

He doesn't move his head at all.

I can feel his dick stiffening, so I know my suggestion has turned him on. My ex-husband would never believe I could be this audacious. I never used to be—until I met Thane.

But I love the new me.

Thane clearly loves it too.

I slide my hand closer to his dick, rewarded by his sharp intake of breath. "Come on, admit it. You've had sex in a moving car while you were driving. I won't tell anybody. My lips will be sealed with crazy blue and duct tape."

"If ye do that, I willnae be able to kiss you."

"Good point." I palm his cock, and even through his pants, I can feel it twitch. "All you have to do is nod. Then I'll know the truth."

He picks my hand up and sets it on my lap. "Enough, Rebecca. I told you from the start that I cannae share everything with you. Accept it, or walk away. Those are your choices."

Damn, he's far more stubborn than I expected. His Buddha attitude isn't an act—of that, I'm sure—but he's hiding something big about his time in the military. Maybe I shouldn't pester him for the whole story, but I need to know more about this man in case I…fall for him.

I give in and change the subject. For now. "Tell me about your family, Thane."

He relaxes visibly and audibly, sighing with palpable relief. "What would you like to know?"

"Everything."

"Dinnae believe in starting small, do you?"

"Nope."

He slings an arm around me, holding on to the wheel with one hand. "My parents are Keith and Elsa Buchanan, both in their seventies. I have a brother, Ramsey, and a sister, Iona."

"Elsa doesn't sound like a Scottish name."

"It isn't. Ma is from Sweden. Da met her when she was an exchange student."

"How interesting. Are your parents retired now?"

Thane chuckles. "Retired? Keith Buchanan won't stop working until his body is dropped into a grave. He loves being a leatherworker. Ma stayed home to care for her children, but once we were adults, she turned her needlework hobby into a business. She sells her creations at fairs and at Kirsty MacTaggart's shop."

"I'd love to see her work sometime. And I'd love to meet your dad too."

He throws me a sly sidelong glance. "But not my siblings?"

"Of course I want to know about them too."

"Ramsay is a blacksmith. He forges every sort of metal object you could imagine, even jewelry. Since his wife filed for divorce, he's been rather obsessed with work. Their two children are adults now." Thane's lips curve into a softer smile. "My sister, Iona, is the baby of the family. She's had various jobs over the years, but none stuck until she took over the *Loch Fairbairn Daily News*, which used to be called the *Loch Fairbairn World News*. It was a scandal sheet when Graham Oliver owned it. But Iona has cleaned up its tarnished reputation."

"Is your sister married?"

"No. She came close a few times, but journalism has always been her passion." He eyes me sideways again. "Aren't you going to ask the obvious question?"

"What?" I abruptly realize what he must mean. "Oh, I get it. Does your sister have any children?"

"Aye, she has two. They're both adopted."

"I'd love to hear her story sometime."

He pulls me closer. "Later, *gràidh*. Look, we're just coming into Loch Fairbairn."

Chapter Nineteen

Thane

When Rebecca and I walk into the café, we need to wait for a wee bit since the premises is brimming with customers. I›ve never seen this place as busy as it is now. While we wait, I entertain Rebecca with a story about the time my brother tried to woo a lass by offering her a handmade *sgian dubh*. The lass did not appreciate being gifted with a dagger.

"How did she react?" Rebecca asks.

"She skelped Ramsay, and he nearly tumbled over backward."

"Um, what does it mean to 'skelp' someone?"

"The lass gave him a right good smack, then she walked away."

Rebecca laughs, then nudges me. "I would love it if a man wooed me with a dagger. That's what *'sgian dubh'* means, right?"

"Aye, it is. How did you know that?"

Our waitress approaches us then, suspending our discussion until we've reached our table. It's in a far corner of the café, just secluded enough to give us a wee bit of privacy. Thankfully, I hadn›t spotted anyone I recognize as we wended our way to our table. I want this date to be something special for Rebecca, with no interfering family or friends causing complications.

Maybe I shouldn't have brought the lass to a popular restaurant. But Rebecca deserves a proper date.

"Do ye need time to browse the menu?" our waitress asks. She's a charming lass with fiery red hair, and she seems very professional. Her name tag identifies her as Bonnie.

I turn to Rebecca. "The café offers all the usual sort of fare. But they also have traditionally Scottish foods, if you›re interested in that. How brave are you?"

She smiles with a mischievous glint in her eyes. "You know the answer to that question. But why don't you order for us both? I trust your judgment."

"All right." I hand the menus back to Bonnie. "We'll have haggis, neeps, and tatties with a side of Scottish porridge. And give us fish and chips too. For dessert, we'll have *cranachan*."

"Would ye like anything to drink in the meantime? Other than water."

I consider her suggestion briefly, then the answer becomes obvious. "No, it'll be local Highland spring water please, for both of us. That is still what you offer here, aye?"

"Oh, aye. I'll fetch you two bottles."

As our waitress bustles away from us, Rebecca lifts her brows. "Local Highland water?"

"It comes from the spring that feeds Loch Fairbairn, the body of water the village takes its name from. You can only get this particular variety of spring water here in the village."

"Nobody distributes it to other parts of Scotland to sell?"

I shake my head. "To preserve the loch, the river that spills into it, and the spring that feeds the entire system, it was decided that only locals can draw water from the loch and only for local use."

Bonnie brings us our bottles of spring water and opens the metal caps for us. Then she tells us to "enjoy the fresh, sweet taste" right before she bustles away again. I take a sip first, in case Rebecca might be dubious about the taste of the water. But she doesn't hesitate at all. As I'm still swallowing my first sip, she has already downed two mouthfuls. She calls the spring water "mm-mm delicious," but she also asks me if the nameless river at Dùndubhan tastes as good as this—or better.

"The river water is better than anything else you'll ever taste. That's why I insisted on using only the spring water from Beann Dealgach as the source for my whisky."

"Is it safe to drink directly from the river? Or does it need to be filtered first?"

As I slide an arm across the top of our curved bench, I tug her a wee bit closer. "That river holds the sweetest, cleanest water on earth. When the weather gets warmer, we should swim in the river. Then you'll understand how special it is. All of Dùndubhan and the surrounding area hold magic within them."

"Oh, come on. You can't seriously be trying to convince me that your friend Rory's castle is on magical grounds."

"You loved my story about the legend of the *Daoine Sìth*."

She takes a sip of water and points the bottle at me. "You know I don't actually believe all that stuff. Legends and myths are fun to read about or hear about, but they're not real."

I down a large swig of my water. "I give up. You American heathens have no imagination."

"You'd better hope that's not true, or our marketing campaign will crash and burn."

"Oh, that will never happen. You're a marketing genius." Before she can complain about what I said, I change the subject. "Tell me more about your children. They're fraternal twins. That's all I know."

Rebecca's expression lights up, as if a bulb has been switched on inside her. She clearly enjoys talking about her children. "Courtney and Eric are twenty-five, and they've been virtually inseparable since birth. Despite being fraternal twins, they behave as if they're identical. Not in their appearance. But in their behavior and the way they often seem to read each other's minds."

"Interesting. I assumed only identical twins did that."

"Have you ever met identical twins?"

"Aye. Richard and Nick Hunter, my British mates, are identical." Cannae stop myself from smirking. "They once played a joke on Maddie, who was Richard's fiancée at the time, by having Nick sneak up behind her and pretend he was Richard. It didn't work. Maddie is far too clever to fall for that trick."

"Hmm. Should I be on the lookout for your Scottish buddies trying to trick me that way?"

I shrug. "Never know what they might do."

Our food arrives, and we spend a few minutes discussing all the dishes. Rebecca is curious about everything, not just food, and I could spend hours just telling her about Scotland and especially the Highlands. But this is meant to be a lighthearted lunch, not a primer of my home country. Besides, I have more questions for the lass.

"You mentioned once that your children live in England. Are they at university? Or do they have jobs here? But you should try some of the food before responding."

She delicately picks up a bit of haggis with her fork and slides it between her lips. As she chews, her expression shifts from wary curiosity to definite interest before she finally smiles and hums with satisfaction. "That's much better than I expected. The way it looks didn't entice me, but I'm glad I tried it anyway. This is good stuff."

"I'm glad you like it. Now, about your children..."

"Awfully nosy, aren't you? Well, you did tell me about your family. It's my turn now." She daintily wipes her mouth with her napkin. "Both Courtney and Eric decided to go to college in the UK so they could see more of the world. Their dad offered to pay for their tuition since I couldn't afford to do that. Gary might have gotten tired of me, but at least he never let his feelings toward me affect his relationship with our kids."

"Sounds like your children are as clever as their mother. What sorts of jobs did they take?"

"They both stayed in the UK after graduation. Courtney is a robotics engineer at a tech startup in London, and Eric is a geologist."

I hesitate to ask my next two questions, but I doubt she'll be offended. If she is, I'll apologize profusely. Get down on my knees and kiss her feet, if necessary. Aye, I would do anything for this woman, despite not knowing her well—yet. "May I ask what your, ah, ex-husband does for living?"

"Of course you can ask. I'm not sensitive about that. Gary has been a personal trainer for as long as I've known him. When we got married, I was happy to work so he could build up his business. But then…" She twists her mouth into a lopsided frown. "Then I got pregnant, and everything changed. I wanted to stay home with the kids, but Gary insisted I had to support him until he had enough clients."

"If he's still a personal trainer, he must have started earning a living from that eventually."

She nods but then rolls her gaze heavenward. "Oh, yeah, he makes a good living now. But I worked my butt off for years to support him and raise our two kids essentially on my own. Once he finally had the clientele he'd always dreamed of, he divorced me."

"What? The *bod ceann* as no scruples, does he?"

She seems to be struggling not to laugh and winds up spluttering. "You're adorable, Thane. And I appreciate that you're offended on my behalf. But I got over my anger years ago."

"I hope your children don't know about how your husband treated you."

"They have no idea, and I want it to stay that way. Courtney and Eric have never been particularly close with their father, but I wouldn't want them to find out about Gary's behavior."

I lay my hand on hers. "I will never divulge that secret. You have my word."

"Thank you. My life must sound like a soap opera to you."

A bitter laugh spills from my lips. "You have no idea what sorts of tawdry things I've experienced."

"You can't tell me about any of that, though."

"Aye, I'm afraid I cannae share the details."

But I'm beginning to realize that I want to share everything with her. I need to do it. But I'm forbidden from doing so. How can I engage in a romance with Rebecca? I should walk away. Dinnae think I can, though. I'm not strong enough to push her away.

We return to enjoying our meal and chatting about which food items she likes. When I ask which ones she didn't like, she shrugs and admits she enjoys all of them. But she's unconvinced that the Loch Fairbairn spring water is the most wonderful water she's ever tasted. Maybe I should give her a taste of the river water from Beann Dealgach. I've never sampled it myself, but maybe it's true after all that fairies blessed the water.

No, that's rot. I'm so enraptured by this woman that I'm turning into a stark-raving bampot. Soon, I'll start seeing *sith* spirits dancing all around me.

We order more food, just so Rebecca can taste every Scottish dish on the menu plus Irn-Bru, a soft drink I've never enjoyed. Rebecca calls it "tasty but not something worth drinking every day." I agree with her assessment, except for the "tasty" remark. I think the drink is rubbish. Fiona likes it, but her sister Jamie absolutely loves it. Her husband, the American Gavin Douglas, cannae stand Irn-Bru. But being hopelessly in love with his wife, he tolerates her addiction to the soft drink.

For her final taste of Scottish food and drinks, Rebecca insists on trying Whipkull. It's a concoction of egg yolks, sugar, cream, and rum.

I lay my hand over the top of her glass. "If you're going to drink this, you should at least say '*slainte*' when you do. And say it with enthusiasm."

Her eyes twinkle in the muted lighting as she smirks and tosses back a sizable mouthful of Whipkull. "*Slainte!*"

"*Mhac na galla*. I said you should say it with enthusiasm, not with ear-splitting volume."

Several adults, men and women alike, raise their glasses and shout "*slainte*" too. Then even more people chime in, and soon, they're laughing and tipping their glasses toward Rebecca. She grins and raises her glass to them.

Once the excitement is over, we finish off our meal and give Bonnie a sizable tip. The lass earned it. We ordered enough food for a small army and asked our waitress to package up what we didn't finish off. We now have two large paper sacks full of leftovers. I commanded Rebecca to take all of it home with her.

"You're commanding me?" she says with a slyly sensual smile as we're walking out of the café. She hooks her arm round mine, bringing her body even closer to me. "I like it when you get bossy in the bedroom. Ordering me to take all this food is kind of hot too, in a strange way." She rubs her cheek on my upper arm—or rather, on the wool coat that covers it. "Thank you for giving me the full Scottish food experience all in one sitting at a cute little Scottish café."

"I'll show you the whole of the Highlands, and the rest of Scotland too. In fact, I would show you the entire world if you asked."

She lifts her head to set her chin on my arm, so she can gaze up at me. "Are you rich? You're so mysterious and secretive that I can't help wondering."

"Wondering what? I'm not a billionaire like Evan MacTaggart or Diana Sangster. She's British, though."

"You know two billionaires? Are they the ones funding your distillery?"

Dinnae mind the lass interrogating me—she warned me she would do that eventually—but I begin to feel an odd sensation prickling my nerves. I recognize this feeling, but I do not want to alert Rebecca to it. I might be paranoid after my encounter with Holden De Boer. I never told the lass about that. Maybe I should do now.

She bumps her shoulder into me. "Well, are they your investors?"

"Who?"

"Those billionaire friends of yours."

"Aye, they have both provided funding, and they're members of the company's board of directors."

Rebecca slips her hand into mine. "You must be the CEO or whatever they call it here in the UK."

"I am. But I prefer to focus on crafting whisky, not attending meetings. Besides, the board members dinnae want to control the distillery. They simply want to help in whatever way I suggest. They also own stock in the company."

"They must really believe in you."

"I reckon…" My words trail off as that prickling at my nape grows stronger. Then I spot a shadow scurrying round the corner up ahead of us. I halt. "Stay here, please. I need to check on something."

"What's wrong?"

"Just wait here."

She frowns.

And I jog round the corner, straight into Holden De Boer.

Chapter Twenty

Rebecca

Thane couldn't have actually expected me to stand here on the sidewalk twiddling my thumbs. Whatever he spotted up ahead of us had spurred him to jog to the corner, then sprint down the side street. Am I going to obey his command? I might like his bossiness in bed, but this is a different situation. Besides, he only asked me not to follow him. He never commanded it.

I race around the corner and freeze.

Thane stands a couple of yards away, having a hushed but clearly heated conversation with a man I've never seen before. Maybe he's one of Thane's MacTaggart buddies or some other Scot he knows.

I walk swiftly to catch up to them, coming up beside Thane.

He scowls at me. "What are ye doing here? I said to stay put."

"No, you requested that I stay put. The word please made it an optional request."

I can tell Thane wants to argue with me, but he gives up on that to focus on the other man. "Are ye stalking me, Holden?"

The stranger puckers his lips and clenches his fists. "Stalking you? Oh, that's rich. You hunted me for weeks and sent me to prison. Fourteen years of living at His Majesty's pleasure isn't a holiday."

"You put yourself there. Go back to England and forget about your petty revenge plot."

I bite my bottom lip as the other man, Holden, glowers at Thane with all the heat of a furnace in Hell. Why does this man despise Thane with such passion? He speaks with a British accent, so I assume he lives in England. He must hold a huge amount of hatred inside himself if he traveled all this way just to harass Thane.

The Brit abruptly veers his attention to me—and smiles with all the wicked glee of a bad, bad man. "Well, who are you, pet? Thane's new bit of stuff, eh? He used to shag shedloads of girls, don't you know? That was his only talent. All that geospatial rubbish was a cover."

"Shut your bloody mouth, Holden," Thane snarls. "Or I will shut it for you, permanently."

"Oh, I'm so fucking scared of you. The computer geek who became a—"

Thane launches himself at Holden, clamping his hands around the man's throat and shaking him violently. "Everything ye just said violates the Official Secrets Act. Ahm taking ye to the police station."

"Don't think so, mate."

Holden slams his knee up into Thane's groin. Thane grunts and stumbles backward, losing his grip on the Brit who spins around to launch himself at me.

I ram my knee into his groin. The second he bends over, I smack my fists down on his neck as hard as I can. That won't stop him for long, but at least it gives Thane a chance to take another shot at the creep.

But just as Thane straightens, wearing a thunderous expression, Holden takes off down the street away from us. He sprints as fast as an Olympic athlete, disappearing before either of us realizes what's going on.

I hurry over to Thane. "Are you okay?"

"Aye, fine." He manages a weak smirk. "You clobbered him good."

"Sorry I couldn't knock him out. The creep got away." I brush hair away from his eyes. "Who was that guy?"

"Holden De Boer. That's all I can tell you about him."

"I understand."

But yeah, my curiosity is desperate for more information. I understood going into this relationship that he had secrets he couldn't share. Now I need to hold up my end of the bargain and not demand more facts. How can I do that now? Knowing a man from Thane's past has a vendetta against him.

I hesitate for about one minute. Then I forge ahead with my questions. "Why did Holden say you're responsible for putting him in prison?"

"Because it's true. I assisted in bringing him in."

"He attacked you, and he saw us together. Will I be in danger now? Sorry, that sounds really selfish."

Thane pulls me into his arms and kisses my forehead. "I'm sorry, *gràidh*. You should never have been pulled into this. You are not selfish to be concerned about our encounter with Holden." He rests his forehead on mine. "Just know that I will do whatever is necessary to keep you out of this and keep you safe."

"Do you think Holden knows where you live?"

"Most likely. I am listed in the phone book." He winces. "Not very clever of me to be listed, considering my background."

I desperately want to ask what he means by that, but I keep my mouth shut. This isn't the time to grill him. "At least Holden can't know where I live. He doesn't even know my name."

Thane's face goes blank. He stares at the empty space beyond my shoulder for several seconds before he squeezes his eyes shut and mutters what sounds like a curse. It must be in Gaelic. "I have royally fucked up this time."

"I don't understand."

"This wasn't the first time Holden cornered me. I saw him on Sunday night when I was leaving your apartment building."

All the blood in my body seems to have frozen solid in an instant. "That creep was hanging around my building? For how long? You knew but didn't tell me? What if he'd gotten into my apartment or caught me in the garage when I was on my way to my car? You should have warned me, Thane."

He scrubs a hand over his mouth. "I assumed Holden was just blowing off steam."

"Clearly, he wasn't. You're so meticulous about your work, but you treat a stalker like he's nothing but a bug on your windshield."

Thane closes his eyes, exhaling the longest sigh I've ever heard. Then he sits down on the curb and rubs his eyes. As he shakes his head slowly, he issues more nasty Gaelic phrases that I can't translate. Even once he's done swearing, he bows his head and slumps his shoulders.

I've never seen anyone look so dejected. And I can't bear to see him like this. The mom in me takes over, and I sit down beside Thane to wrap my arms around him.

He stiffens. "What are ye doing?"

"Comforting you."

"Why? I've dragged you into the quicksand of my past and exposed you to someone I never wanted to see again."

"But you can handle that Holden guy. You aren't a child. You're a mature, intelligent, strong man."

He sighs heavily once again, just before he slings an arm around me to hug me firmly. "You are far too forgiving, Rebecca. We barely know each other. You should run away now."

Maybe I should walk away now and forget I ever met Thane. I'd have to quit my job too. Then what? Do I move in with my kids? No, I won't do that. I might have met Thane a few weeks ago, but I cannot abandon him when he's in trouble. Am I crazy to stick around? Possibly. Behaving like a sane adult hasn't exactly made my life better. Might as well go down the dark alley with Thane Buchanan.

"I'm not leaving you, Thane. So, you might as well tell me what you can about Holden and his 'revenge plot.' That's what you called it."

"Aye, I did say that." He pushes his face into my hair and inhales deeply. "Never wanted to drag you into this rubbish, but you might as well know. When I saw Holden on Sunday, he gave me a warning. About what, I dinnae know. But he assured me that when I saw him again, he would reveal what my punishment will be."

"Punishment for getting him thrown in prison?"

"Aye. That must be what he meant."

I wish I could push for more answers from him, but I get that he had some kind of top-secret job when he worked for the DIO. That means I can't press him on the issue too much. But I have a legitimate reason for questioning him about something else.

"You said you first bumped into Holden in the parking garage of my apartment building. He made threats then, right? But you never mentioned any of that to me."

He scrunches up his whole face. "I realize now that I should have told you at the time. But we weren't officially a couple yet, were we?" He shuts his eyes and bows his head briefly, then meets my gaze again. "That's no excuse. I regret hiding that encounter from you, but I honestly believed Holden would bugger off for good."

"I thought you were some kind of computer expert when you were in the military. Now it sounds like you were a secret agent who caught the bad guy."

"Technically, I wasn't any sort of agent. My job was classified, but not covert."

No matter how I phrase my questions, I can't get a concrete answer from him. Might as well give up for now. "We both have jobs to do, and we need to get back to work."

"Aye, we do."

He sounds defeated. That makes me want to hug him, but I'm too confused right now to know what I should do.

Thane leads me to the parking lot where he'd left his truck, and we don't speak to each other during the thirty-minute drive back to the distillery. Though I've developed strong feelings for this man, I have no idea how to respond to the bizarre and abruptly violent events that unfolded on that side street in Loch Fairbairn. My life had never been this exciting or terrifying before I moved to Scotland.

As we enter the main building, Thane holds the door open for me. Once we're both inside, he leans toward me as if he wants to kiss me goodbye before he heads for other parts of the complex. But he pulls away before he gets close enough to kiss me. His pained expression makes me feel anxious too.

"Have a good afternoon," he says. "Will I see you after work?"

"If you mean will you see me in the parking lot, the answer is yes. If you mean any other way...I don't know."

Thane nods once sharply, pivots on his heels, and stalks off down the hall.

Is he mad? No, I doubt that. He must be anxious and probably feeling guilty too. After all, he neglected to warn me about his dust-up with Holden De Boer. I'm suffering from a bit of anxiety too. Okay, maybe it's more than a little. Just a touch more. I've never been involved in a physical fight between two men. I've definitely never kneed a man in the nuts before, but I don't regret what I did.

For the rest of the day, I behave like a mature, professional woman and just do my job. I've been playing around with several options for the marketing campaign, though I haven't yet found anything that goes "zing" for me. My mom likes to tell me that, if I'm stumped at work, I should sit back, relax, and let my mind wander wherever it likes until something zings. That usually does the trick. But today is no ordinary day.

Thinking about the phrase ordinary day reminds me of one of my favorite Duran Duran songs, "Ordinary World." So, I pop my earbuds in and crank up that song. It's rather melancholy but beautiful and emotional. I listened to it on repeat for days after my husband announced he was filing for divorce and moving out of our house. But I hadn't been as anxious then as I am now. Worrying about Thane affects me far more deeply than losing Gary had.

As the song ends, another begins—"Come Undone."

No, I will not fall apart. As much as that encounter in Loch Fairbairn had shaken me up, I never felt panicked. Upset, yes. But not terrified. I was worried about Thane more than anything else.

I close my eyes and let the music lull me into a state of pure relaxation. I wouldn't call it meditation. My favorite songs can both relax and revive me, so I let my thoughts drift away. I often get ideas for campaigns because of my relaxation technique. Images float through my mind.

A bottle of whisky. Blue eyes. A kilt. It's the Buchanan tartan. Lips brushing against mine. The whispering of breaths. Rough hands touching me. Thane's voice whispers to me. *I am not the focus of this operation. The whisky is.*

I jerk upright, which sends my chair rattling across the floor with me still sitting cross-legged on it. I set my feet down and roll the chair up to my desk. An epiphany slammed into me a moment ago. Without Thane Buchanan, this distillery would never have gone anywhere. I know it's true. The whisky isn't the heart and soul of this operation. Thane is.

How can I convince him of that?

For several minutes, I sit here with my arms on my desk, tapping my pen on the surface. Ohhhh, I've got a fantastic idea. Thane will hate it—at first. But I have to try. If I can't seduce him into climbing on board for this marketing train, I don't deserve my job. No one else can convince him the way I can.

Okay, that sounds awfully arrogant. But I don't see it that way.

In my career, I'd created or helped create hundreds of campaigns for the agency's clients. None were as perfect or as racy as this one. Whisky is for adults, after all. I can push the envelope like never before—if my boss will go along with this idea. Fiona will agree, for sure. The boss I'm referring to is the man I spent the weekend with while naked and moaning.

Our mutual attraction is the key to my whole plan.

I straighten, turn up the volume on my earbuds, and get to work.

Chapter Twenty-One

Thane

I've been avoiding Rebecca as much as possible since our barnie with Holden De Boer on Monday. That means I've alternately been holed up on the malting floor, in the still room, in the dunnage warehouse, or in my hothouse. The new flavors I hope to glean from this crop of plants might become the best I've ever crafted. But I can't focus on anything long enough to do my work.

Thoughts of Rebecca consume me.

Well, thoughts and fantasies. Aye, for the past five days including Monday, I've taken matters into my own hands, literally, to relieve my lust for the lass.

A self-made orgasm isn't as fulfilling as fucking Rebecca.

But I need to stay away from her. What happened on Monday should never have happened, and all I can do to protect Rebecca is to keep my distance. Naturally, Fiona has other ideas that involve meddling in my relationship with the American lass. Whatever we had is over now, thanks to Holden.

Fiona stalks into the hothouse and slams the door shut. Then she sets her hands on her hips, lifting her chin in a defiant pose. "You are behaving like a flaming ersehole, Thane Robert Buchanan."

"Only my mother calls me that. But it doesn't intimidate me no matter which woman in my life uses my full name."

"Rebecca is working all day on your marketing campaign, and she keeps working after she goes home."

"That's not my fault." But I do feel a twinge of…something in my chest. "Order the lass to take the weekend off."

Fiona marches up to me and rolls her eyes. "Oh, aye, that will do the trick. She's as stubborn as you are."

I focus on pruning a plant to avoid looking her in the eye. "Did ye want something specific? Or is this strictly a verbal lashing?"

"Both." She stabs her finger into my chest. "You and Rebecca are perfect for each other. Whatever's fashing you, get over it right now. Fall to your knees and beg Rebecca to forgive you."

"Maybe it's best if our dalliance doesn't become a relationship." It already has become that, but Fiona shouldn't assume such a thing.

The stubborn lass gives me a mulish look. "You weren't like this when you and I were dating." She tips her head to the side and narrows her gaze on me. "You know what that means, ye pigheaded *cacan*."

Aye, I'm well aware of what it means. But with Holden plotting who knows what, I cannae keep romancing Rebecca. And I won't discuss my feelings with Fiona.

She wags a finger at me. "Dinnae bollocks it up with Rebecca. She's a wonderful woman, and she's perfect for you."

I cannae deny she's right about that. What I want doesn't matter anymore. I need to push Rebecca away for her own safety. That means I need to pretend I'm a *bod ceann* in the hopes that will silence Fiona and convince Rebecca to stay away from me. "Haud yer wheesht, ye *siursachd*. Dinnae need anyone telling me how to live my life, ye *phitean*."

Fiona shakes her head. "Calling me the C-word and a whore proves how desperate you are. That's not a good sign."

Before I can open my mouth to spew a litany of even worse Gaelic insults, Fiona spins around and marches out the hothouse door. She attempts to slam it shut after her, but the door isn't sturdy enough for that.

Aye, I'm bloody brilliant at cocking up my life. It's not a skill I ever wanted to acquire. But if my display at least convinces Fiona to tell Rebecca that I'm a worthless *riatach*, I will have accomplished my task. Protecting Rebecca means chasing her away.

Only a worthless bastard would do what I've done.

For the remainder of the week, I focus on whisky. Though I see Rebecca in the cafeteria every day, I do not speak to her or acknowledge that I see her. This is not the adult way to handle the situation, but I can't think of anything else to do to keep Rebecca safe. Holden can't possibly find out who she is or where she lives. He was never a computer wizard or that good of a spy. That's how he wound up in prison.

I try to relax over the weekend, but I only make it until two o'clock on Saturday before I can't stand it anymore. I need to distract myself. That means I go back to the distillery and let myself in with the master key.

On Monday morning, I bump into Rebecca as I'm heading for the dunnage warehouse, though I haven't stepped out of the main building yet. I've just turned the knob on the door when Rebecca rushes up from outside and yanks it open. When she sees me, her eyes fly wide open.

"Thane, hello, how are you?"

Aye, she seems a wee bit confused or perhaps anxious about seeing me. I haven't given her any reason to believe I'll be anything but curt with her. I am a bastard, for dead certain.

"I'm well enough," I tell her. I'm bloody awful at lying, and I feel bloody awful overall, but she doesn't need to know that. The lass is too kindhearted to understand why I'm behaving in this way. "Shouldn't you be working on the marketing plan?"

"I am doing that. But I'll need to visit a few local businesses to put the finishing touches on the campaign." She stares at me for a moment as if she's sizing me up. "Would you like to come with me?"

"No, I'm far too busy."

She twists her mouth into an expression I've seen a fair bit lately. It means she's disappointed and slightly irritated. "Okay. See you later, then."

I feel oddly uncomfortable as I watch her walking away. Once the door shuts behind her, I turn round to watch her shapely figure receding down the main hallway. I scratch my arm vigorously. Why? I haven't a clue. Aye, I'm in denial about the fact that I've hurt a woman I care about more than I expected I would. I should run after her. Beg the lass to forgive me.

But instead, I jog to the dunnage warehouse.

And I spend the remainder of the day trying to banish all thoughts of Rebecca from my mind. It doesn't work. By the end of the afternoon, as the other employees are leaving, I go to Rebecca's office to see if she's there. She isn't, of course. The lass had said she wanted to visit some local businesses.

What had I meant to do if I found her in this office? I have no bloody clue.

I'm shuffling across the car park toward my truck when a familiar figure steps in front of me. His bulk blocks my path. When I try to sidestep around him, he seizes me by the shirt and hoists me off the ground.

Now, I'm staring directly into his squinted gaze. "Put me down, Cormac. Ahmno in the mood to wrestle with you."

"Ye think I mean to wrestle?" My cousin laughs, and his deep, rough voice always reminds me of how I imagine a giant from folklore might sound. He looks the part too. And now, he gives me a hard shake. "Everyone has heard about your barnie on West Cameron Brae."

"Aye, I was on that street. How did you know? Must have seen me with Rebecca, walking down the high street. Eh?"

Cormac shakes his head slowly. "We know because a man called Holden De Boer walked into the Loch Fairbairn Police Station and started shouting about how you need to be arrested for false imprisonment."

What the sodding hell? I never imprisoned anyone, not even Holden, who deserved it. A jury decided his fate.

"Let me down, Cormac. Dinnae care what Holden said. It's no one's business but my own."

My cousin is twenty-eight, younger and stronger than I am, not to mention much larger and heftier thanks to an abundance of muscles. But I have my ways of getting around him.

Cormac hoists me higher, so that now my head lies above his. "How could ye hurt that sweet lass, Thane? Rebecca is a good woman, but ye tossed her away like rubbish."

How does he know about that? Rebecca wouldn't tell anyone.

My cousin smirks. "I met the lass this afternoon in Kirsty MacTaggart's metaphysical shop. Rebecca never said a word about what you did, but after she left the shop, Kirsty told me. Her *dà-shealladh* showed her."

"Ye dinnae believe in that second-sight rubbish."

He shrugs, making me sway in his hold. "Why shouldn't I believe it? Kirsty is clever and sweet. She wouldn't lie."

I do not believe a word of that psychic bollocks. Cormac is only trying to convince me I'm a heel for pushing Rebecca away. Dinnae need him to tell me that. But if Cormac and Kirsty know what happened on West Cameron Brae, then everyone else will know by now too. The MacTaggarts have a grapevine vast enough that it could choke the whole Highlands.

Cormac shakes me again. "Last chance. Will ye make it right with Rebecca? Or should I toss you into the river?"

"Let me down. I promise I will speak to the lass."

"And treat her kindly."

"*Mhac na galla*, Cormac."

He narrows his gaze to mere slits. "Thane—"

"Aye, all right, I swear to be kind and make things right with Rebecca."

"Good." Cormac drops me, and I fall into a heap on the ground. "Maybe I should drive you to the lass's apartment, just to make sure."

I clamber to my feet and brush the dirt off my clothes. "Dinnae need to drive me there. I will go straight to her apartment building."

Cormac nods curtly. Then he pats me on the head. "Good boy."

"I'm nearly two decades older than you. Dinnae treat me like I'm a wee bairn."

"Then dinnae act like one." He pats my cheek this time, and his grin has a touch of menace in it. "Go on, then. I filled up the petrol tank for you."

"What? You broke into my truck?"

"No. I brought a full petrol can and poured it into your truck's tank."

Everyone I know is insane. Maybe I didn't mind when Domhnall and Fiona were the object of their meddling, but now I'm caught up in their web. Dinnae like that at all.

But I dutifully trudge to my pickup truck and climb inside. In the rear-view mirror, I can see Cormac still standing there, wearing his most menacing expression. He bloody well knows that won't intimidate me. I start up the engine and drive out of the car park. When I glance back again, Cormac is climbing into his vehicle. He follows me until we reach the crossroads that's halfway to Loch Fairbairn, then he turns off to head toward the far side of the loch itself. That's where Cormac lives.

I drive straight through Loch Fairbairn and continue into Fort William, turning down the street where Rebecca's apartment complex lies. As I pull into the underground garage, I see Rebecca's car further down the aisle where residents park. At least I know she's home.

After a brief hesitation, I leap out of the truck and race to the lift. I ride up to Rebecca's floor in the company of an elderly couple who want to chat. I politely respond to their queries, but I'm in no mood to blether. Fortunately, I'm good at faking interest. They seem like a lovely couple, and I don't want to insult them.

The second I step out of the lift, I burst into a sprint.

Seconds later, I knock on Rebecca's door.

A moment that feels like an eternity passes while I wait. Then, finally, the door swings open. The lass maintains a neutral expression.

"*Feasgar math*, Rebecca. How are you this evening? The weather is pleasant." Could I have thought of a stupider thing to say? I want to kiss her, not blether about the weather. "I said good evening, by the way. May I come in?"

She clasps the doorknob, twisting it this way and that. "You've been ignoring me. 'Running away' might be a more accurate description."

"Aye, I've done that. I'm sorry. After our encounter with Holden, I thought what I needed to do was keep you at a distance. I was wrong."

"No shit."

"Please, *gràidh*, give me another chance."

She chews on her bottom lip.

This isn't the time for me to be measured and calm as usual. No, I need to prove to her that I regret shunning her more than she could possibly know. That means I need to grovel.

I fall to my knees and clasp my hands. "Please forgive me. I will never again push you away, no matter what happens. You mean more to me than even I realized."

She blows out a breath and waves her hands. "Get up, Thane. Unless you're proposing marriage, you don't need to drop to your knees."

I wince as I rise. "Thank you, *gràidh*. My knees are a wee bit arthritic these days."

"Didn't notice that when we were having sex."

"The weather affects my knees. And spending the afternoon in the dunnage warehouse didn't do them any good. It's chilly in there." I wince again. "Not that I'm whingeing. I was only explaining that—"

She seals my lips with two fingers. "Shut up, Thane, and get in here."

I surge forward, pushing her backward with me as I wrap my arms round the lass and kick the door shut. Before she can speak another syllable, I claim her mouth. She exhales a soft wee sigh. But when I push my tongue between her lips, she sags against me and reciprocates the kiss. Soon, we're groping each other with abandon. Her breasts are mashed to my chest. She wriggles her erse, then shoves a hand between our bodies to mold her palm to my cock.

This wasn't how I intended to apologize to her, but it will do.

Chapter Twenty-Two

Rebecca

The moment Thane Buchanan fell to his knees and begged my forgiveness, I gave up any pretense of being angry with him. Yes, he hurt my feelings. But I'm a grown woman who can handle that sort of thing. Right now, though, all I can think about is getting him inside me as soon as possible.

But Thane pulls away, stumbling backward. "We shouldn't shag yet. I need to explain—"

"Explanations later. I need you inside me right now."

"Dinnae ye want to curse at me?"

"Maybe later." I start unbuttoning my shirt. "Get naked, Thane. That's an order."

He grins and chuckles. "You are the most wonderful woman."

"Ditch the compliments and talk dirty to me."

Thane grins and chuckles again. "We can do that after. Right now, I need to talk to you about Holden and my connection with him. It's time I cleared the air."

"You said your past was top secret and you couldn't tell me about it."

"After Holden's little visit to the police station, I dinnae give a toss about the Official Secrets Act. Let them arrest me."

I take his hand, leading him to the sofa where we both sit down. "I don't want you to go to prison, Thane."

"Neither do I. But I doubt it will come to that." He slings an arm across the sofa's back, turning toward me. "After my first exchange with Holden,

I rang my old handler at the DIO. She said she can no longer help me. But maybe I can change her mind if I can get proof that he's been blethering to everyone about his time in MI6."

"He was a spy?"

"That's right. A ruddy awful one, as it turned out. He had gone over to the other side and became a double agent."

I can't deny that I'm getting excited—in a nonsexual way—simply because he's sharing more of himself with me. More of his covert past. "You must have been the one who captured Holden, right? He said you got him sent to prison."

"Aye, my handler ordered me to track him down and bring him in." He gazes directly at me while he speaks, clearly no longer burdened by the need to keep mum. "I wasn't an intelligence officer, but I was asked to become an agent. That means I secretly passed information to an intelligence officer. That person operated under deep cover, as an illegal, meaning that she had none of the protections that regular intelligence officers had."

I sit up straighter, my curiosity piqued by one word he spoke. "She? Your contact was a woman?"

"Aye. The same woman I rang immediately after Holden made his first appearance."

"Did you sleep with her?"

Thane screws up his mouth and swerves his attention to a spot somewhere behind my shoulder. "Aye, we had a poke now and then."

"Why so shy about giving me the details? I hardly expected that you'd been a monk."

"But lasses don't usually like to hear about a man's former lovers."

"You know I'm not that judgmental."

He smiles, though it's soft and somewhat melancholy. "Aye, you would never rebuke me for my past lifestyle. You're a kindhearted woman."

"Mess with my kids and you'll find out just how tough I can be."

"I'm dead sure you would turn into a lioness in that sort of situation. But I would never interfere with your family."

"Yeah, I know." And I love that about him. He's respectful and sweet, but he knows when to get tough, like on that side street in Loch Fairbairn. "You tell me you were never a spy, but you were an agent. That means you were passing information to your handler. Doesn't that also mean you were secretly collecting evidence?"

He scratches his cheek, and his expression tightens. "Aye, you're right about that. But I wasn't James Bond. I wasn't even like Logan MacTaggart, who was in MI6. His job involved serious covert operations. I did most of my spying from the comfort of a desk at the DIO. Only on certain occasions did I go out into the field."

"I realize you can't tell me everything. And I don't want you to risk getting in trouble for what you've already said."

"Dinnae fash. This is between you and me. But if it ever should come out that I told you these things, I will be the one in trouble, not you."

"But I don't want you to go to prison."

He slides closer, wrapping his arm around my shoulders. "Relax, *mo chridhe*. From this moment on, your safety is my number-one priority."

No one has ever given me that kind of vow. He means it too. I can hear the truth of it in his voice and see it on his face.

Thane lays a hand on my cheek and gently turns my face toward him. "I want you to come to my house. You'll be safer there."

"Where is your house?"

"On the outskirts of Loch Fairbairn."

"This building has security guards and electronic surveillance, plus electronic locks. Wouldn't we be safer here?"

He rubs his thumb on my cheek, smiling in that same soft yet melancholy way as he had a moment ago. "Holden knows you live here. But I doubt he managed to find out where I live."

"Why not? He used to be a spy, after all."

"Aye. But my house is not listed under my name. I created a sort of shell game to keep villains guessing about who owns the house. It's very complicated. Two of my mates, Evan MacTaggart and his cousin Logan, arranged it all for me."

"You're very paranoid, huh?"

"It isn't paranoia. It's insurance."

Considering the kind of life he used to lead, I guess I can understand why he feels that keeping his home a secret is necessary. But I think there's a flaw in his plan. "Don't all your friends and relatives know where you live?"

"They do. But none of them would ever reveal that information."

"But a bad guy could spot you in town and follow you home."

He shakes his head slowly. "I'm always watching the vicinity, even when I'm driving. It's instinct. Years of working as a geospatial analyst taught me to pay close attention to details, especially in the environment."

Okay, maybe he actually can protect me better at his house. I'd rather stay with him, anyway—wherever that might be. If he believes his home is the best place, I'll go there with him. Heck, I'd go anywhere in the world with Thane.

"I agree. We should move to your house. But it's dark out, so maybe we should wait until morning."

"No. Nighttime is better. Pack up what you'll need for tonight, and to-morrow we can come back for the rest."

He's really serious about this. I had no idea the Holden incident was such a big deal, until he explained it to me this evening. Holden De Boer isn't just a whackjob with a grudge. He's a former spy and a traitor.

So, I quickly pack what I need for tonight and the morning. Then we walk out of my apartment. Instead of going down to the parking garage, however, we detour around that, heading outside via a door that's marked "employees only." Thane pulls out a set of what looks like lockpicking tools. I've only seen those in movies, but he actually owns a set.

This is no movie. It's a genuine dangerous situation.

But I feel safe as long as Thane is with me.

We skulk out of the building on the backside and then skulk down an adjacent street until we reach Thane's pickup truck. As he starts up the engine, I have to ask a question.

"The apartment complex has electronic locks, electronic everything. Yet there was an old-fashioned door hidden in the corner of the garage."

"Aye, that's right. Clearly, the architect didn't think the employee exit needed such tight security. I've seen things like that before."

"I guess that makes a kind of sense. The cheapskate kind."

Thane takes us through a maze of houses and other buildings on our way out of Fort William, and he does the same thing once we reach Loch Fairbairn. By the time we get to his house, I have no idea how I might ever find my way back to my apartment without the maps app on my phone. Even then, I couldn't be sure I'd find my way. A digital map isn't foolproof.

As it turns out, Thane lives in the middle of nowhere, just far enough away from Loch Fairbairn that I can't see the lights from that little town. His house is dark. The only illumination comes from the sky and the truck's headlights, which he quickly shuts off, leaving us with only the stars and moonlight.

Thane climbs out of the truck and rushes around to my side to open my door before I've even grasped the handle. He offers me both his hands as I climb out. Then he shuts the door.

And he tips his head back to gaze up at the night sky. His lips curl into a sweet little smile as he closes his eyes.

What is he doing?

Thane clasps my hand, tugging me closer. With his eyes still shut, he tells me, "Shut your eyes, lass, and enjoy the ambient sounds of the natural world."

"Um, shouldn't we go inside? It's cold out here."

"Listen with me for a wee bit. I'll keep you warm." He proves that claim by hugging me tightly to his body. He feels warm all right. "I won't ask you to do this again. Just give it a go and see if you like it. This is my version of meditation." He opens his eyes just long enough to wink at me before he shuts his lids. "If you don't like it, I'll never ask you to do this again."

His version of meditation seems innocuous enough, and it's oddly important to him that I try it. Why not? Might as well give it a go. I tip my head back and close my eyes.

"Relax, and let your thoughts fly away. Don't try to hear the natural sounds, just let them sink into your psyche."

His calm and soothing voice makes it easy for me to do what he suggested. I focus on the feel of his body hugging mine and the masculine scent of him. Soon, I forget about the truck, the gravel driveway beneath my feet, and everything else except the natural world. Then, I begin to notice little sounds. The rustling of the leaves on the trees. The whispering of Thane's breaths.

"Do ye hear that sound?" he asks. "It's grasshoppers."

"What sound?"

"Let your ears guide you."

Not sure what that means, but I relax and roll with it. Soon, I do hear a noise. "What's that clicking sound?"

"Grasshoppers."

"Oh. I've never heard that sound before. Had no idea grasshoppers made any kind of noise."

Thane opens his eyes and smiles in that serene way I've seen him do often. "Let's go inside now, eh? You must be getting cold."

I rub my hands together, trying to warm them up. "It is chilly out here. I forgot to bring my mittens. They're back in my apartment."

"We'll get them tomorrow."

He keeps his arm around me while we cross the gravel driveway and step up onto the porch. I can't see much in the darkness. My eyes haven't adjusted yet. But the outlines of the porch suggest it has pretty architecture. I'd love to see it in the daylight. But right now, I just want to get inside and get warmed up.

Thane throws the door open and ushers me inside, kicking the door shut behind him. Then he flips a switch, and a lamp comes on in the living room.

"Wow, Thane, your home is beautiful."

"I appreciate the compliment, but Fiona and her sisters are responsible for the interior design."

"Those ladies have excellent taste. Mind if I have a good look around?"

He smiles. "Go on, lass. Have your fun while I get the wood stove started up."

I wander around the living room, admiring the furnishings that are attractive and country-ish but not feminine. The woodsy colors and styles are a combination of soft and manly. Fiona and her sisters must know Thane pretty well to decorate his home this way. It suits him perfectly.

"Mind if I go into the other rooms?" I ask. "Don't want to invade your privacy."

He glances at me over his shoulder from his squatting position. He's been fiddling with the wood stove. "Invade all ye like, love. I've only had a woman in my house twice, not counting when the sisters decorated my house."

"The other woman was Fiona, right?"

"Aye."

While he goes back to fiddling with the stove, I wander toward what looks like the kitchen doorway. I take a quick peek at his ass along the way. Can't help it. He's squatting there in a way that highlights his taut bottom. When he catches me admiring is glutes, he smirks and winks.

The kitchen is amazing, though not overly fancy. I can picture Thane whipping up a Scottish breakfast in here and delivering it to me in bed. My ex-husband never treated me that way. If he made breakfast, it was scrambled eggs and buttered toast, nothing else. I would have to go retrieve my favorite strawberry jam from the refrigerator myself.

I know Thane would never make me do that.

But I would gladly serve him breakfast.

My perusal of the kitchen is now complete, so I walk away from the window that must give Thane a beautiful view of his property in the daytime. I've just turned away from the window when I hear an odd noise outside. It sounded like…a humming cow. No, I must have imagined that. I won't mention my humming-cow delusion to Thane.

By the time I've inspected the one and only bedroom, my tummy has started to grumble. I take a gander at the bathroom too, which is part of the bedroom. I hadn't expected Thane to have a spacious and fancy bathroom, but of course, Fiona and her sisters are responsible for that. They gave Thane a huge king-size bed too.

When I return to the living room, the fire is already burning and producing enough heat to warm me up.

Thane could do that all by himself, no stove required.

Chapter Twenty-Three

Thane

No man could wake up in the morning to a better sight than what I have before me. Rebecca lies beside me, naked, with her torso exposed. She had fallen asleep with the blanket covering all of her, but during the night, she had somehow moved about enough to pull the blanket down to her waist. Maybe she did that on purpose. I hadn't noticed any of her movements.

Ah, but I love drinking in the vision of her bonnie tits.

We both slept naked. It had been Rebecca's idea.

No, I didn't argue with her about that.

Now, the lass's eyes flutter open, and she yawns. I can see all her teeth and get a wee glimpse of her tonsils. Aye, that was quite a yawn.

When her gaze lands on me, she smiles lazily. "Good morning, Mr. Bond."

"My surname is Buchanan. Have ye already forgotten who you slept with last night?"

"You were a spy. That makes you James Bond in my book. Only you're much sexier than even Sean Connery was, and that's a high bar to vault over."

"As a veteran of multiple rounds of Highland games and a strongman competition, I feel quite certain of my status as tougher than a film star. But I am not a spy."

She rolls on top of me, then sits up to straddle my thighs. "You worked for a covert agency, right? That makes you a spy. Give it up, Thane. You'll never convince me you weren't a secret agent."

"I was an agent, but in the MOD, that doesn't mean what it sounds like."

"Yeah, I know. You explained that last night." She draws circles on my chest with one finger, leaning forward a wee bit. Her hair falls over her cheeks. "You will always be a secret agent to me."

"But I can't do any karate kicks, and I don't have a cyanide pill embedded in one of my molars."

She straightens and spreads her arms out to stretch. Her lips curve into a sensual smile. "Let's have sex before breakfast."

"First, I'd best check the wood stove. Cannae have you getting a chill."

"You think of everything. Hard to believe you haven't dated much. I mean, you're the perfect boyfriend, so attentive and thoughtful, but tough when you need to be."

She stretches again, shutting her eyes briefly. Then the lass veers her gaze toward the window above the bed.

And she yelps, leaping backward. "What is that?"

Before I can respond, a loud honking noise erupts just outside the window. Rebecca scrambles backward, leaping off my lap to huddle beside me.

I sit up and turn around, then wave at the furry beast who is staring through the window. "Go on, Odin, back to the coop. The hens need you, but I can take care of Rebecca."

Odin nods his head as if he understands me. Then he saunters away, toward the backyard.

"Where did that thing come from?" Rebecca asks in a tone that's higher pitched than her normal voice. "What was that horrible noise it made?"

"That was Odin, my llama. He guards the chickens and the homestead at large."

Her brows crinkle in the sweetest way. "Llama? You have those in Scotland?"

"Aye. There are a surprising number of llamas and alpacas in this country. They were imported here, naturally. Their hair makes good yarn, but Odin is strictly a pet with a job."

Rebecca leans to the side, peering anxiously out the window. "But that horrible noise…"

"That's his alarm call. I should go out and check what's the bother." I hop off the bed and gather my clothes, while Rebecca still seems skeptical. "Relax, *gràidh*. Odin won't hurt you, especially once he sees that you're with me."

She twists her mouth into a strange expression that I take for anxiety.

I toss the lass her clothes. "Get dressed. Then I'll introduce you to Odin and the chickens."

"Um…okay."

"Don't you trust me?"

"Of course I do." She slides off the bed, conspicuously keeping her back to the window. "I've never seen a llama in person, and I've never heard that they make frightening noises."

I chuckle. "Once you meet Odin, you won't think he's terrifying anymore. I predict he will fall for you instantly."

"Uh-huh. Can we eat breakfast before I meet your critters?"

"Aye. But I need to check on what Odin was making a fuss about first."

I dress quickly and rush outside to check on the "critters," as Rebecca called them. The chickens aren't upset, and when I speak to Odin, he doesn't behave as if anything unusual happened. Well, other than Rebecca yelping. I think Odin was just surprised to see another person in my home.

When I walk back into the house, I can hear the sounds of food cooking. I jog into the kitchen. "Are ye making breakfast for me?"

"For both of us. Your llama will have to feed himself."

"I'll feed him after we eat." I approach the wee island. "May I help with the meal?"

"Sure. You can crack some eggs." She opens the refrigerator door and points toward its interior while giving me a cheeky look of disapproval. "When was the last time you went grocery shopping? You don't have much in the fridge."

"Ah, sorry about that. I've been distracted."

She pats my cheek. "Poor baby. Avoiding me all week was so stressful for you."

"Cheeky lass." I grab a carton of eggs from the refrigerator and flip the top open so I can pretend to study the brown eggs. "Twelve might be enough for me, but you'll need to harvest more from the chickens."

"I have never done that. Don't know how."

"Oh, it's incredibly difficult. You shove your hand under the hen's erse and pull out the eggs."

Rebecca squints at me. "You don't seriously expect me to shove my hand under a hen's bottom. I think you're lying about how to collect eggs."

"You caught me. I enjoy teasing city lasses."

"I grew up in the country, but my mom always collected the eggs. I was, um, afraid of chickens."

"Hmm." I scratch my chin as I study her. "Afraid of llamas and chickens. We'll need to desensitize you."

Rebecca slumps her shoulders. "Can we do that later? I'm starving."

"Aye, later." I pat her erse. "And I was joking about me eating a dozen eggs. There's plenty for both of us."

"Oh, good." She puckers her lips and glances toward the windows. "Do you have any other animals out there?"

"Just Odin and the chickens."

"So, no geese."

Cannae help laughing. "Geese? No, lass. Dinnae like to eat goose eggs."

"Whew. That's a relief." She makes a sheepish face. "I'm afraid of geese. One bit me in the ass when I was five years old."

I set the egg carton down and grasp her hands. "Dinnae fash. I vow to protect you from rampaging geese."

"Ha-ha." She grabs ingredients from the refrigerator, then we both begin working on our breakfast. But she pauses briefly to gaze up at me through her lashes. "Is there anything you're afraid of?"

"Everyone is afraid of something."

"I meant animals or insects. Stuff like that."

"Oh, I see. No, I'm not afraid of wee beasties or any other sort of creatures."

She raises her brows. "Wee beasties? Do I need to be looking out for tiny elfin geese?"

A chuckle spills out of me. "We do not have tiny animals in Scotland. 'Wee beasties' are insects."

"Well, that does make more sense. I hate bugs."

"Everyone does, except for the entomologists."

Making breakfast with Rebecca is more enjoyable than I expected. For me, cooking is a necessity rather than something fun to do. With her as my partner, though, creating a meal becomes a treat. I love making her laugh, and she makes me laugh too.

After enjoying our food at the kitchen table, I need to go out and take care of the chickens and Odin too. Surprisingly, Rebecca volunteers to go with me.

"Might as well start my desensitization," she announces. "Don't want to be a scaredy-cat forever."

"You are not a scaredy-cat. Only a brave woman would knee a traitor in the bollocks."

"I assume you're talking about the time I slammed my knee into Holden's private parts."

"Aye, that's what I meant."

We exit out the back door, heading for the chicken coop. Rebecca holds an empty egg carton that we will put more eggs in shortly. The rooster crows, almost as if he's welcoming Rebecca.

"Do you name your chickens too?" she asks. "Or are they all anonymous?"

"I've named them." As I kneel, the rooster approaches us. " This handsome fellow is Wallace."

"Why did you name him that?"

"Because of William Wallace, the great Scottish hero."

"Ohh, I get it." She folds her arms over her chest as she studies the rooster. "Is he going to be drawn and quartered like his namesake?"

I rise and shake my head at her. "Dinnae say things like that in front of Wallace. He's a sensitive laddie."

Rebecca bends over to stare directly into the rooster's eyes. "I apologize, Wallace. Didn't mean to insult you."

The rooster meanders away.

"Now, it's time for you to meet the lasses." I lead Rebecca to the coop. "I'm going to introduce you to the hens, but be advised that I let Malina MacTaggart choose the rooster's name."

"Is she one of your ex-lovers?"

"No. The lass is sixteen and the daughter of Iain and Rae MacTaggart. When she heard I was getting chickens, she begged me to let her name the rooster, but I couldn't let the poor laddie be called Clucky McCluckster."

"I can't picture you patting his head and saying 'good boy, Clucky Mc-Cluckster.' That's not your style."

"What a dead stupid name. Dinnae tell Malina I said that. She's a sweet lass, but her taste in animal names leaves much to be desired." I wave at each hen in turn. "Rebecca meet Agatha, Prudence, Ginger, and Henrietta."

"Let me guess. Ginger is called that because she has reddish feathers."

"Aye. The others are named after women I met at the MOD."

"Ones you screwed?"

I strap my arms over my chest. "No, not the women I screwed. One was a civilian driver, another was a pharmacy technician, and the third was an administrative officer."

"But you just admitted you slept with women at the MOD."

"No, I did not."

I realize my tone was irritated, but that's not like me. I might be slightly annoyed because she implied I shagged women I worked with. So, I tip my head back, shut my eyes, and take a few slow, deep breaths.

"Not made of Teflon after all, huh, Thane?"

Since I feel more myself now, I face her again. "I have never been made of Teflon. But I've cultivated a mindset that prevents me from lashing out. Dinnae like to get angry."

"Neither do I." She glances at the hens and winces. "Guess you better show me how to harvest eggs."

"You could try assuming it won't be an awful task."

I open up the coop and wait until Rebecca has come up beside me. Then I tell her to flip the lid up on the empty carton, and I gently push Henrietta away from her nest. She clucks softly, inspecting Rebecca's hand gently. The lass doesn't shy away. I set one egg in the carton.

"Your turn, *gràidh*. Let's move over to Agatha's favorite spot."

She hands me the carton and follows me to another part of the coop where one egg lies on the straw bed. The lass lifts it out and sets it in the carton. "Are they supposed to have more than one egg?"

"No. A hen can only produce one per day. That's why I mostly get my eggs from the store. The ones from my backyard are a special treat."

"You could get more chickens."

I shrug one shoulder. "Too much bother. I mostly have chickens to give Odin some company."

As if on command, the llama ambles up behind Rebecca and nuzzles her cheek.

She jumps, but this time, she does not yelp. The lass lays a hand on her chest. "Jeez, this guy knows how to sneak up on you."

"Aye. The noise you heard him make earlier was an alarm call. Anytime a new person appears in his world, he will alert me."

Odin nuzzles her cheek again.

She smiles and laughs, then rubs his forehead. "Good boy, Odin. You are beautiful. Look at all that thick, curly hair. Makes me a little jealous."

Odin kisses her cheek in his llama manner.

Rebecca laughs again. "You're the sweetest animal I've ever met. But you probably just like the way I smell, huh?"

"Odin has a crush on you, *gràidh*. He likes people, but he has never reacted to a newcomer this way." I scratch behind the llama's ear. "But I can't deny he has excellent taste in women."

And I also can't deny that I'm a wee bit jealous of how much Rebecca fusses over Odin. Women usually love animals, though. Malina thinks Odin is "the most adorable critter in the world" and that he has "the most gorgeous eyes ever." Apparently, even her father can't compete with a llama.

Now that we've gathered our eggs, I lead Rebecca back into the house. We need to talk about the Holden problem for one, but I'm certain Rebecca also wants to discuss her marketing plan. I stash the eggs in the refrigerator while she waits for me in the living room. Then I bring a tray of tea and shortbread, setting it down on the coffee table, and take a seat beside her.

She eyes the tray with a hint of suspicion. "More food? Are you trying to fatten me up for the winter?"

"Thought you might like a wee piece, especially since I made the shortbread myself. Dinnae have to eat it if you're too full."

"Never said I wouldn't eat it."

I pour us each a cup of tea, though I only add one spoonful of honey to mine. Rebecca puts three spoonfuls of sugar and a large amount of honey too. Before she tastes the shortbread, she takes a few sips of her tea and seems to relish the flavor of it. At last, she plucks up a rectangular slice of shortbread and takes a dainty bite, chewing it slowly.

Her face lights up. "This is wonderful, Thane."

I sit up straighter, suddenly feeling so good that I might float away on a cloud.

Chapter Twenty-Four

Rebecca

Thane looks adorably pleased with himself simply because I complimented his shortbread. I hadn't lied. It's delicious. I could eat the stuff all day long. But I'd get very nauseous if I did that, not to mention very bloated. This man feeds me the most amazing foods and beverages and gives me the best orgasms I've ever experienced.

I love being with him.

Once I've gobbled up three slices of shortbread, it's time to get more answers out of him. "Why do you have a llama?"

"To protect the chickens from predators."

"Is that the only reason?"

He rests his elbow on the sofa's back and props his head up with his fist. "I had a feeling you would ask me that. No, protecting the chickens isn't the only reason I have a llama. Odin has another job too. He's my security system."

I stare at him for a moment, sure I've misunderstood. "You mean because he watches out for the chickens. I'm asking about your home security system, the kind with keypads and cameras and all that jazz."

"You won't find any of that here. Odin is my only security system."

"Huh?" I glance around the living room but don't see anything that resembles an electronic system. "You can't be serious. A llama is not a reliable means of protecting the property or yourself."

"You don't know Odin. He might be a charming and affable fellow, but if anyone invades the property, he will alert me."

"But he made those honking noises at me."

"Aye, because he didn't know you. Now he does."

This is insane. A llama security system? Nobody does that. Some people have Rottweilers, but they have huge teeth and massive jaws that could rip a person apart. Odin the llama is friendly. His only defensive weapon is, apparently, the weird noises he makes.

"You're skeptical," Thane says. "I understand why. But believe me, if anyone tries to hurt either of us, Odin will step in to help."

"Uh-huh. This is all very bizarre, but we need to talk about other things right now." Before I tell him about the marketing campaign, I need to ask him about something else. "Holden has harassed you once and attacked both of us once. What if he comes back? Have you even tried to find out where he is? I'd rather not get ambushed again."

He moves closer, gently wrapping an arm around my shoulders. "I haven't tried to find him. But you're right, I should do that. I'm just not sure how to track him down since my only contact at the DIO told me she can't do anything to help."

"Can't you tap into your old skills? That geospatial whatsit stuff."

"I no longer have access to the technology needed for that 'geospatial whatsit stuff.' "

"You can't do it without computers? I thought you said you have friends who are techno-wizards."

"I do but—" He runs a hand over his face and sighs. "They don't understand the intricacies of geospatial analysis."

"Thane, you are a very smart man. Surely you can figure out how to track down Holden without computers."

He stares into the distance behind me, and I swear I can almost hear the gears clicking in his brain. "Maybe I could do that. Charles Picquet, a French geographer, was the first to employ spatial analysis in the nineteenth century. He tracked cholera outbreaks in Paris that way. Two decades later, John Snow expanded on Picquet's idea by bringing in the concept of spatial analysis. And then in the early twentieth century, photozincography was developed. That's a process that made it possible to isolate the layers of a map."

"They did all that without computers."

"Aye. But it wasn't until the nineteen-nineties that true geospatial analysis began to be created. Even then, no one could have imagined how much and how quickly the technology would evolve."

The look on his face tells me that he's getting more ideas.

He faces the coffee table, setting his feet atop it. "I might not have access to the most high-tech geospatial platforms. But I can certainly dig up some publicly available data to give me an idea of where to find Holden. He doesn't know the area, so I have an even greater advantage over him. And I could use physical maps to assist me."

I smack a kiss on his cheek. "I knew you'd figure it out. You're not just a hot body and a pretty face. You've got the brains to back it up."

He laughs softly. "Going a wee bit overboard, aren't you? I'm no genius."

"Au contraire. It's not possible to go overboard when I'm complimenting you."

"*Gràidh*, you are quite a woman."

No other man would say the things that he says about me. Thane isn't afraid to sound mushy or to admit when he's stumped or he's screwed up. The man fell to his knees to beg my forgiveness when all he did was ignore me for a few days. I can't imagine how he might apologize if he actually hurt my feelings.

I sit up and set my feet on the floor, clasping my hands as I turn toward him. "You must want to get started on finding Holden. But could I give you the abridged version of my marketing campaign first? It won't take long."

"Of course. I'd love to hear about it." He settles a hand on my thigh. "Dinnae need to abridge your plan. Tell me all of it now."

"Some of the details need fleshing out, but here's the gist of it." I used to always get a little bit nervous before a presentation, and I would relax once I got started. But here with Thane, I don't feel even a tiny twinge of anxiety. "This whole campaign relies on one simple fact. You are the distillery, Thane. Without you, everything would fall apart. Not only are you the master distiller, but you're also the master maltster. You craft every new variation with exquisite care and attention to detail. I want everyone to see just how brilliant you are."

"I reckon that makes sense, even if I don't like being the focus of a promotional plan."

"You aren't just the focus, Thane. You *are* my campaign."

"What? Dinnae understand."

I slide a little closer to him. "This campaign will feature you. Every print ad, every radio ad, every bit of marketing material, it will all showcase you—the handsomest, sexiest, smartest, most innovative whisky maker in the Highlands and possibly the whole of Scotland."

His face goes blank. He stares at me without even blinking, and his lips have fallen open a little bit too. "Ye cannae be suggesting that you'll put my face on everything."

"That's exactly what we'll do. Print ads will feature your gorgeous face. Radio ads will feature your smoky voice. The creative for social media ads will also feature those two elements. It's all about you, Thane."

"Mhac na galla." He whispered that phrase as if it were an incantation to ward off evil.

I shimmy even closer and grasp his face with both hands. "Do you trust me, Thane?"

"Aye."

"I mean all the way."

"Your plan might have shocked me, but I do trust you implicitly. If you believe this is the right way to promote the distillery, I'll do whatever you suggest."

He says that now, and I know he means it, but I have one more element of my campaign to share with him. This one just might be the deal breaker.

"If you really trust me implicitly..." I hesitate for precisely two seconds. "We need to change the name of the distillery. No more unpronounceable Gaelic phrase. From here on, it will be called the Thane Buchanan Distillery. And your original single-malt will be renamed Thane Black Label."

He seems only slightly less shell-shocked now, but I can see the beginnings of understanding in those beautiful blue eyes. His posture softens. Then he sighs and...kisses me.

"You are the genius, *mo chridhe*. This is a bloody brilliant plan."

I can't stop myself from grinning. "You like it?"

"Aye, lass, I do. Naturally, I should be the face of the distillery, and it should be named after me." He scrunches up his face and scratches the back of his neck. "I hope my mates and my family won't think that's too pretentious."

"They'll love it. Trust me."

"What about the other two whiskies? You didn't like the Triple Threat version, and I never did name the third one."

"Let me think about those two for a while."

Thane rises and heads for a desk in the corner of the spacious living room. It's an old-fashioned roll-top desk, and the top is down right now. I watch as Thane pulls out the chair that was tucked up against the desk and takes his time getting settled in. Finally, he rolls up the top, revealing a number of drawers as well as a computer monitor.

"Where's the computer?" I ask. "Don't see anything."

"It's a small model that fits under the desk, up against the wall."

"Oh. That's a big monitor you've got."

He glances at me over his shoulder and smirks. "Everything I have is big, lass."

"Not your chickens."

"Come over here and sit on my lap." He pats his thigh. "You can help me with the hunt for Holden De Boer."

I hop off the sofa and trot over to him. When he spreads his arms, I climb onto his lap. "What am I going to do? I know nothing about geospatial stuff."

"You have eyes. Your vision is good, aye?"

"Uh-huh."

"So, you can help me search. Geospatial analysis is a visual task." He turns the monitor on and navigates to…a maps app. "You seem skeptical. Dinnae trust my skills after all, eh?"

"No, I trust you. But this is a public app, and I don't think it has up-to-the-minute data."

"That's true. But right now, I'm simply going to navigate to the spot where we last saw Holden. Then I'll expand the search area gradually and make note of locations where he might possibly have been." He hooks an arm around my waist. "Let's both study the map. I'll use the mouse to move around on the screen. If anything jumps out at you, speak up."

We both scrutinize the images, beginning on that side street where we'd run into Holden after our lunch at the café. No matter how hard I squint at the images, I can›t see anything that might give us a clue to where Holden went after he ran off. I suck at geospatial analysis.

Thane rubs his eyes. "This isn't working. We need real-time data."

"Can't any of your friends help? Some of them are computer wizards, right?"

"Aye. But I can't explain to them why I'm searching for Holden."

"Maybe they won't care. Why don't you call one of them and find out?"

He scrunches up his face again. Thane often does that when he doesn't like one of my ideas. In this case, I think he's embarrassed to ask for help. But finally, he sighs and nods. "If you can get my mobile out of my pocket, I'll ring someone."

I wriggle around until I find his phone in his jeans pocket, then offer it to him. "Here's what you wanted."

Thane is wincing.

"What's wrong now?"

"You were rubbing your erse into my *slat*."

"I don't know what that means."

"The word *slat* is Gaelic for 'cock.' Understand now?"

Ohhh, I get it. I hadn't realized I was doing that, but at least I now understand why he's wincing. "Yeah, I understand. Sorry I was making you uncomfortable."

"No worries." He takes the phone and dials a number, then turns on the speaker so I can hear the conversation too. The phone rings five times before a gruff male voice mumbles hello. "Logan, it's Thane. Were you up late satisfying your wife?"

"Why the bloody hell are you calling me on a Sunday?"

"Just so you know, Rebecca is with me and we're on speaker."

"Oh, aye, your new lass. We've heard about her. Dinnae care if she listens."

"Good. We, ah, need your help. I have a wee problem."

"Holden De Boer."

Thane's brows lift the tiniest bit, but otherwise, he doesn't show any surprise on his face. "Aye. How did you know about that?"

Logan grunts. "You're talking to a former MI6 operative. I know everything about everyone. Now, what do you need from me?"

"Access to up-to-the-minute maps data as well as street cameras and any other types of video feeds you can get. I realize that's a tall order."

Logan grunts again. "Try giving me a hard task. This one is child's play. I'll have everything you need within the hour."

I can't restrain my excitement. "Really? It's that easy?"

"Did I claim it's easy, lass? No, I did not. First, I'll ring my contact at the MOD. If he can't help, I'll contact Evan and also Errol Murdoch, possibly Grey Dixon too."

"Those are the computer wizards in your family."

"Evan and Errol are my cousins, but Grey is no relation. He's a Brit."

"But you're sure you can get Thane what he needs."

"Aye, lass, I'm positive of that." Logan pauses for a few seconds. "Rebecca, do you have any family in the UK?"

"Both my children live in England. They're adults. Why do you ask?"

"Just thinking maybe we should take your children to a safe house."

"What?" I jerk upright. "You think they're in danger?"

"No, but I like to be thorough when a former double agent is after Thane and you. I'll ring again once I have the information."

Logan disconnects the call.

Thane pulls me close and hugs me firmly. "Try not to worry yet. Logan will gather all the necessary information and get back to us within the hour, I'm sure."

"Do you think Eric and Courtney might be in danger?"

"Let's not jump to the worst conclusion just yet."

Thane always remains calm. Right now, I'm grateful for that. My kids mean everything to me, and I can't help freaking out a little bit. But as long as Thane isn't worried, I'll do my best to stay calm.

I trust Thane with my life—and the lives of my children.

But God, I hope it doesn't come to that.

Chapter Twenty-Five

Thane

We have nothing to do except wait for Logan's call. I can tell Rebecca is anxious, with good reason, and I'm doing my best to ease her worries. To distract her, I suggest we go outside to say hello to Odin and the chickens. Rebecca does seem less anxious after that. Odin is very friendly, and he adores the lass. She even laughs a wee bit when the llama nuzzles her cheek. She feeds him a treat and tosses some feed to the chickens too.

All of that expended about twelve minutes.

I take Rebecca back into the house and try another tactic to distract her, after we've sat down on the sofa. "Tell me more about your marketing strategy."

"You probably won't like some of it."

"Tell me anyway. I might surprise you."

"Okay." She wriggles about until she has her feet tucked under her cross-legged. "I want to hold an event at the distillery for Valentine's Day."

"What sort of event? A whisky tasting?"

"That's part of it. But the main event will be a party with dancing and music, though I might move that to a bigger venue. You will wear your formal kilt. I'll wear a gown. The guests will all dress in fancy clothes too."

"A ceilidh at the distillery could be enjoyable. It might also bring in more of the public."

"Exactly. But I'm not done yet. I also want to highlight the romance aspect of Valentine's Day with appropriate decor as well as guided tours of the whole operation." She holds up a staying hand. "Let me finish before you grouse about it. Once people see the process of making your whisky, they'll realize how unique and amazing your distillery is."

"Why are you tying my company to Valentine's Day? The two have nothing in common."

She wags a finger at me. "You need to broaden your mind, Thane. Valentine's is the perfect platform for launching your products to the broader market. Right now, you mainly sell to friends and relatives, right?"

"Aye."

"We have three weeks to get this campaign moving. By the time I'm done, everyone in the Highlands will know about the Thane Buchanan Distillery and how deliciously spicy and sweet and exciting your whiskies are."

I sink back into the sofa, resting my head on it which means I'm staring up at the ceiling. "Three weeks doesn't sound like a great deal of time. Your plan seems quite complicated."

"Not really. I've already booked a recording studio so we can get your radio ads running right away. And I also booked a photography studio."

"Where did you find either of those? We'll need to drive three hours to Inverness, I imagine."

She shakes her head. "You hope it will be impossible, but you're wrong. We only need to go to Loch Fairbairn and maybe Fort William."

I jerk my head forward to gawp at the lass. "I have never seen any such things in Loch Fairbairn."

"Fiona suggested I should talk to Kirsty about it."

Now I jerk my whole body upright and twist round to scrutinize the lass. "Kirsty MacTaggart? She's Fiona's cousin."

"Yep. Turns out Kirsty wants to start her own podcast to promote her metaphysical shop. Her husband, Luke, bought all the equipment, and he'll be acting as her producer." Rebecca leans toward me. "So you see, there's no wriggling out of this. Luke will be the producer for your radio and TV ads."

"Television? You never mentioned that."

"Just now I did." She climbs onto my lap, straddling my thighs. "I promise I'll make it all worth your while."

"You're going to shag me until I'm so enthralled by your sensual skills that I'll do anything you want."

She sinks deeper into my lap and brushes her lips across mine lightly. "I can already make you do whatever I want. The shagging is a freebie."

I link my hands behind her erse. "I'll need a down payment on that."

We're mixing metaphors, but who gives a toss?

Rebecca begins to unbutton her blouse.

And my bloody mobile rings.

I unleash a string of Gaelic curses as I struggle to extricate my mobile from my pocket while Rebecca is on my lap. By the time I say hello, I'm a wee bit winded. The caller ID tells me who it is. "Logan, do you have what I need?"

"Aye. I've sent it to you via encrypted email."

"How do I decrypt it?"

"You'll see. Evan and Errol will be coming your way shortly, and Grey Dixon will join in via video call. And please let Rebecca know that her son and daughter are safe, and there's no sign Holden even knows about them. But a mate of mine will keep tabs on them covertly."

I can't believe Logan could arrange all of this in such a short time. It's been forty-two minutes since I called him. "Dinnae know what to say, Logan. I appreciate all the help, but that doesn't seem like an adequate response."

"Good luck, Thane. If you need anything else, just let me know."

I toss my mobile onto the coffee table. "No time for a poke, I'm afraid."

Rebecca slides off my lap. "Oh, well. There's always later."

Someone bangs on the front door. "Wakey-wakey, Thane! The reinforcements have arrived."

"Who is that?" Rebecca asks. "Errol or Evan?"

"It's Errol. Evan MacTaggart never uses the term 'wakey-wakey,' and he also never bangs on doors." I jump up and hurry over to the door, swinging it open. "Come in, laddies. Evan, can you swear to me that Errol doesn't have any explosive devices on his person?"

Evan pushes his glasses up with one finger. "No one can guarantee that. For all I know, he's dropped miniature land mines throughout your property, and he'll detonate them via the app on his mobile."

Rebecca springs off the sofa and races over to me. "Land mines? Are you serious?"

"Unfortunately, yes. Errol is a bampot of the first order."

Errol feigns shock. "Who, me? I'm the gentlest person on earth."

The other MacTaggart, Evan, rolls his eyes heavenward and sighs.

I swing the door all the way open. "Hurry up and get in here. Dinnae want Odin to become agitated and think you lot are attacking me."

The two laddies amble into the house. Rebecca and I head for the sofa, but only Evan follows us, and he takes the desk chair. Errol detours over to the window.

He opens it up and waves while grinning. "No worries, Odin. It's just me, Errol. Evan is here too. We're all mates, and I promise to go out there and have a chat with you later. Brought some treats for you too."

Errol shuts the window and saunters over to the armchair, dropping onto it with one leg slung over the side. "Sooo, what should we do first? Dinnae reckon you've got any explosives on hand."

Rebecca, who sits beside me on the sofa, glances back and forth between me and Errol. "Is he insane?"

"Aye." Evan and I say that at the same time.

Errol clutches his chest. "I'm wounded. My mates think I'm a bampot." He winks at Rebecca. "Ye haven't lived until you've experienced my remotely detonated land mines. It's better than a fireworks display. I could show you right now. Wouldn't ye love to see that? You can tell your son and daughter that you witnessed a unique explosives display."

Rebecca looks completely flummoxed. "Uh, no thanks. Maybe some other time."

"Aye, just let me know."

Evan steeples his fingers as he rocks his chair gently. "Perhaps we should get to the geospatial data."

"That's my cue to visit with Odin," Errol says. "Be back in a wee while."

I rise and approach the desk, leaning my hip against it. My focus remains on the computer screen as Evan downloads the compressed files and opens those up so we can peruse the contents. I recognize that we're looking at geospatial data, but it doesn't seem to be in any particular order. In my job at the DIO, I never needed to unpack a data dump. I received the files already cataloged and ready to go.

I rest my palm on the desktop and speak in a hushed voice. "Do you know how to sort through all of this data, Evan?"

"Afraid not. I design security systems. This is a wee bit out of my wheelhouse." He sits back in his chair and rubs his neck. "It's time to bring Grey Dixon into the discussion. I'll start the secure chat interface."

Whatever the bloody hell that means. But I trust Evan—and aye, even Errol—to get me what I need to track down Holden and not attract the attention of the MOD. Dinnae think they would appreciate what we're doing.

"The secure chat is online," Evan announces. "Now just let me ping Grey Dixon."

"What does he do for a living? I've only heard that it's very technical."

"Oh, aye, it is. Grey is a business intelligence analyst. Basically, he sorts through data to find out how best to help companies do better business." Evan shrugs. "I can't say I understand it completely. Grey explained it to me once, but I wasn't very interested, to be honest."

"Then how do you know he can help us?"

"Because I understand some of the skills that are required for a business intelligence analyst." He ticks them off on his fingers as he recites them. "Problem-solving. Critical thinking. Creativity. Data visualization and interpretation. Attention to detail. Programming skills. Data mining and modeling—"

"Aye, fine, I get the idea. Grey is very clever with computers."

Evan smirks. "You always have a way of boiling things down to the most essential elements."

"I assume that's a compliment."

"Of course it is." Evan glances at the screen, where some sort of notification has appeared. "Ah, yes, Grey is online. I only need to start up the video feed."

Evan taps keys on the computer keyboard.

Grey Dixon appears on the screen. He's much younger than I am, younger even than Errol and Evan. "Good morning. I hear you have a problem, Thane, and my skills might be useful. Happy to help."

"I appreciate that."

Errol returns from his chat with Odin with a conspicuous amount of dirt on his hands and shirt. He comes up behind Evan's chair, setting his hands on the back. "We need you, Grey, because Thane isn't smart enough to sort through the data packet on his own. Apparently, geospatial analysts are rather finicky. Can you unravel all of it for him?"

I am the least finicky person in the Highlands. Errol is being cheeky, as usual.

"Give me a moment," Grey says. "I'll get everything filed and alphabetized for you, Thane."

"Map data doesn't need alphabetizing."

"Can't hurt, can it?" Grey winks, then focuses on his computer. "I'm diving into the packet right now."

I narrow my gaze on Errol. "What were you doing outside?"

"Planting mini mines. You can thank me later."

Rebecca shuffles over to the desk too, slipping her arm around mine. I glance at her and manage a tight smile. She hoists herself up onto her toes to kiss my cheek.

Errol grins. Evan gives me a lopsided smirk.

Rebecca rubs her cheek against my upper arm.

Grey chuckles. "Getting cozy with your girl, eh? Can't blame you. She's a beautiful woman." He twists his head around to shout at someone behind him. "You'll never believe it, Jess. Thane Buchanan finally fell in love."

Why is that news worth broadcasting to his wife and everyone in this room?

Jessica Dixon comes up behind Grey's chair. She grins. "I'm so happy for you, Thane. Ooh, is that your girl right beside you?" She sits down on Grey's lap and rests a hand on her very pregnant belly. Then she waves at Rebecca. "Hello, I'm Jessica Dixon. Are you American too? Seems like all the men in the Highlands marry Americans."

The lass throws me a sideways glance before she responds to Jessica. "Yes, I am American. My son and daughter have jobs in England."

"Oh, how wonderful! You aren't far from your family."

I slap my palm down on the desk. "Are we done blethering yet? I do have a serious problem, ye know."

"Sorry. I got excited because we've all been betting on when Thane Buchanan would finally get hitched. Won't be long now, for sure." Jessica waves at Rebecca again. "It was nice to meet you. Bye."

"Great to meet you too."

Jessica climbs off Grey's lap and walks away.

I squint at Grey. "Who is betting on my personal life?"

"The American Wives Club, of course."

While Grey goes back to fiddling with the data packet, I interrogate Evan and Errol. "I want to know what your wives have been havering about that has to do with my life."

Errol grins and punches my chest, though not with any real force. "You know what they've been talking about. How can you be shocked that the American Wives Club is plotting against you? After all, you took part in the shenanigans they arranged for Domhnall and Fiona."

"Aye, but that was different."

Evan arches one brow. "How, precisely, was it different?"

"Because—Well, it just was."

Errol laughs heartily and even lays a hand over his belly as if his guffaws have strained his abdominal muscles. "That's what every bloke says right before he finds out the American Wives Club is on the case. Just ask Domhnall, Munro, Jack, Magnus, even me. No point in fighting it."

"Those barmy lasses can't harass me now. I have bigger problems."

"Here it comes," Grey declares. "Should be coming up on your screen at any second."

Just as he predicted, a map appears on the screen.

I squint at it. "Not sure a point map is the right tool."

"Sort through it yourself. That's your specialty, isn't it?"

"Aye. But it's been years since I did this sort of thing."

Rebecca gazes up at me with the sweetest look of admiration. "You can do it, Thane, I know you can."

I wave a hand at Evan. "Let me sit in the chair. It will be easier for me to do this when I'm right in front of the data with a mouse in my hand."

Evan stands up and moves to the side of the desk.

I begin to comb through the first map. "This has geocode location data. That's good. Grey gave me a GIS application too, which ought to make things a wee bit easier."

Rebecca stands behind my chair and massages my scalp. At first, I din-nae understand why she's doing that. But then I realize the lass is trying to help me stay focused and relaxed. She's a clever woman.

I switch to a cluster map but get nothing useful from that. Then I decide a heat map might be more meaningful. It gives me deeper data, but I switch to a data space distribution map for even more points of reference.

And then I see it.

Chapter Twenty-Six

Rebecca

Thane has stopped in the middle of whatever he was doing, and though he still holds the mouse in his hand, he doesn't move it or click on anything. He simply stares at the screen. Whatever it shows looks very strange to me, but then, I'm not a geospatial analyst. The map has a dark-blue background with black lines that I assume represent streets. Several lines in various brighter colors look like paths that lead to…somewhere. Most of them just stop in the middle of the map. I also see gray blocks with numbers in them.

Though I desperately want to ask Thane what he's doing, I don't want to interfere with his analysis of the data. He swiftly flips between various layers of what I assume is a map, but I can't keep track of any of it.

"How's it going?" Errol asks. "That rubbish looks like something a nauseous bear coughed up."

Thane grits his teeth. "Haud yer wheesht, ye *cacan*. I'm trying to concentrate."

I kiss the top of his head. "Take it easy. Get back into the groove and you'll find what you're looking for." I begin to massage his scalp again, moving my fingers in slow, swirling patterns. I also soften my voice. "Relax, Thane. What you need is in there, you just have to stop trying so hard to find it. Take a deep breath, close your eyes, and release that breath slowly. When you open your eyes again, you'll see the clue you've been searching for."

Thane does exactly what I suggested, and I keep massaging his scalp.

When he opens his eyes, he smiles. "Of course. How did I not see that before?" He closes the map he'd been pondering and instead brings up what looks like satellite imagery of a small town. "Here we are. This is Loch Fairbairn, and right there"—He scrolls his mouse until he has zoomed in on a precise spot that I recognize—"is the location where Holden ambushed us. See? There he is, there I am, and Rebecca is a few paces away."

"That's amazing," Errol says in a sarcastically hushed voice. "She's the Thane whisperer."

"Who is?" Evan asks.

"Rebecca. The moment she laid her hands on him and whispered to the laddie, suddenly he got his eureka moment." Errol slaps my arm. "Good job, lass."

Thane grumbles out a sigh. "Dinnae get excited yet. I found the last location where we know for sure Holden was. But I still need to track his path forward from there."

"Remember the video feeds, gents."

That voice, emerging from the computer, makes all of us exchange confused glances. Yeah, everyone forgot that Grey is still on the other end of the video call. Thane's maps cover up the whole screen.

"We forgot about you," Evan says. "Sorry, Grey."

"No worries. I can watch everything you're doing onscreen, which means I can also provide advice as necessary."

"Excellent," Thane tells him. "How about some advice right now? Can I overlay the video on top of the still images?"

"You bet your arse you can. And if you need help, just speak up."

I feel rather superfluous at the moment, despite Errol's claim that I'm the Thane whisperer. That sounds ridiculous. "I'll go outside and talk to the animals while you boys do your thing. I'm just getting in the way."

Thane jerks his head up to gaze directly at me. "Please stay, *gràidh*. I need your magical skills to get me through this."

Errol smirks. "Thane whispering. That's the official term I just invented."

Thane reaches up to touch my face. "Will you stay?"

"Absolutely. If that's what you really want."

"It is." He takes hold of my hand and kisses it. "You are my lucky charm for certain."

"Aw, that's so sweet."

I did not speak those words. The voice emerged from the computer.

"Quiet, Jess," Grey admonishes. "You'll ruin Thane's vibe."

"But he's got Rebecca to keep him in the groove. I'll go back to the kitchen and call the ladies of the American Wives Club British Branch. They need an update."

"She's gone now," Grey says. "Let's get to work on tracking that knob Holden."

Thane gets back to work analyzing all the data, but now he has the added advantage of seamlessly switching back and forth between a static map and video footage. I go back to massaging his scalp, since it seemed to help before. I'm curious about how this whole geospatial stuff works, and especially how videos can be integrated with flat maps. But I don't want to distract Thane. He's focused on his task, only speaking when he needs to ask Grey to assist him or confirm something.

After about ten minutes, Thane slumps in his chair and shuts his eyes. "Need a wee break from staring at the map layers. How about you, Grey?"

"Yes, I am going a touch crosseyed."

"Let's leave the screen as-is. We'll come back to it shortly."

Grey hums as if he's thinking. "You know, I believe Evan and I could come up with a self-running program that would alert us to any movement or updates on the geospatial data. That way, we could all get a bit of rest. Scouring the maps for hours might make us all barmy and cross-eyed."

Thane glances up at Evan. "Do you think Grey's idea might work?"

Evan rubs his chin, nodding slowly. "I believe it just might be possible. Why don't you and Rebecca go outside and get some fresh air? Errol can keep an eye on the perimeter while Grey and I work on creating that program."

"Aye, we'll do that." Thane stands up and stretches his entire body, releasing a groaning sigh. Then he abruptly freezes. "How precisely will Errol 'keep an eye on the perimeter'?"

The man in question slaps a hand on Thane's shoulder, giving it a hard squeeze. "Dinnae worry, mate. My methods are strategic and smooth."

I can tell Thane wants to complain about what Errol said, so I seize his hand to drag him away from the desk and toward the front door. He doesn't fight it.

Errol races ahead of us to swing the door open. "Ladies and master distillers first."

"He's also a master maltster," I say. "But that's more of a tongue twister."

Thane grips my hand firmly as we walk out of the house. Errol shuts the door, then trots off to do whatever it is he's going to do. I hope it doesn't involve land mines. Thane and I head for the backyard where the chickens and Odin live. The llama greets us, nuzzling my cheek and licking Thane's. The chickens are milling around, eating whatever feed lies on the ground, sprinkled here and there.

After spending some time with the critters, we go out to the front lawn. Thane has a porch swing, so we cuddle up together there and just appreciate the beauty of the Highlands, on full display thanks to the fact that no one else lives within sight of Thane's home. At least now I'm beginning to understand why he's cagey about his past and why he was reticent to get involved with me. But I will not let fear guide me. I will follow my heart—and it leads me straight to Thane Buchanan.

He stretches an arm across my shoulders, and I snuggle even closer to him. Then he nuzzles my cheek and whispers, "What are ye thinking of, *mo chridhe*?"

"The past, the present, the future." I lay my hand on his arm, where it's draped over my shoulders, and thread our fingers. "The truth is, I never had this kind of relationship with my ex-husband. But despite his behavior, I can't wish I'd never met him. He gave me two wonderful children who became amazing adults."

"You're very proud of them. They must be proud of you too."

"Not so sure about that. I got fired from my old job."

"But it wasn't your fault. You are an incredible woman, and I know you'll take our company to new heights and make it the most popular whisky in Scotland, probably the UK too." He winks. "Who knows? Maybe it will take over the world market."

"Let's not go crazy with our sales projections right off the bat."

"I believe in you, Rebecca. That's what I meant."

His statement stuns me so much that, for a moment, all I can do is gape at him. Then I blink rapidly as I rouse from my shock. "No one has ever told me that before. I—I don't know what to say."

"Dinnae need to say anything. I wanted you to know how much I respect and admire you, that's all." He gets up and holds out his hand. "We best go back into the house. Evan and Grey must have come up with a solution by now."

I accept his hand, letting him help me get up even though we both know I could've done that on my own. Thane is just that kind of gentleman. When he turns toward the front door, I lay a hand on his arm to halt him.

He turns toward me.

And I splay a hand over his cheek. "I believe in you too, Thane."

I swear his eyes are tearing up just a little. He swallows hard, trying to smile but too choked up to do it. Then he clears his throat and faces the door again, grasping the knob with his free hand.

"That's the sweetest thing I've ever seen, Thane. You and Rebecca expressing your admiration for each other. Should I set off a land mine in celebration?"

With a sigh, Thane glances at Errol. "No, ye barmy *cacan*. But thank you for the offer."

I can just see Errol's face peeking around the corner of the house. He really is a strange man. But from what Thane and his friends have told me, Errol Murdoch is also brave, selfless, and kind. I gave up on judging other people based on superficial things a long time ago.

"Are you coming in too, Errol?" Thane asks.

"No. I'm staying out here with Odin. He's a brilliant conversationalist."

Uh, sure, whatever. Errol must be joking, but it's hard to tell with him.

Thane and I return to the living room just as Grey shouts, "I pulled a blinder! It's bloody brilliant! Wish Jess hadn't gone to the loo. She would love to see what I just did."

We come up behind the desk chair, where Evan sits. The tech billion-aire leaps out of the chair and waves for Thane to take the seat. "Grey and I finished coding that program. And as Grey just shouted to the entire universe, he came up with the final bits of code that made everything fall into place. He did indeed do a blinder."

"It's 'pull a blinder,' Evan. Your cousin Cat married a Brit, so why don't you know all the slang yet?"

"Because I am not married to Alex Thorne." Evan rolls his eyes. "Thank heavens for that."

I raise my hand. "Um, what is a blinder?"

On the computer screen, Grey grins. "It means I accomplished some-thing bloody amazing without any cock-ups."

"In that case, congratulations."

"Thanks, Rebecca." Grey puckers his lips and raises his brows. "I notice that none of you blokes had enough manners to congratulate me."

He's being sarcastic, of course. But the boys lavish phony praise on Grey, which makes him laugh.

Thane sits down in the desk chair. "You can go now, Grey. I'm grateful for all your help, but the new program will take over now. You must have other things to do."

"Good luck, mate. Ring me if you need anything else."

He waves goodbye, then his video feed cuts off.

Thane glances up at Evan. "You can go home too. Keely and Joy must be anxious to have you back and vice versa."

"Aye, I miss them already." Evan pats Thane's shoulder and nods to me. "Remember, Errol is still prowling around out there with his land mines."

With that, Evan strides out of the house. A moment later, I hear a car engine starting up, followed by the crunching of gravel.

Thane rises and gestures toward the chair. "Sit down here, *gràidh*. I'll go check on Errol and try to talk him into going home. Ashley must want her husband back. The lass is pregnant, after all."

"I haven't met Ashley yet. Or hardly any of your family or friends."

He bends over to kiss my cheek. "I will remedy that situation soon. And I'd like to meet your children too."

"Yeah, I'd love to introduce you to them."

Thane ambles out of the house while whistling a cheerful tune.

He can't be that happy just because I offered to introduce him to my kids. When I think about meeting his family, I feel a mixture of excitement and anxiety. What if they don't like me?

Oh, for pity's sake. I'm a grown woman. I can handle meeting my boyfriend's family. It does feel a little weird to call a mature, middle-aged man my boyfriend, though.

Out of the corner of my eye, I notice Thane standing outside the living room window. "Go home, Errol, ye bampot. I can protect my home and my woman without your barmy devices."

"All right, all right. I'll go. But if you need my land mines, just give me a ring."

Errol walks past Thane, who follows him out to the front yard. Soon, another car starts up and drives away.

Thane clomps up the porch steps and pushes the door open. He takes one step across the threshold before the sound of yet another car engine becomes audible. It's coming this way, not heading down the road, away from the house.

I can't see around Thane, whose body blocks the doorway. But his brows crinkle, and his jaw drops.

"What's wrong?" I ask as I hustle over to him. Still, all I can see is the little car that just pulled into the driveway beside Thane's pickup truck. A figure sits in the driver's seat, though I can't tell if it's a man or a woman.

Thane urges me to back away from the door. "Wait here. Please."

I nod my agreement.

He marches out the door and slams it shut. Then I hear his boots clomping down the steps.

A car door slams shut.

I can hear voices, but I can't understand the words they're saying.

Oh, screw this. I am not going to stand here waiting to find out what's going on. I shuffle over to the porch window and finally get a look at the visitor.

She's a beautiful redhead. And she just mashed her lips to Thane's.

Chapter Twenty-Seven

Thane

I peel the woman's mouth away from mine and grasp both her wrists, raising them between us. The shock I'd experienced when she stepped out of her car hasn't quite worn off yet. And I dinnae know quite how to respond to this situation, especially since I can see Rebecca watching us through the window. "What the bloody hell are you doing here, Ava?"

"You asked for my help. I'm here to oblige you."

"Oblige me? Yer bum's oot the windae."

Ava cants her head to the side, which makes her short haircut sway a wee bit. Her dark-brown eyes always have a canny glint to them. "I discussed the problem with my superiors, and they agreed that I should indeed race to your rescue. You could at least thank me. It was a bloody long drive from the Inverness airport to this depressing little backwater region."

Backwater? Depressing? Most folk tend to become kinder as they age. Ava has not softened one iota.

She tips her sunglasses down to appraise my hovel. "Dear lord, please tell me that you at least have indoor plumbing."

"Oh, aye, and we discovered the telephone a few weeks ago too. But we're still working on that newfangled thing called the internet."

Ava pushes her sunglasses up again and sashays past me. "Let's go inside, darling. We have a great deal to discuss."

I move in front of her to block the way. "Tell me why you're here, Ava, or I'll toss you into the boot of your car and drive you back to the airport. Then, I'll put you in a box and send you home."

Ava removes her sunglasses and shakes her head. "You've changed, Thane. What happened to the man who would discover a geospatial anomaly and race out into the field to gather more intel? You were fearless, and it was such a turn-on. I remember all those times when we would get so randy that we would shag anywhere, anytime."

A throat-clearing behind me makes me wince—because I know who made that sound.

Naturally, Ava peers past my body to see the lass who has just walked out of the house. "Well, well, what do we have here? Must be your older sister."

"Haud yer wheesht, ye *phitean*."

Ava laughs. "Honestly, Thane, I'd hoped you might grow out of that Gaelic gibberish eventually. An intelligent man like you shouldn't speak in such a crude manner."

"Are ye labeling me crude because I called ye the C-word in Gaelic?"

Rebecca leans over my shoulder, so she must be standing on her tiptoes. Then she whispers, "You can't use the C-word, but you'll call her that in Gaelic?"

I respond in an equally soft voice, speaking out of the side of my mouth. "Aye. What's wrong with that?"

"Nothing, I guess. It's just kind of weird."

I return my attention to Ava. "Or are ye upset because I'm daring to speak the mother tongue of Scotland?"

"Why must you always revert to the heathen language? It's so…distasteful." She settles both her palms on my chest, and her tone becomes huskier. "Get rid of your housekeeper. Then we can fuck anywhere you like in this tiny home."

"No thank you." I walk up the steps backward, halting just in front of Rebecca. "For the last time, Ava. Tell me why you're here."

"Have you lost your hearing from listening to bagpipes for too many years? I told you, I'm here to help. Your intelligence officer has come to bring you back into the fold, darling, as my covert human intelligence source."

"That phrase is too much of a mouthful. I was your agent, that's the common term for it. You turned me into a spy just so you could move up the career ladder at the MOD."

Rebecca comes up beside me. Chin lifted, she gazes steadily and coolly at Ava. "So, you're Thane's handler. I suppose we should introduce ourselves. I'm Rebecca Taylor."

The lass offers her hand to Ava, who glances at it haughtily. "And what do you do for a living, pet? Cleaning Thane's house can't be a full-time job."

"I'm the marketing manager at Thane's distillery. And what's your job, sweetie? Wiping babies bottoms in a daycare center?"

Ava huffs. "You have no idea who you're dealing with. I am Ava Marston-Baines, daughter of Sir Richard Marston-Baines."

"Uh-huh. Is that supposed to mean something to me?" Rebecca slips an arm around my waist. "Thane, do you know this Sir what's-his-name?"

"Aye, unfortunately. He's a right *riatach*. The man never met a kickback he didn't take. But I knew nothing about that until long after Ava had pulled me into her covert world."

Rebecca sets her hands on her hips. "Did you take the kickbacks, Ava? Like father, like daughter?"

Ava lifts her chin. "I have never been corrupt."

But I noticed she didn't say her father hasn't been. "Tell me the real reason you came here, Ava. Tell me now, or I will ring my mate Logan MacTaggart and have him lock you up in the dungeon at his cousin Rory's castle. It's a fine spot for an interrogation, Roman-legion style."

That sounds like a nasty threat. The Romans weren't known for their civility during wartime—or anytime. But Ava isn't stupid, and she knows me better than I wish the lass did.

She puckers her lips and taps her fingers on her hips. "All right, have it your way. But I insist upon speaking to you alone. For five minutes, that's all. If I can't convince you in that time, I'll drive away and never bother you again."

I glance at Rebecca. The lass exhales a gusty breath, and her shoulders flag. "Go on, talk to her alone. She's the one I don't trust, not you."

"Aye, Ava is a slippery sort."

"But you can handle her."

Rebecca steps aside to let me and Ava walk into the house. I stand on the threshold to watch Rebecca approach the porch swing and settle onto it. Then I go inside and shut the door.

"Explain yourself, Ava."

"Come closer, darling. I'm about to reveal state secrets to you."

I realize she means to try to seduce me, strictly to solidify a connection between us. That was how she roped me in back in the day. The technique no longer works on me. Even before I met Rebecca, I'd become immune to the erotic techniques employed by covert agents like Ava.

But out of the corner of my eye, I can see Rebecca sitting on the swing, hands clasped on her lap, head down. Suddenly, I want to get this over with as soon as possible. So, I stride over to the island, seizing Ava's arm to drag her along with me.

I shove the lass against the island. "Talk, Ava."

She reaches for me, preparing to set her hands on my chest.

But I push her backward, caging her with my arms and my hands on the island. "No more rubbish about how you've missed me." I glance up at the clock above the stove. "You have less than five minutes left."

Ava hugs herself and rubs her arms. "All right. Here's the truth. I have missed you, Thane, but that's not the reason I'm here. You got out of the game, but I had nowhere else to go. I've stayed with MI6. It's all I know."

"Dinnae care about catching up on your life story."

She bites the inside of her lip, hunching her shoulders, and glances round as if she expects a sniper to take her down at any second. "We've known for some time that Holden De Boer has a grudge against you. It's rubbish, of course. You were doing your job—the one I convinced you to take on. You would've been quite happy to remain at the DIO as only a geospatial analyst. I…" She hugs herself more tightly. "I used sex to get what I needed from you. But I did care for you. That was never a lie."

"Says a lifelong spy. Pardon me if I cannae believe that."

"I don't blame you. I deserve your scorn."

As I study Ava's face, I can't figure out if she's trying to win me over, or if she honestly despises her job and the things she's done for her country. It's true that I got out mostly unscathed. But Ava had stuck with it. What horrific things has she witnessed? Or done? I never believed she was a killer, but I don't really know her anymore. I think I never did.

Aye, that's the quicksand of covert operations.

I take two steps backward. "What do you know about Holden? I'd had no contact with the scunner until a few weeks ago."

"Yes, I know. When he was released from prison, he made a beeline straight for you." She holds up a hand. "Please, hear me out before you ask more questions."

I lean against the island beside her. "Go on, then."

"My current agent was meant to be keeping tabs on Holden, but he lost track of De Boer."

"Not much of a geospatial analyst, eh?"

"You were the only agent I ever had who possessed that skill set. My current agent is a civilian who works for a defense contractor in England. He knows how to play the game with contractors, but he lacks the strategic and emotional expertise you displayed."

I have emotional expertise? The lass must be off her head.

"You don't believe me, do you? That your talents were more than technical. You still think your only value to MI6 was as a computer specialist." She shakes her head slowly. "Thane, I chose you because you are a good man with a conscience and empathy for others. That's what made you such a bloody brilliant covert human intelligence source."

"Stop trying to worm your way back into my good graces. What I need from you is information about Holden."

Ava hops up onto a stool and rests her elbow on the island. She lets her head fall into her upraised hand. "I'm sorry, Thane. The way things went down during our last mission... I understand why you needed to escape from my world."

"Four people died, Ava. Civilians who had nothing to do with your 'op.' They were innocent people just out for a walk in the park and who got caught in the crossfire." Literal crossfire. I will never forget that day as long as I live. "The only information I need from you is what you know about Holden."

"Of course." She straightens and faces me. "After Holden was released, I asked the DIO to have their best geospatial analyst keep track of him. We followed him as he procured a vehicle and began his journey north toward Scotland. We still had him in our sights at Glasgow."

"And then what happened?"

She glances away. "We lost him. Even our best geospatial analyst couldn't find Holden."

At last, I begin to understand the reason for her sudden reappearance in my life. "You paid me a visit because you hope I can find Holden for you."

"Yes."

For a moment, I study Ava and try to deduce how much I should trust her. Very little, that's how much. Yet I believe some of what she's told me. No MI6 veteran would come crawling to me for assistance unless she were desperate.

"Can you help, Thane? Or should I say, *will* you help me?"

"Aye, I'll find Holden for you."

The tension evaporates from her posture. She leans against the island as if she might melt into a puddle on the floor without the counter holding her up. "Thank you, Thane. You have no idea what sort of bind I've been in."

"Dinnae care about your bind. I'm doing this because it's the right thing." I march over to the door and yank it open. "Come in, Rebecca. You need to hear about this."

The lass leaps off the swing and races up to me. I sling an arm round her waist, and we walk into the living room together. Ava remains on her stool, though her haughtiness is now long gone.

I gesture for Rebecca to sit on the sofa, then I join her. "Come over here, Ava. We still have things to talk about."

She kicks off her high-heeled shoes and carries them as she shuffles over here and drops onto the armchair. Fortunately, the computer screen is turned off. Ava won't get any information from me unless I decide to share it.

Rebecca gives me a sly smile. "Did you smack her around good? She went from arrogant and rude to demure in five minutes."

"We had a good chat. She understands the situation now."

"Sure she does."

I set my ankle on the opposite knee, then drape my arm over Rebecca's shoulders. "Go on, Ava. Tell my girlfriend everything."

Ava's eyes go wide. "Girlfriend?"

"That's right. Rebecca and I are in a relationship. A serious one."

"Oh." Ava wriggles in her chair, staring down at the floor. "That's none of my concern. But I know you want me to explain to Rebecca everything I've just told you."

"Aye. So go on."

She relates all the details to Rebecca, leaving nothing out, and then collapses against her chair. "So you see, I know as little as you do."

"Wrong. I know more than you do."

Ava's eyes flash even wider this time, though only for a second. "How could you—I assumed you—"

"You assumed I'm a hick and that I've lost all my geospatial expertise after returning to the Highlands."

"Well, you do sell whisky for a living."

"And what's wrong with that? I craft whisky, though. I'm not simply a salesman."

Rebecca wraps her hand around mine and smiles with pride. "Thane creates the most innovative and original whiskies you'll ever taste."

I can't stop myself from smiling. Rebecca's endorsement means more to me than any award or review of my whiskies. The woman I worship loves my single malts and believes in me the way I believe in her. After all these years of shying away from romance and hiding my past from everyone, I finally understand that's exactly how my life needed to unfold. I met the perfect woman at the perfect time.

And I am in love with Rebecca Taylor.

The realization hits me so hard that, for a moment, I can't breathe. I stare at Rebecca as if I've never seen the lass before, as if I've suddenly been dropped into an alternate universe. Thane Buchanan in love? No one would believe it. I've dated occasionally, though I only made it beyond the first date with Fiona. Our two weeks had been my longest relationship, and that wasn't serious for either of us.

Rebecca has changed my life.

Chapter Twenty-Eight

Rebecca

I study the man sitting beside me, worried about his abrupt shift from smiling to staring blankly at me. Thane seems to have frozen up, like an old computer that needs a tune-up. Did I blurt something out that shocked him? All I remember saying was that he makes the most amazing whiskies. But I've told Thane the same thing before, so I doubt he's shocked that I repeated my statement in front of Ava.

Oh, yes, Ava. That woman makes me feel like a teenager defending her boyfriend from a cheerleader who wants to poach him.

I've never met a man who made me want to get catty just to protect him from another woman's advances. But I will gladly get in a chick fight with this wannabe man-stealer. Who does she think she is? No less than ten minutes ago, she called me a housekeeper and flirted with my boyfriend right in front of me. Maybe I am too old to behave this way, but who cares? Thane would fight for me, for sure, and beat the crap out of any man who tried to steal me away. I'll do the same for him.

Ava with the snooty hyphenated name has zero chance of seducing my man. Well, I assume her name is hyphenated. That's a common British thing, at least in movies.

Wow, I'm actually on board for a chick fight. My kids would be shocked to see me like this. Hell, I'd even mud wrestle to pry that woman away from Thane.

Okay, maybe I should cut Ava a sliver of slack. She has been much less arrogant since she and Thane had their private chat. Errol had called me the Thane whisperer, but my man cowed this haughty spy in five minutes flat. He's the Ava whisperer.

Thane's phone makes a bleeping noise, indicating a new text or some sort of notification. He digs around in his jeans pocket until he extricates the phone. With a few swipes of his finger, he brings up the notification. And he freezes again. "We've got him."

I slant forward to squint at the tiny screen. "Holden? You've got him? That was amazingly fast."

"Dinnae get excited yet. I need to verify this." He hurries over to the desk and pulls up the information on the computer screen. Thane's expression falls. "No, it was some other bloke. The program misidentified him."

Damn. I was hoping this ordeal would be over soon. "Evan and Grey seemed so sure it would work."

"They might be miracle workers, but they aren't infallible. Besides, this is bleeding-edge technology."

Ava sits up straighter and clears her throat. "I almost forgot about the gift I brought for you."

She jumps up and hurries outside.

Thane and I exchange confused looks.

Ava returns carrying a black box the size of an average laptop computer. She hands the item to Thane. "You were incorrect. The program your mates created was incredible, but it's hardly the most cutting-edge option available. This is the bleeding edge."

He gingerly accepts the box. "What is it?"

"Something my current agent heard about during his surveillance of a Russian miscreant who kept it on a computer that's cordoned off from the rest of the world." She glances sideways at Thane's computer, then returns her attention to him. "This box contains a copy of a program that will make the one your mates created seem like child's play."

"How do I access the data?"

"Only via biometrics. In this case, that means facial recognition."

"Do I look anything like this bloke?"

Ava rolls her eyes. "Of course not. Did you think I wouldn't have brought a decryption app that would confuse the facial recognition software?"

"Why would I know that? I wasn't a spy, Ava, not the sort you and Holden were."

"Yes, all right, I'm sorry." She pulls another item out of her pocket, handing it to Thane. "This is the decryption key. It should grant you full access to the laptop's contents. Feel free to contact your mates if you need help. This is a bit far from my wheelhouse."

I wish I could help Thane, but my expertise with technology goes only as far as creating social media graphics. But maybe I can help him in another way. Ava watches me closely while I amble up to Thane's chair, halting behind it, and settle my palms on his head. He smiles up at me and touches my hand.

Ava's lips pucker again. That woman needs to expand her repertoire of annoyed expressions.

Thane gets to work, easily unlocking the laptop with the decryption whatsit Ava gave him. I massage his scalp the way I'd done earlier when he was trying to find Holden via that geospatial gobbledygook. My touch seemed to relax him, which might've made his task less stressful. He told me he believes it did. That's why I decided to try it again.

Ava's brows draw together over her nose.

While Thane taps away on the keyboard and swirls his mouse around, I keep up my massage. At the same time, my attention becomes riveted to the computer screen. I have no idea what he's doing, but watching him work makes me feel closer to him. I love this man, and I would do anything for him.

Holy shit. Did I actually think those words? I haven't known him for long, but I suddenly realize it's true. I am in love with Thane Buchanan. I need to tell him that, but not in front of Ava the Hyphenated Princess. Okay, my opinion of Ava might be slightly colored by the fact that she flounced onto the scene and started insulting me while getting handsy with my man.

I bend my head down to murmur into Thane's ear, "How long do you think this will take?"

"Ten to fifteen minutes, I'd wager. This is an unfamiliar program."

"In that case, I'm going to have a little chat with our guest."

His mouth kinks up at one corner in a sly smile. "Dinnae rough her up too much, *gràidh.* She needs to be conscious to answer any questions I might have for her."

"In other words, you don't mind if I rip her hair out and slug her in the jaw, just as long as she stays awake."

He winks, then goes back to studying the new program.

And I approach Ava's chair. "Let's go outside and have a little girl talk."

She lifts her brows, then pushes herself up and out of the chair. Then she smooths out her designer clothing with both hands and reasserts her haughty demeanor. "Yes, let's do that."

Her snooty tone of voice has returned as well.

But I suspect that's a facade.

I lead the way as we step outside and tromp down the porch steps, halting in front of Thane's truck. "I want the truth, right now."

Ava huffs. "I've already told both of you everything."

"Not quite." I fold my arms over my chest and keep my gaze leveled on hers. "Thane told me that he called you after the first time Holden came after him. But you refused to help him. Now I want to know why you waited so damn long when you knew a dangerous ex-con was on the loose and itching for some payback."

"It wasn't within my remit."

"Thane was your agent."

"Years ago. He's been a civilian for a long time, and I have not been his intelligence officer for equally as long."

That's pretty much what I expected her to say. But I have an ace up my sleeve that I'd bet will shake her up just enough for me to dig the truth out of her. "Even if it wasn't in your 'remit,' you would've wanted to help him because you are in love with him."

Ava stops blinking. Stops breathing, I think. And she definitely goes pale underneath all that makeup. She swallows hard enough that I can see the movement in her throat. "Why would you suggest such a thing?"

"Because it's true." I lean toward her a little bit. It's enough to make her cringe. "I don't care if you'd rather Thane never finds out how you feel. I am going to tell him. We're a couple, and that means we need to be transparent with each other. I'm giving you one last chance to confess."

She bites her upper lip and glances around as if she's looking for an escape route. Finally, she slumps against the truck and bows her head. "Yes, I've been in love with him for a long time. I knew Thane didn't feel the same way. When he announced he was leaving the DIO and the army, I knew I'd lost him forever."

"Until he called you for help."

"Yes. I had no idea he'd become involved with you in the meantime." She squirms and curls her fingers around the truck's grill, refusing to look at me. "Hearing from Thane again... Well, I can't deny it gave me a thrill. I did a bit of digging and managed to find out where he lives now."

"Stalking isn't sexy, Ava."

"I have not stalked him." She snaps her spine ramrod straight and lifts her perky little nose. "I had a legitimate reason to come here. You know as well as I do that I'm in a far better position to help him resolve the Holden situation."

"Bullshit. You're here because you've been obsessed with him for years. Isn't that right? Or do you honestly believe you're in love with him?" I tip my head to the side and narrow my gaze on her. "Give it up, Ava. Thane doesn't want you."

"I'm aware of that. But I can be far more useful—"

The door bangs open behind me.

While Ava gapes at Thane, I whirl around and race up the steps. "What's wrong?"

"Not a bloody thing." He grins. "I found Holden. He's in Oban right now, and he's heading this way."

"And you're thrilled about that?"

Thane slings an arm around my waist, tugging me close. "Aye, lass, it is. We can lay a trap for the *riatach*. That means 'bastard,' by the way."

I smack a hard kiss on his lips. "You're a genius, Thane."

"Best wait until my plan works—if it works—before you praise me." His attention veers to Ava, who still stands in front of his truck. "We could use your help, but only if you can work together with Rebecca."

"I can do that."

"Good. Then let's go inside and talk about my plan. We won't have much time."

Thane keeps his arm around me as we hurry back into the house with Ava scurrying after us. The black box she had given Thane sits on the coffee table with the lid open and the built-in screen ready to go. I notice it's displaying a map of what I assume is the area around Oban, wherever that is, and also Loch Fairbairn. The screen faces the sofa.

Ava drops onto the chair she'd sat in earlier.

Thane and I settle onto the sofa.

I glance at the screen, then look at Thane. "What's the big plan?"

"We need Holden to believe we're unaware that he's coming this way. But we also need defensive measures, the sort Holden would never expect."

"Do you want to activate your security system?"

"Aye."

"Okay. Just tell me what I can do."

Ava surveys the living room with her brows pulled together. "What security system do you have? I can't see anything of that nature."

"That's precisely the point. No one expects to run into my type of security."

He's talking about Odin, but Ava clearly hasn't met the llama yet. Ohh, I'd love to see her reaction when Odin starts screaming at her.

That brings up a question, which I whisper into Thane's ear. "Why didn't Odin make any noise when Ava arrived?"

"He must not have seen her. I put him out in the pasture after Errol and Evan left so he could browse."

Not sure if I believe Ava the stone-cold spy would freak out at the sight of a llama, but my impression of her might be inaccurate. Maybe she does have a girlie streak hidden under that iron-maiden facade.

Ava compresses her lips and snorts a breath out through her nostrils. "If you lot are talking about me, I should be included in the conversation."

"What makes you think we're talking about you?" I ask.

"Because I am not a moron."

She has a point. Ava might be obnoxious, but she clearly has a functional brain.

Thane finally aims his gaze at her. "I need you to stay here and monitor the data on this black box. It's tracking Holden's movements now, but if he should fall off the radar, I'll expect you to alert me."

She flicks her gaze between me and Thane before settling on him. "Where will you be?"

"Outside. I need to check the perimeter and…a few other things." He pushes up off the sofa, gesturing for me to stay put. Then he aims a hard look at Ava. "I will expect you to obey Rebecca. Whatever she says, you will do. Full stop."

Ava wants to complain. It's obvious. But she keeps her trap shut and moves onto the sofa to sit beside me.

Fantastic. I get to babysit the smug Brit.

She wriggles to get a little bit further away from me while still having a good view of the computer screen. She clasps her hands on her lap.

Thane walks out the door.

Ava tilts forward a little, squinting at the screen.

I keep watching it too. No, I don't trust Ava Marston-Baines to keep her eye on the map on the computer screen. I don't trust her, period.

Peripherally, I see Thane marching down the side of the house on his way to wherever he's going. I know he has a good reason for keeping me in the dark right now. Probably because he doesn't want the British snoop to overhear our conversation.

"Bloody hell," Ava whispers as she points at the screen. "Look how fast Holden is moving. He must be violating all the speed laws."

"He's got a serious hard-on for harassing Thane." I lean forward to study the screen too. "Looks like an hour might be an overly generous estimate of when Holden might get here."

"Yes, I'm afraid it is. One of us needs to go out there and warn Thane."

"Why don't you do that? He would want me to watch the screen."

That's true, since he doesn't trust Ava. But it's not the main reason I want to send her outside. I feel slightly guilty about playing a trick on her.

Ava jumps up. "Try not to lose track of Holden while I'm gone. I know you're only a marketing manager who got sacked from her last job. But do try, darling."

Nope, I don't feel guilty anymore.

Chapter Twenty-Nine

Thane

I jog through the fenced yard, heading for the pasture gate, where I'll find Odin. Though I dislike using him as my security system in this instance, when a dangerous man is coming for us, he is the best and most reliable alert system I have. He'll know what to do. Once I reach the gate, I whistle for Odin to come inside. He trots through it without hesitation.

I've just shut the gate when I hear the sound of someone approaching. The noises are subtle—soft grunts, wee hissing sounds, shoes sliding across grass. Then I hear a sound no one could miss.

"Ah! Fucking Scottish mud."

Odin's head shoots up. His ears prick up.

Just as Ava rounds the corner of the house, Odin sounds his alarm call. And she jumps backward, shrieking. Odin rushes toward her.

I shout to him, giving orders in Gaelic. He halts, but keeps his head up and his ears pricked—and his attention squarely on Ava.

She holds a hand to her chest, eyes wide, breathing hard. "What the bloody hell is that…thing?"

"Meet Odin. He's my security system." I stride up to the llama and scratch behind his ears. "Good laddie."

Ava eyes Odin with suspicion and a hint of fear. "Will that thing bite me? Or kick me?"

I scratch my chin, pretending to contemplate her questions. "Aye, he might do both of those, if you annoy him. You shouldn't have come through the gate and invaded his home. Best back away slowly."

She remains immobile.

I whisper more Gaelic to Odin, and he ambles back toward the chicken coop. I approach Ava. "What are you doing out here? You're meant to stay with Rebecca and obey her every command."

"Rebecca thought you would want her to stay inside to monitor Holden's progress. So, I came out here to inform you."

"Of what?"

"Holden is driving very fast and might be here much earlier than expected."

I have my suspicions about why Rebecca told Ava that I would want her to stay inside while the other lass came out to find me. Dinnae blame Rebecca for wanting to harass Ava. She deserved it.

"Go inside and help Rebecca," I tell her. "I need to call for reinforcements."

"But I can help you."

I glare at her. "Go inside, Ava. Now."

She pouts, then scurries away.

And I can't resist harassing her a wee bit more. "Hurry, Ava! Odin's coming your way."

The lass shrieks and leaps over the gate. She sprints back into the house.

Who knew a tough-as-nails intelligence officer would turn out to be afraid of a llama. Odin had surprised Rebecca the first time she saw him, but she recovered from the shock quickly.

I pull out my mobile and ring Errol. "Might have a use for your land mines after all. When can you get here?"

"Dinnae need me. Just access the app on your mobile."

"The what? I don't have an explosives app."

He chuckles. "Aye, ye do. I installed it on your mobile phone while you lot were arguing about whatever it was."

"I haven't noticed a new app."

"Look for one called MacFlynn. Open it up, and you'll see the locations of all the mines I planted around your property."

"You did what?" I shouted those words loud enough that everyone in Loch Fairbairn probably heard it. "Ye bloody *cacan*. Planting explosives in my yard without my consent is—"

"You're welcome. I'll get the gang ready, and we'll fly out to your place."

"I hope you don't mean that literally. I do not want Marilyn landing in my yard and scaring the chickens to death."

He clucks his tongue. "Chill out, Thane. Those are words I couldn't have imagined I'd speak. The man who never gets upset about anything is 'freaking out,' as my wife would say. But no, I will not fly my plane there."

"Goodbye, Errol."

I hang up on him and rush back into the house, where Rebecca and Ava are sitting on the sofa together, with a discrete gap between them. I crouch beside Rebecca. "Where is he now?"

"Approaching Loch Fairbairn. You better get reinforcements quick."

"The laddies are on the way, but I can't guarantee they'll get here in time."

"Oh, great. Do you have a gun or a knife or any kind of weapon?"

"Nothing but kitchen knives. It won't come to that, though." I lay my hand on her knee. "Relax, *mo chridhe*. Errol left us a gift that he just told me about."

"What kind of gift?"

I pull out my mobile and bring up the app Errol had mentioned. The name "MacFlynn" tells me I have the right app. Why Errol called it "Mac-Flynn" is beyond me. On the wee screen, I see a map of what I assume are Errol's mines. The *cacan* planted them all around the front yard and the house, not to mention the driveway. Fortunately, he left the backyard alone. Even Errol doesn't want to hurt my animals.

Right now, my only concern is protecting Rebecca and Ava.

My mobile rings.

The caller ID tells me it's Magnus MacTaggart calling. "Hello, Magnus. I take it Errol contacted you."

"Aye. Logan and I are on the way to help with your villain problem."

"Might be too late. Holden De Boer has a significant lead, and he's driving dangerously fast."

"The program Evan and Grey created is working, then."

"Aye, it's brilliant. But Holden is off his head and clearly doesn't give a toss about speed laws or safety."

Magnus chuckles. "Villains rarely do."

"No offense, but I was hoping for a bigger contingent than the two of you and Errol, who's getting here by means I probably don't want to know about."

"The laddie is barmy, but he has a good heart and a fearless nature that has served him well. And it's also saved the lives of several MacTaggarts."

"Aye, I know that. Thank you for calling."

We hang up, and I suddenly realize Rebecca and Ava are both staring at me as if I've turned into a human-size eggplant. "Why are you gawping at me?"

Rebecca raises her hand slowly and points one finger at the screen on the black box device. "I don't think your friends will get here in time."

I follow the track of her finger and study the imagery on the screen. "*Mhac na galla*. He's driving like his car is a rocket ship."

"What should we do?"

"You lasses go hide in the bathroom and shut the door."

"No way. You can lock Ava in there if you want, but I'm staying with you."

Ava bristles. "Lock *me* in the loo? I'm an intelligence officer. She's just a saleswoman."

"Haud yer wheesht." I wipe a hand over my mouth while my pulse accelerates by the second. I need to protect the women, but I have no weapons—except for Errol's mines. "We have only one option, and it's dangerous."

Ava makes a derisive noise. "I am an MI6 agent, for pity's sake."

"Who is afraid of llamas. For all I know, you'll panic when a mine goes off. Have you ever seen that happen?"

She squirms and makes a pained face. "Not in person."

"Then you'll do as I say. Understand?"

"Yes, all right."

I stand up. "Please would you both hide in the kitchen behind the island. When I shout for you to take cover, I want you to crouch and shield your heads. Plug your ears too."

Both lasses nod their agreement. Ava stopped complaining. It's a bloody miracle.

I watch as the lasses move behind the island. Then I tuck my mobile into my shirt pocket, with Errol's app still open, and pick up the black box device. I cradle it with one arm as I patrol the house from the inside, checking the windows with every pass round the living room and through the bedroom. How clever is Holden? I'd never gotten the impression that he's a genius, but he is vicious and conniving.

Even a dolt can cause serious harm if he's determined and off his head.

"Are you really going to use Errol's mines?" Rebecca asks, though I can't see her face. She's following my orders by staying low.

"I'll only use them if it's absolutely necessary."

"Won't that scare Odin and the chickens? They might panic and get themselves hurt."

"The chickens might be upset, but they won't injure themselves. Odin has heard all manner of loud noises, and it doesn't fash him. Besides, these are relatively small mines, the sort Errol brings out at large outdoor gatherings to impress everyone."

"Oh, good, I'm glad Odin will be okay." She peeks at me over the countertop, though only her eyes and forehead are visible. "Sorry I'm being a pest. My defensive mom instincts kicked into high gear."

"Dinnae mind your questions."

She sinks below the counter again.

I set the black box on the wee table beside the door, where I can keep an eye on the screen. I have my mobile in my hand, ready to tap the button that will set off a land mine. Cannae believe it's come to this. Setting off explosives outside my house? It's insane.

On the computer screen, the blip that represents Holden's vehicle is barreling ever closer. Less than a mile separates him from us.

Abruptly, the blip stops moving.

What in the world? Why is he sitting there? Must be waiting for something, but I can't fathom what it is.

Holden's car begins to move again, but now it's virtually flying down the road at such a high rate of speed that it might flip over if the tire hits a pebble.

To the lasses, I whisper, "He's coming fast. Dinnae think he can keep control of his car at this speed, so be prepared for a crash."

Both lasses give me the thumbs-up sign while keeping the rest of their bodies hidden below the counter.

Now, I begin to hear the snarl of a car engine pushed to its limits. I peek out the window, searching for the object that must be hurtling toward us. All I can see is a billowing cloud of dust. That must be Holden.

"Get ready," I call out to the lasses. "Cover your heads. He's here."

I see the car only a split second before the calamity strikes, and I don't have time to sort out what's happening. It's all a blur of motion and sound. I grab the black box and run for the sofa, just in case Holden's vehicle crashes through the front of the house, and throw myself over the sofa, onto the floor, shielding my head with my arms.

A horrendous racket erupts. The engine screams. The tires squeal. Metal crunches on metal. Then it's over. The silence deafens me almost as much as the concussion of the vehicle striking who knows what.

I peel my arms away from my head, rising slowly until I'm standing upright. As I glance around the area, I breathe a sigh of relief. The house appears to be intact, though I can't swear the porch hasn't suffered any damage. Now that I know the immediate danger has passed, I call out, "Lasses, you can come out. But watch for a *cacan* creeping about outside."

I kept my voice semi-hushed, so Holden wouldn't hear. Of course, the concussive power of that crash might have left him with ringing ears, anyway.

Rebecca stands up cautiously, surveying the area.

A few seconds later, Ava pokes her head up and flicks her gaze left and right, up and down. When she finally rises, she keeps her arms wrapped round herself.

I skulk toward the door. With my hand on the knob, I pause to glance at the lasses again. "I'm going out to see what's happened. Stay here."

Rebecca races over to me and grasps my hand. "Where you go, I go."

"But Holden might have a weapon."

Ava trots over to us, offering two kitchen knives. "Here. You should at least have these for defense. My Glock is in my car, in the glove box, otherwise I'd give you that."

I accept the knife. "Best get one for yourself too, Ava."

Though I would prefer for the lasses to stay inside, I know that won't make them safer, not after the way Holden announced himself a moment ago. Once both women have knives in their hands, I cautiously turn the doorknob, opening it only enough that I can peer through the crack with one eye.

"*Mhac na galla*," I hiss. "He thrashed those cars good."

Ava sidles up to me, trying to push me away from the door. "Whose car? Yours? Holden's?"

I shove her away. "Dinnae know yet. You stay behind me while we sneak out there to assess the situation. I'm counting on you both to watch out for me and shout if you see or hear anything unusual."

The lasses stun me by nodding their agreement. I'd expected that at least Ava would complain. She's been so bloody annoying overall.

I stay low as I carefully walk down the steps, which are intact. A quick glance backward confirms the lasses are moving just as cautiously. The pick-up truck has been pushed forward just enough that the front bumper hovers above the bottom step of the porch. As I inch forward, I continue scanning the vicinity, though I don't see Holden yet. The rear bumper of my truck suffered moderate damage, but Ava's car didn't fare as well. The front has been crushed, though I'm sure it can be repaired. She should have chosen a tougher vehicle instead of the fashionable tin can she's been driving.

Holden's vehicle, a four-door model, suffered the most damage. The entire front end has collapsed into itself, and the remnants of the air bag are visible inside.

But where is Holden De Boer?

I hurry back to Ava's car and manage to open the door. The vehicle is so small that I need only lean across the center console to retrieve her weapon from the glove box. I've just extracted myself from the tin-can car when I hear Odin issuing his alarm call.

That tells me where Holden might be.

Ava and Rebecca approach me, and I give them the kitchen knife I'd been holding. "I have your Glock, Ava, so I don't need this anymore. Holden is somewhere in the vicinity of the fenced yard."

"How do you know that?"

Rebecca smirks. "He knows because Odin is announcing it with his alarm call."

"You mean that horrible noise the creature makes."

I hand Rebecca my mobile phone. "Drag Ava back inside the house with you and keep Errol's app open. If you think it's necessary, I want you to fire off a mine. You can see where they are on the screen. Just tap one, and boom. It will go off. That should give me an advantage over Holden."

Rebecca accepts the mobile. "I'll do that. Be careful, Thane."

The lass grabs hold of Ava's arm and hauls her into the house.

Now, it's time to confront Holden.

Chapter Thirty

Rebecca

I watch out the north windows, cracking one open so I can hear what's going on out there better and keep an eye on Thane. He treads cautiously around the side of the house in search of Holden. Odin makes that odd loud noise again. The chickens become upset too, squawking and flapping their wings loud enough that I can hear it.

A faint creaking sound draws my attention to the front door.

Where Ava is sneaking out.

Oh, that woman is ticking me off big time. I race after her, snagging her arm just as she jumps off the second step and onto the ground. She stumbles but catches herself. And then she glowers at me.

I give her a hard shake. "What is your problem? Are you trying to get Thane killed?"

She tries to wrench her arm free but can't do it. "Let me go."

"Not until you tell me what you're up to."

"I'm doing what you can't because you are too nice."

"And you're a jerk, that's what you mean. But it doesn't explain what in the world you're doing."

"Gah!" a male voice shouts with so much volume that it echoes off the house. "I won't let you do this to me again."

That must be Holden. His British accent gives it away.

Ava wrenches out of my grasp and sprints to the backyard gate. But just as she attempts to scramble over the obstacle, I race after her. I know how to open the gate, unlike Ava who falls down twice while trying to get over the gate. She finally tumbles over the barrier just as I swing the gate open and sprint toward the corner of the house. Veering around it, I finally see what's happening.

Thane has Holden pinned to the ground with one knee on the jerk's chest and both his hands fastened by one of Thane's. Holden's face is red. He snarls words through his clenched teeth, like a rabid dog.

"Release me, you wanker!"

The chickens are huddled inside their coop while Odin shuffles around, clearly agitated. He makes his alarm sound occasionally.

I halt beside Thane and his captive. "Looks like you've got things under control."

"Aye, for the moment. He's a wriggly snake, though."

"Should we call your friends? Maybe they could help."

"They're already on their way." He swerves his attention away from Holden and straight to me. "Go inside and find something to restrain him with."

Ava finally rounds the corner of the house and reaches us. "Thane, are you all right? At least you've got the knob in hand. I can get those restraints for you."

I raise my brows at her. "You don't know where anything is in Thane's house."

She huffs. "How difficult can it be to find a rope or…something."

"Fine. You go hunt around for 'something' while Thane and I do the real work. Try opening the gate this time instead of making pitiful attempts to climb over it."

Ava scowls at me, then stomps off like a toddler who didn't get her way.

Thane winks at me. "You're a force to be reckoned with, *mo chridhe.*"

"What does that Gaelic phrase mean?"

He opens his mouth to speak, but Holden rams his head into Thane, knocking him off balance. He teeters and almost falls over, flailing a hand out to stop his tumble. Just as Thane regains control of Holden, the bastard knees him in the balls.

I point the gun at Holden. "Stop now! I *will* shoot you."

Holden freezes, though he has a sneaky glint in his eyes. "Oh, I'm terribly frightened of your girlfriend, Buchanan."

"Ye did stop trying to get away. So, I'm thinking she does scare you."

Ava comes racing out the back door of the house, which I had completely forgotten existed. It's a narrow doorway that opens off the kitchen. The most annoying woman I've ever met halts beside me, though she focuses on Thane.

She holds up a leather belt. "This ought to do."

Thane scrunches up his mouth as he studies the item Ava has brought for him. "That's not long enough, and the buckle doesn't look sturdy enough to restrain this *cacan.* Nice try, but I doubt it will work."

Ava's entire demeanor deflates. She really must have hoped to impress Thane with her gift. Her bottom lip quivers the tiniest bit. I swear her eyes seem to be tearing up too. Does she have genuine feelings for Thane? I'd assumed she was being bossy and annoying because she feels like she owns him, since he was her agent for years. But I'm beginning to reassess that assumption.

I think Ava wanted to save Thane from Holden.

She thrusts the belt at Thane. "Try it. He could hurt you if he keeps thrashing."

Thane stares at her with confusion riddling his expression. But he reaches up to take the belt, almost as if he doesn't want to offend her by refusing the gift. He wraps the belt around Holden's wrists, cinching it up as tightly as he can. Holden's ankles remain free, though Thane still has them pinned with his own legs.

When the prisoner thrashes again, the belt loosens.

Ava falls to her knees and starts fiddling with it. "You haven't done this up tight enough. Let me try."

Thane swats her hands away. "Stop interfering."

"But the belt—"

"Quit your havering. I know what I'm doing."

Ava reaches for the belt again, and Thane tries to push her away which causes him to lean over a bit too far.

Holden slams his head into Thane's.

Ava frantically tries to get control of the belt, but it's too late. It all happens so fast that I have no chance to intervene. Thane seems slightly dazed by the head butt, and Ava finally gives up on the belt. Holden kicks out with both legs. Ava tumbles over backward with her ass in the air while Thane gets thrown to the side.

Holden leaps up, punching me in the gut in his haste to sprint toward the back door. The gun drops out of my hand. I lose my breath for just long enough that I'm too late to stop the bastard.

Thane leaps to his feet, roaring like an enraged beast as he barrels toward Holden. When the jackass realizes he's ticked off the wrong Scot, he seems to panic, suddenly veering toward the front gate.

Odin races after Thane, moving faster than I ever imagined a llama could. The animal's alarm call echoes off the house.

Where's the gun? I glance around but can't see it.

Then I turn to watch the men racing toward the gate. Holden has the gun in his hand. If I shout to Thane, Holden might shoot him. But I have another option.

I pull my phone out and punch a button on the screen.

Boom!

The sound reverberates in my ears as earth sprays up from the spot where the land mine had gone off. Thane was too far away and off to the side to be affected by the blast. Holden freezes for just long enough that Thane can catch up to him.

Ava and I hurry after the men and the llama. Poor Odin seems frantic and more concerned with Thane than with the small explosion I detonated.

Thane seizes the back of Holden's shirt collar, effectively snaring the creep. He pins Holden to the gate. Odin comes up beside Thane and spits in Holden's face, releasing a greenish goop. Holden cringes. Whether it's because Odin terrifies him or Thane terrifies him, I can't say. Maybe he doesn't like being spit on by a llama.

Holden's lips peel back from his teeth, and his pathetic moans are interspersed with tiny sobs. "Get that thing away from me. What sort of pathogens has it spat on me?"

"Pathogens?" Thane chuckles. "No, you aren't in any danger of catching Ebola. Odin spat out saliva and a wee bit of undigested hay."

Holden turns his head to the side, avoiding the llama. "Make it go away."

Odin spits on the creep again and stomps his feet.

"Ah!" Holden tries to wipe away the bit of undigested hay Odin just deposited on the creep's lips, but Thane slugs him in the gut. "Don't let that beast touch me. What if I catch a disease from it?"

Thane grunts. "You can lap up the llama spit with your tongue. After the way you punched Rebecca, you'll get no sympathy from me." He shakes Holden so hard that the man's head snaps backward. "I should kill you right now for what you've done. Assaulting women is a capital offense in my book."

His nasty tone gives me a warm shiver.

Odin stomps his foot and clucks his tongue.

And our captive whines. He wilts like a flower, his knees buckling.

Thane drops Holden on the ground, eying him with a mixture of disdain and bafflement. "Who knew a former spy would have the spine of a jellyfish."

Ava throws herself at Thane, forcing him to catch her. "Oh, I'm so glad you aren't injured. I was desperately worried for you."

Thane sets her down on her feet and gives the annoying woman a gentle shove away from him. "But you weren't worried about Rebecca, aye? Not sure you're much better than Holden."

Her joy crumbles away. "What? But I came here to save you."

"Save me?" Thane sighs. "Get it through your head, Ava. I do not want to be with you. Rebecca is my girlfriend."

Ava straightens and lifts her chin. "I had you first. You belong to me, Thane."

"No one owns me."

"I meant you belong *with* me."

He straps his arms over his chest. "But that's not what you said. Your subconscious got the better of you, eh? The truth will always out."

Our prisoner moans.

Thane, Ava, and I glance at the slimeball. He's crying now, wiping his face off with his shirtsleeve while sniffling.

A car roars up the road, screeching to a halt at Thane's driveway.

"The reinforcements are here," he says. "Ye won't get away from these blokes, Holden, that's a dead certainty."

Odin nuzzles Thane's cheek.

I move closer to pet Odin's head. "Are all llamas this affectionate toward people?"

"No. But Odin was raised differently than most of his kind. His mother died shortly after giving birth, and his original owner decided to give him to someone else. I took Odin in and raised him in my own way."

Though I'd love to hear more of the story of Odin the llama, we don't have time for that now. Thane's friends have arrived. I recognize Errol, but the other individuals aren't men I've met before.

Errol and his friends halt at the gate. He glances at the pothole where I'd set off one of his mines, and he grins. "Needed the Fire Starter's expertise after all, eh?"

Thane still wears a ruthless expression, and his tone remains equally cold. "Rebecca set off the mine, and it's a bloody good thing she did. You lot took a long time to get here."

I sidle closer to Thane. "Who are the other two? I know Errol and Domhnall, but not the others."

One man holds out his hand to me across the gate. "I'm Logan Mac-Taggart. You heard my voice on the phone earlier."

"So I did.." I shake his hand. "Nice to meet you in person. You're the former MI6 agent, right?"

"Aye."

The man beside Logan also offers me his hand. "Magnus MacTaggart. I'm a private investigator, though I prefer the term bounty hunter. My wife and I catch villains together."

"How romantic."

Domhnall glances at the hole where the land mine had been, and he gives me a wry smile. "I could tell the moment we met that you'd be a force of nature, Rebecca. It's no wonder Thane fell for you."

"That's a wonderful compliment, Domhnall. I'm surprised Fiona didn't come with you."

"My wife wanted to come. I convinced her otherwise."

"Fiona doesn't seem like the type who shuts up when her husband says so."

Domhnall sighs. "You're right about that. But I asked her to get my warmer jacket. Then I jumped into Logan's car before the lass came back. Dinnae want her getting injured, so I felt justified in tricking her."

Thane slips an arm around my waist. "I didn't want Rebecca to be here either, but I couldn't very well banish her since I brought her here in my truck."

Errol smiles. "Shared jeopardy is a bonding experience for couples."

Well, I can't deny that. I do feel closer to Thane after what we've been through today. Still, I have no desire to replicate this experience.

Odin pushes his head between mine and Thane's, resting his chin on my shoulder.

I pet the llama's nose. "Does this mean he approves of me?"

"Aye. Odin is only this friendly with people he's known for months. You've captivated him after one day."

While Domhnall, Magnus, and Logan open the gate and haul Holden away, Errol wriggles his fingers at Thane in a gimme gesture.

But Thane simply gazes calmly at Errol.

I whisper to Thane, "I think he wants you to give him your phone."

"Aye, that's right," Errol says. "I assume you'll want the land mines app removed from your mobile. Or would you rather keep it just in case?"

I expect Thane to want the app erased, but he surprises me.

"Leave it on there for now," he tells Errol. "Just in case Holden escapes again, though I cannae see Domhnall, Logan, or Magnus letting the *cacan* get away from them."

Errol shrugs. "You never know. Sometimes the villains can be bloody determined. For all we know, Holden might have an accomplice."

Oh, perfect. I needed another reason to feel anxious.

"I should go with the other laddies," Errol announces. "Looks like Odin and Rebecca are all the security you need."

He jogs out to the road, joining the others in the car with Holden. Soon, their vehicle disappears from view and the rumble of the engine fades away.

Ava has been standing behind us to sulk in silence. Now, she moves in front of us. "If you mean to drive me away, it won't work."

I lift my brows at her. "Why on earth would you want to hang out here with me and Thane? We'll be screwing each other's brains out, and you are not invited to the party. But if you want to hang out with Odin and the chickens..."

She acts like I never spoke. "Thane, darling, we need to have a serious conversation."

"If you want to discuss your obsession with me, I am not interested."

Thane ushers me through the gate and waits for Ava to follow. She stands there with her nose in the air for about seven seconds. Then Odin approaches her and starts sniffing her hair. She cringes a tiny bit. But when the llama licks her hair, she jumps and rushes through the gate.

As Thane shuts it, he shakes his head at Ava. "Dinnae understand you at all these days. Not that I ever really understood you back in the day. But you used to be a tough intelligence officer, the sort of strong woman any wee lassie would want as a role model. What happened to you?"

"Nothing that I care to discuss in front of *her*." She jabs a finger toward me.

"In that case, we have nothing to talk about."

Thane and I walk away.

Chapter Thirty-One

Thane

As we enter the house, I can still see Ava standing there. Once I've shut the door behind us, I peek out the window—and Ava is still waiting. For what, I have no ruddy idea. Rebecca comes up beside me to gawp at Ava too. We exchange baffled looks. I shrug. Rebecca shrugs. Neither of us has an explanation for why Ava wants to loiter out there.

When Ava wanders over to her wrecked tin-can vehicle, Rebecca smacks her palm on her forehead. "Duh. She can't leave even if she wants to because her car is smushed between your truck and Holden's vehicle."

"Smushed?" I say with a slight chuckle. "The only person I've heard use that term is Malina MacTaggart." I scratch my chin. "Though I might have heard Rory's wife say it once. Emery is American, after all."

"Are you implying that all American women use the same words?"

"Well, no. I've gotten myself into a fankle, haven't I?"

"If you tell me what a fankle is, I'll answer your question."

"A fankle is a tangle or confusion."

Rebecca rolls her eyes in a deliberate attempt to harass me, affectionately. "Oh, so it's like 'hot mess.' That's another phrase a teenager might use. Care to comment on my use of it?"

"Wouldnae dare. Have all the smushing and hot messes ye like."

"I actually learned that phrase from my daughter."

I gaze out the window at Ava, who is now shuffling about, apparently analyzing the condition of her car. She hugs herself, bowing her head.

Rebecca groans. "Oh, jeez, we can't just leave her out there. She looks pitiful, like a lost puppy in a rainstorm."

I blow out a big sigh. "Aye, you're right. As much as I would love to ignore her, I can't do it. She can come in, but only until a tow truck arrives. I can go out there and move my truck to make room for that."

"Want me to go out with you?"

I kiss her forehead. "No, *gràidh*. You stay inside and relax. Ava is my problem."

"Our problem. We're a couple, and that means we share everything." She winces. "Even annoying MI6 agents who are infatuated with you."

"You're wonderful, Rebecca."

She struggles not to laugh, but that results in a snort. "Why am I wonderful? Because I haven't murdered Ava yet?"

"Aye, exactly."

I walk out the door. As it shuts behind me, I catch Rebecca peering out the window. I can't blame her for wanting to observe my interaction with Ava, though I know Rebecca isn't jealous. Not in the least. She's fully aware of the fact that I have no romantic or sexual interest in that woman.

I leap over the bumper of my truck to get off the steps and approach the lass. I whistle. "Your car is in worse shape than I thought. It would take a magic wand to fix it."

She scowls at me. "Thank you ever so much for the useless advice."

"Calm down, Ava. I'm here to help."

"Then do something, please. I have no transportation."

I walk all the way round her car to study its current condition. But the news does not get better. Holden did quite a number on the car. "Why are you driving such a small, thin-skinned vehicle? I would have thought MI6 could find you a more appropriate model."

"What does that mean?"

"This is clearly not a new car. And it would fly to pieces in a strong breeze. But that's not the point." I return to where she stands, or rather slumps, beside the dilapidated machine. "Something about you isn't right, Ava. I knew you for years, and the woman I'm looking at right now hardly resembles the strong, confident lass who talked me into becoming her agent."

Ava rubs her arms.

I study her again, still feeling like I've missed an important clue.

She bows her head, then snaps at me, "I'm so terribly sorry that my behavior doesn't match your expectations."

"Ava—"

"Shut up, Thane." She covers her face with her hands. When she peels them away, tears shimmer in her eyes. "I was demoted last year. I'm no longer an intelligence officer. Now I spend most of my time filing things and fetching coffee."

"But you told me you were still with MI6. It was all you knew, that's what you said."

"And that much is technically true." Her lips tremble, and she avoids looking at me. "I lost my edge. You know as well as I do what that means. I am of no further use."

"But I contacted you for help on your MI6 number."

"Don't you remember? I always rang you on my burner phone, and you always rang me at the same number. That was to protect your identity."

I do remember that now. It's been so long since I left the army that the details had become fuzzy over the years. Honestly, I never wanted to reminisce about those days, and I preferred to forget all of it once I returned to civilian life. "Why would they let you keep your burner phone after you were demoted?"

"Because no one knew about it. I was in deep cover, Thane. Only I knew about you. The DIO wouldn't have liked to know that one of their people had become a mole."

I only did that because Ava seduced me into it—literally. She used sex to pull me in and keep me in for a long time. Once I was free of her, I realized our relationship had never been more than shagging.

Ava shuffles a wee bit closer. "I love you, Thane. That's why I rushed to your rescue." She lifts her head, and her tone turns sour. "I'm a bloody fool. Of course you found someone new, and of course she's far better than I ever was. I'm sorry I lied to you."

"I understand why you lied about being an MI6 operative. But that doesn't explain what happened to the iron-hard intelligence officer I used to know. You panicked when you saw a llama."

"All I can tell you is that I fucked up horribly. It involved a terrible car crash and three deaths." She closes her eyes for a moment. "I lost my nerve. That's the worst thing that can happen to a spy."

Finally, all the pieces have fallen into place. I feel bad for Ava, but it's just the way she said. I have a new life. Ava Marston-Baines has no place here.

I touch her arm. "Go home, Ava, wherever that might be. I have nothing to offer you."

She nods. That's all the response she gives.

"Let me ring for that tow truck, and in the meantime, come inside and get warm."

Ava follows me into the house, shuffling her feet even once we've gone inside. She flops down on the armchair. Rebecca and I take the sofa. And we wait. I turn on the TV, but none of us really watches the home improve-ment show that's playing on the screen. This has been a bizarre and stressful day, full of unwelcome surprises. All I want right now is to crawl into bed with Rebecca and sleep for three days.

Eventually, the tow truck arrives with two men inside. Once they've gotten her crushed car hooked up to their vehicle, Ava rides into the village with the laddies. I should have called it a "smushed" car. That's the word Rebecca likes. But no, I wouldn't say that to a pair of tow truck drivers.

Rebecca and I go straight to bed, though it's only five in the afternoon.

A wee nap does refresh us, and we collaborate on whipping up a meal. After dinner, we sit on the sofa together to discuss this wild day.

"Your friends are incredible," Rebecca says. "You needed their help, and they flew into action without any hesitation."

"Aye, they did. But that's what we all do for each other whenever someone needs a hand." I rotate toward her, laying an arm across the sofa's back. "What you did for me today, I will never forget that."

"Don't know what you mean."

I smile as I recall the incident. "You set off one of Errol's mines and stopped Holden from getting away."

"First, I got punched in the gut. I'm no hero."

"Of course you are. Not only did you stop Holden from escaping, but you stood up to Ava and never cowered in the face of danger."

She bites her lip, averting her gaze. "It was all instinct."

"You are my hero, Rebecca."

Her cheeks have turned slightly pink.

The house phone rings, and I jump up to retrieve it from the kitch-en. Then I glance at the caller ID. "It's Logan. He must have an update about Holden." I answer the call while trotting back to the sofa. "Hello, Logan. What news do you have?"

"Holden De Boer is snug inside his holding cell. The laddie was so shellshocked by the land mine explosion that he won't even speak now." Logan grunts. "I doubt that will last long, though. He seems like the whingeing sort."

"Aye, he loves to complain."

"The Loch Fairbairn police will keep him until someone arrives to arrest him and drag the *cacan* back to England for trial. He won't bother you or Rebecca again." Logan pauses, then adds, "Your lass is quite the explosives expert. Errol will be proud to hear that."

"Aye, she saved my life."

Logan and I say goodbye, and I turn to Rebecca—who is now grin-ning. "I'm glad you're happy, *gràidh*. But what brought about this abrupt change in your mood?"

"You told Logan I saved your life."

"Because it's true."

"I wasn't sure if you'd want everyone to know that a woman saved you. Most men wouldn't like it." She shimmies closer to me. "I should've guessed you wouldn't care. You're the least offendable person I've ever met."

Now my lips curl into a grin. "I don't think 'offendable' is a real word."

"No, it's my word. I invented it a minute ago."

"I do love your playful language. It's one of your most endearing qualities."

For the rest of the evening, we share a bottle of whisky and watch old TV westerns. I learn that Rebecca loves the shows that have "sexy men wearing tight pants and a gun belt" and also that she wishes she had learned to ride horses. She just never had the time for it.

Maybe I can remedy that for her. I'll need to think on it. Valentine's Day is coming up soon, and I do want to lavish her with gifts. The woman who set off a land mine to protect me deserves the world and more.

At bedtime, we crawl under the sheets and go to sleep.

The next morning, we drive into Loch Fairbairn so the gent who keeps my pickup running can examine the damage to the rear bumper. He checks out the vehicle from stem to stern. Fortunately, the damage isn't severe. All I really need is a new bumper. While my mate orders the part, I can still drive my truck in the meantime.

Rebecca and I go to the café for a late breakfast—and receive a surprise. We've just entered the establishment when it happens.

Everyone rises and claps. A few people whistle.

"Why are they doing this?" Rebecca whispers to me.

"Dinnae know." I shove two fingers into my mouth and blow, releasing a piercing whistle much louder than anyone else's. Everyone quietens down. "What is going on here? We came to have a wee breakfast. You lot are acting as if a rock star just walked into the café."

Jack MacTaggart and his wife, Autumn, leave their table to approach us. He shakes Rebecca's hand. "We're all congratulating you, lass, for your bravery and fortitude in a frightening situation. You saved Thane and stopped a criminal from escaping."

Her eyes bulge. "This is all for me? That's crazy."

I hug her to my side. "*Mo chridhe*, you deserve all the accolades."

Autumn turns to speak to the crowd. "Okay, we showed our appreciation for Rebecca. Now it's time to go back to enjoying breakfast."

The crowd settles down, and everyone goes back to eating.

"Would you like to share our table?" Jack asks.

I glance at Rebecca, and she nods. "Aye, we'll join you and Autumn."

As we sit down at the table, Rebecca leans toward the other side where Jack and Autumn sit. "This is all very strange. I mean, Thane did a lot to stop Holden too. It wasn't just me."

"Doesn't matter," Jack informs her. "Your legend has been created. Everyone will tell the story for years to come, maybe even centuries."

Rebecca's face goes blank.

Autumn pokes her elbow into her husband's side. "Don't scare her, Jack. Can't you see she's uncomfortable? Let the poor girl eat in peace."

Our waitress is Bonnie again, and she remembers both me and Rebecca. The lass has enough common sense not to bring up the issue of Rebecca's heroism. Instead, she cheerfully takes our orders and bustles away.

Lunch with Autumn and Jack is enjoyable, and Rebecca especially loves to hear the stories the couple tell us. Jack and Autumn had married impetuously in Las Vegas, then divorced a few months later. But two years after that, they realized they belong together—with a bit of meddling from the rest of the MacTaggarts.

Once Jack finishes the story, Autumn folds her arms on the table and speaks to me and Rebecca in a fake whisper. "Jack left out the best part. His cousins and their wives conspired to trick us into meeting here at this café. Then we wound up going back to my hotel room and having sex for two hours."

"*Mhac na galla*, Autumn," Jack hisses. "Haven't you heard of too much information?"

"Yep. But I ignore that." She reverts to her fake whisper as she faces us again. "I got pregnant on that afternoon. Two months later, when I found out I was having a baby, I flew to Scotland and shocked Jack with the news. That's when the meddling began."

"No one has meddled in my life," Rebecca says. "I think I'd know if they had."

"Sometimes it's very subtle."

Before Rebecca can ask any questions about the MacTaggarts' penchant for mucking about in other people's lives, Jack and Autumn announce they need to pick up their wee bairn from his parents' home.

For the rest of the day, I keep wondering what my friends might be plotting.

Chapter Thirty-Two

Rebecca

Sunday with Thane was blissful. But now, I have work to do. Lots of work. All the upheaval lately distracted me from my job and the marketing campaign I need to get rolling immediately. So, I spend all of Monday finalizing the details. That means not only fleshing out my calendar for the campaign but also buying ads and arranging the finale. It will be incredible—if I can get it all set up in time.

At lunch, Thane and I eat in the cafeteria. That gives me a chance to explain all the upcoming events and advertising campaigns. He winces the entire time, as if I'm discussing how to erect a gallows and when he will be hanged from it. I understand that he's never needed to think about marketing before. But I'd hoped he would be more comfortable with it by now.

"Do what you believe is best," he tells me. "Since I know nothing about marketing, I'm relying on you to handle everything."

"Oh, great. No pressure there."

He squeezes my hand. "You can do this, *mo chridhe*. Listen to Duran Duran while you work, and I'm sure that will give you the momentum you need to race through the preparations."

This man really does know me like nobody else could.

He pops a cheese curd into his mouth and speaks while chewing. "Have you spoken to your children lately?"

I wag a finger at him. "What horrible manners you have. Talking while you chew."

"Feel free to spank me for my poor etiquette."

Spank him? Did I hallucinate that he said that? It must've been a joke. "Ha-ha. To answer your question, I talked to Courtney and Eric last night. They really want to meet you."

"I'd love to meet them too, anytime."

"You aren't in the least anxious about that possibility, are you?"

He shrugs. "Why would I be?"

I love this man. But I haven't told him that yet. I know I should, but after lunch, I have to get back to work. I spend the entire week arranging ads on TV, radio, and social media. This campaign matters more to me than anything else I've ever done in my whole career. I want to make Thane's distillery a worldwide sensation, but I'll start with impressing everyone in the Highlands.

By the time the weekend rolls around, I have great news to share with Thane. I already told Fiona, and she agreed with my plan. I've added one element that might make Thane scrunch up his face. But I have tools for pacifying him. Sexy tools. And I will use everything at my disposal to ensure he's happy with what I've done.

I've invited Thane to my apartment.

He arrives at six o'clock on the dot, just as I'd told him to do.

The second I hear a knock at the door, I fling it open. Yes, okay, I was standing right in front of it waiting for him to get here. I haven't had much time alone with him this past week. "Thane, you're here."

"As commanded." He bows deeply. "How may I serve you tonight, *mo chridhe*."

"Come in. I have a lot to discuss with you." I lead him to the sofa, where we sit down, side by side. "Before we get started, I need to ask you a question. What is that phrase you keep using? 'Mo' something."

"*Mo chridhe*. It's Gaelic for 'my heart.' You have captured my heart and my soul, for sure. Can't picture my life without you anymore."

"I love you, Thane." *Shit*. I hadn't meant to blurt that out. My heart overrode my common sense, and those three words came tumbling out. I don't regret saying them, just the way I said them.

He cups my cheek with one hand. "I love you too, Rebecca."

Relief rushes through me, and I sag against the sofa's back. "I'm so glad I told you that. I've wanted to say it for a while now, but I wasn't sure how you'd feel about it. We haven't known each other for very long."

"Aye, that's true. But I trust my instincts. You are the only woman for me."

I grasp his face and plant a hard kiss on his lips. "I hope you'll still feel that way after I tell you about my plan."

"Dinnae worry about that. I won't toss you out the window."

I pick up my leather portfolio, which I'd left on the coffee table. "Sure you're ready for this? It's all marketing mumbo jumbo."

He breathes words into my ear, tickling my lobe. "Any mumbo jumbo you speak will be highly sensual, and I will need to make love to you afterward."

"But you haven't even heard what I'm going to say."

"Doesn't matter. Your voice is all it takes."

"If I'd known it would be this easy, I wouldn't have bothered to dress sexy on our first official date." The tone of his voice and the sensation of his warm breaths on my earlobe turn me on. But I have important information to convey, and I will not let him derail my speech. Not even if he licks my lobe. Nope, doesn't matter how hot he is. "Try to concentrate on what I'm going to tell you, okay? It's all about your business."

The rat pulls my lobe into his mouth and suckles it. "Mm, I will pay attention, *gràidh*. You have my word." He skates one finger across my bottom lip. "But I can't promise not to arouse you."

"You're going to tease me the entire time, aren't you?" So much for my plot to get my way by seducing him. He beat me to the punch.

Thane grins. "What else would I do?"

"Listen carefully to what I'm saying, that's what you're supposed to do. But never mind that. I can resist your charms for at least ten minutes."

He gives up my earlobe, and instead, rests a hand on my inner thigh.

I can play this game too. If he wants to get naughty, I'll go tit for tat. "We've discussed the basis of my campaign a few times. It centers on you, the man behind the whisky, the master distiller and master maltster. The Thane brand doesn't exist without your sexy self."

"You want pictures of me for adverts."

"Pictures, videos, audio recordings, everything. Your inimitable sex appeal is the cornerstone of our promotional efforts."

He laughs softly in that smoky, sensual way. "I've never been called inimitable before. I like it."

"Phase one of the campaign involves getting the word out. Once people know your company exists, we'll move on to phase two." I flip my portfolio open and lay it on my lap so he can view all the data I've collected while I talk. "With the right brand positioning, we can show everyone how unique and incredible your products are. But we also need to engender brand awareness. If nobody realizes your company exists, they won't know they need your products. We want the Thane brand to be foremost in everyone's minds when they think of single-malt Scotch whisky."

He glides his hand lightly up and down my thigh. "I'm listening, Rebecca."

Oh, that sneaky man. He knows his voice affects me more powerfully than any aphrodisiac. "I need your full attention, Thane. Stop staring at my tits and look me in the eye, please."

He slowly raises his focus to me while he continues petting my thigh.

"Demand generation is vital." My voice has grown sultrier, thanks to his efforts to derail me with sexy teasing. "We won't have customers unless we can convince them that they need the product. I've already run two surveys to find out how many people in the Highlands have ever heard of your whisky. The combined results show that less than eighteen percent of respondents have heard of *Collaidh Sgeul-Rùin*. Only two percent have bought your whisky."

"You were right. It's a bloody awful name."

"Rebranding ought to alleviate some of the name recognition problems. That's why I also stopped in at more than a dozen restaurants and bars in the Western Highlands, from Loch Fairbairn to Fort William and even Kyle of Lochalsh in the north."

Thane stops teasing my thigh and stares directly into my eyes. "When did you do that?"

"During the week when you were avoiding me."

He winces. "I'm sorry about that."

"It's okay, water under the bridge."

"What did you learn from your travels?"

"That although most people haven't heard of your whisky, they would be interested in trying it. I took a few bottles with me—Fiona approved that—and gave out glasses of one-sip samples."

His lips twitch, almost a smile, and his blue eyes shimmer in the muted lighting. "That was a brilliant idea. What was the result?"

"Everyone loved the taste tests. I've been working on some contextual marketing too, but I believe we don't need to go overboard with this stuff. The ads will be what initially draws people to the product." I slide my finger under the page's corner, preparing to flip to the next page. But I hesitate. "Before I show you the next part, I need you to promise you'll give it serious consideration and not simply scoff at it."

"You have my word. Should I cross my heart too?"

"That won't be necessary. Would you mind closing your eyes? I want to get your honest first impressions."

He holds a hand over his eyes. "I'm ready."

I flip to the second page. "Okay. You can look now."

Thane opens his eyes, and they gradually widen while his mouth slowly slides into a smile. "You are a genius, Rebecca."

A laugh splutters out of me. "Hardly. This was the obvious choice for an event. I kind of assumed you wouldn't like it."

"This isn't my usual sort of gala, but I love anything you come up with."

We're both studying the mini poster I created as a test. The headline reads, "Thane Buchanan Distillery presents a Valentine's Day to dazzle your taste buds. Enjoy the romance of Highland whisky with a guided tour of the distillery, then join us at an ancient medieval castle for a ball worthy of Cinderella."

"What do you think?" I ask. "The vibrant red background and red rose petals evoke romance and sensuality. The ball will be for adults only, and the dress code will be formal. We're sending out invitations to everyone you know via mail, then I and my army will pound the pavement to offer full-size posters to businesses."

"This is beautiful and sexy, just like you."

"You were the inspiration for the entire campaign. Now that I know you're okay with the ball, let me show you the ads." I flip to the next page and let him drink in the information without me reading it aloud. "What do you think? Are you comfortable with my plans for you?"

He scratches the back of his neck. "Ah, not sure. I am not a professional model."

"That's the point. You are the brand. People need to see you, not some preening, pouting model." I lay a hand on his cheek and gently push him to turn his head toward me. "They want a real man. The kind men will admire and want to emulate. The kind women adore and wish they could sleep with."

"Do I really want lasses feeling that way about me?"

"You know what I meant. I wasn't suggesting women will be ripping your clothes off." I flip to the next page and hold up the portfolio so he can get a good look at the information there. "This is the itinerary for the big event. I've emailed you a copy, so just print that out and study it. You'll feel better about the whole thing if you understand the timeline."

He takes the portfolio and reads every bit of information on the page. I can tell he's absorbing all of it because I watch his eyes moving as he pores over everything. When he's done, he hands the portfolio back to me. "I will memorize the details. You have my word I will do whatever you believe is best for promoting the distillery."

"You'll do anything?"

"Aye." He seems to abruptly realize what he just promised, and he rubs his jaw. "I stepped into that quagmire, didn't I?"

I bite my upper lip. "Are you sure you're ready for this? If you're calling it a quagmire—"

"Relax, *gràidh*. I won't back out, and I trust you to handle the marketing efforts. Dinnae need to ask me again if I'm sure." He takes my hands, folding his around them. "I am fully committed to your plan—and to you."

"Monday morning, we will shoot all the ads for TV, print, and social media. You'll get to see them before we release the ads and ask for any reasonable changes." I start to bite my lip again but then realize that's dumb. He's all in, and he wouldn't lie about that. "You are about to become a celebrity, Thane. Locally, at least."

"If I can handle rogue spies, I can certainly survive a marketing blitz."

"Yes, you can." I kiss him. "Never imagined that getting a new job would change my world forever and bring new joy into my life. Thank you for showing me what real love looks like."

"No, lass, it was mutual. We taught each other that lesson."

We spend the night in my apartment but then head for his house on Sunday. Thane doesn't like to leave Odin and the chickens alone for too long, especially after the debacle with Holden. That jerk is locked up in England now, awaiting his trial. No bail for him. A convicted double agent who tried to kill a former fellow agent isn't likely to get a commuted sentence. I hope they lock Holden up for good this time.

I love hanging out with Odin and Thane. I've even gotten to like the chickens, and my egg-gathering skills are improving.

Monday morning arrives, and it's time for Thane's big close-up.

Chapter Thirty-Three

Thane

I turn my body to the left and swivel my head to the right while lifting my chin just a touch. For over an hour, I've done this repeatedly. Being a male model is not the lifestyle for me, but this is for my company. That's the only reason I'm enduring this photo session and obeying the ridiculous instructions from the photographer. A moment ago, he told me, "Let your inner light shine through so everyone can see it. Don't be shy."

Dinnae have an inner light, and ahmno shy. That's rubbish.

When I glance at Rebecca, she smiles and gives me the thumbs-up sign.

I smile and wink at her. Why? Because I love that woman, not because I enjoy the dull and annoying experience of having my photograph taken over and over for an hour. I think I've assumed every sort of pose imaginable by now. Cannae be much left to do.

The photographer sets his camera down. "That was perfect, Thane. You're a natural in front of the camera."

"Are we done? I could go for a piece."

"So could I. Our session is over, anyway."

I glance at Rebecca, who's still smiling at me. Then I ask the laddie, "Why don't you join us for lunch?"

Rebecca is clearly surprised by my offer. We both wind up having a meal with the man who told me that rubbish about my inner light. He's not a bad bloke, just a bit too artsy for me. My mates are mostly tough men.

After lunch, I'm taken to a video studio in Fort William. Rebecca accompanies me, of course. I can't decide if she escorts me everywhere because she worries I'll run away or if she simply wants to be intimately involved in every aspect of the advertising campaign. Either way, I'm glad to have her nearby. She is my muse.

When the lass who films me announces she wants to shoot me outdoors too, Rebecca loves the idea. Since I've been wearing my kilt all day, I'm skeptical of the outdoors idea. It's chilly outside.

But then Rebecca sidles up to me and whispers, "You're a strong, virile man who can handle anything. A chilly breeze won't bother Thane Buchanan, and besides, I'll warm you up anytime you need it."

I know she will. The heat of her luscious body could melt the polar ice caps.

At the end of the day, we go home—to my house. Rebecca intends to give up her apartment in Fort William on Monday. Only a few minutes after we've walked into the house and sat down on the sofa, the doorbell rings. Rebecca is jeeked, so I shuffle over there to find out who's come to see us.

I swing the door open.

Two young people, a man and a woman, stand there grinning at me. The lass peers around me and grins. "Whoa, Mom, you weren't kidding. Your new boyfriend is sizzling hot. No wonder you haven't visited me and Eric in England." The lass eyes me with clear appreciation. "I mean, if I had a boyfriend who walked around in a kilt, I'd hold him hostage to make sure he couldn't get away."

Rebecca races up beside me. "Courtney? What are you and Eric doing here?"

These are her children. I'd figured that out a moment ago, but I wasn't one hundred percent certain until now.

Eric rakes his gaze over my kilt and rolls his eyes at his mother. "If I'd kept a secret like this, you would read me the riot act. Why didn't you tell us about this guy?"

"Well, it's, um…" Rebecca pushes me aside, waving for her children to enter the house. "Come inside, you must be cold."

"Nah, this isn't cold weather," Eric says as he ambles into the house. "I've been living in England for four years. Chilly is normal."

Courtney and Eric sit on the sofa with Rebecca, who's sandwiched between them. She has a new glow about her now. The lass must have missed her children more than she wanted to let on.

I take the armchair, lodging one ankle on the opposite knee.

Courtney's eyes widen a touch, and her gaze is riveted to my lower body. Eric smirks and glances away. Rebecca grins.

"What are you lot staring at?" I ask. "Does my kilt have mud on it?"

Eric tries to stifle a laugh and ends up spluttering. "Dude, you aren't wearing any briefs."

Courtney bites down on both her lips while furtively glancing at the area between my thighs. "Don't point that out, Eric. I'm hoping he'll spread his legs more, right when the furnace comes on, and the breeze from that might flutter his kilt."

Rebecca's eyes bulge as she swivels her head toward her daughter. "Courtney, for heaven's sake. That's a completely inappropriate thing to say to someone you just met thirty seconds ago."

I lower my leg so now both feet are on the floor, and my kilt hides my dangly bits. I hadn't noticed I was flashing everyone.

Eric smirks, but to his credit, he looks me in the eye now. "Guess we never did formally introduce ourselves. I'm Eric Taylor, and this is my sister Courtney Taylor. We're fraternal twins."

"Aye, Rebecca told me about you two. She's very proud of her children." Since he introduced himself and his sister, I feel obliged to do the same. "I'm Thane Buchanan, by the way. Your mother works for me at my distillery."

"Yeah, she told us about that. Courtney got all excited, hoping Mom would marry a Scottish guy. My sister's had a thing for kilts ever since she read her first Scottish historical romance novel."

Courtney sits forward, her attention focused on me. "Do you always wear a kilt?"

"No, lass. It's for special occasions."

"Thane has two kilts," Rebecca announces. "One is for casual use, and the other is his formal kilt with all the trimmings."

She described me somewhat like a turkey dinner. Not that I mind. The lass can talk about me however she likes, and she knows I will never be offended.

"Which kilt are you wearing now?" Courtney asks.

"The casual one. It has an elastic waistband. My formal kilt is one large piece of plaid that I wrap round myself in a particular fashion. Then I add the trimmings, as your mother called it, which includes a sporran, a *sgian dubh*, formal kilt shoes, plaid socks, a kilt pin, a belt, a kilt flash, a formal shirt and tie, and a brooch to hold up the shoulder section of my plaid."

Courtney's eyes flare wide. "Wow, that sounds amazing. How often do you wear that outfit?"

"Only on very special occasions. I wore it at my brother Ramsay's wedding. His wife divorced him a few years ago, though."

She gives me a mischievous wee smile. "And you'll wear it again when you and Mom get married."

Rebecca rolls her eyes at her daughter. "Tap the brakes, honey. It's too early to talk about marriage."

"But you really like Thane a lot. I can tell. You never looked at Dad the way you look at your Scottish hottie." Before her mother can respond, Courtney turns to me. "How old are you, anyway? I'm just curious because you're dating my mother. Eric and I are twenty-five, and Mom is forty-nine."

If she expects me to be shy about my age, the lass will be surprised. "I'm fifty-one, and I've never been married. I used to date Fiona MacTaggart, who works at my distillery with your ma, but I haven't had a serious relationship until now. Your mother means a great deal to me."

Courtney clasps her hands, holding them to her chest. "Oh, that is so sweet. I can tell you mean it, and I also can tell you'll treat her right. We love our dad, but he's kind of an asshat. We were glad when they got divorced, because now Mom can finally find the right guy and not be lonely anymore."

Rebecca's jaw drops. "I was never lonely. You make me sound like a spinster."

"All I meant was that we're so happy that you're happy now."

Eric squints at me. "We'll be watching you, though. One false move, and I'll be coming for you Mr. Whisky Man. Nobody hurts our Mom and lives to talk about it."

Rebecca covers her face with her hands and exhales a gusty sigh. "Honestly, you two, you're being ridiculous. Thane probably thinks you're insane."

"Not at all," I tell her. "Your children are devoted to you, and I have no doubts they would do anything to protect you. I feel the same way about you, *mo chridhe*. A family should stick together."

She raises her head to look at me. "Is your family like that?"

"Oh, aye. The Buchanans are a close-knit clan, and we fight for each other whenever it's necessary. That includes not just my immediate family but also cousins, aunts, uncles, everyone. It's the same with the MacTaggarts and the Sterlings, even those barmy Murdochs."

"Errol Murdoch is a hoot. I love all the Scots I've met. But you are my favorite by far."

"And you are my favorite American, *mo chridhe*."

Courtney clasps her hands over her chest again. "Awww, you two are completely adorable. I can't wait to have Thane as my stepdad."

"Step-what?" Rebecca almost shouts. "Forget about tapping the brakes. You need to slam those suckers and yank the key out of the ignition."

Eric laughs. "Enough with the automotive metaphors, Mom. You're about as car savvy as a two-year-old."

"Gee, thanks a bunch, sweetie." Rebecca glances back and forth between her son and her daughter. "How did you two know where I was?"

Courtney laughs. "You'll never believe it. A hot British guy stopped by my house and told me my mom needs me. The same guy went to Eric's flat too. Turned out his name is Kendall Halfenaked, and he's the butler for a guy called Lord Sommerleigh."

Rebecca's brows shoot up. "Did you say Kendall's last name was Halfenaked?"

"Yeah. Isn't that crazy? Anyway, Kendall said we should go to the airport because a jet was waiting to take us to Inverness. He claimed you wanted us to come see you."

"I was kind of skeptical," Eric says. "But Kendall suggested we call Fiona Sterling for confirmation. Since we knew your boss was called Fiona Sterling, we figured the deal was legit."

Rebecca's mouth falls open. "Honestly, I thought I raised smarter children. How could you take a stranger's word?"

"Was it all true?"

She squirms. "Well, yes. But still…"

Courtney pats her mother's hand. "Relax, Mom, we aren't stupid. Eric's best friend escorted us all the way, and he didn't leave until we walked into the house. Now he's on his way to visit his sister who lives in Inverness."

"You're talking about that bodybuilder guy, Russell."

Courtney nods. "See? We aren't as gullible as you think."

"That's a relief."

"You know, if anyone's irresponsible here, it's you, Mom." Courtney bumps her shoulder into Rebecca. "I mean, you're shacking up with a Scottish guy you met a few weeks ago."

"It's not like that."

Eric grins. "What is it like, Mom?"

"I—Well, it's, um…"

Courtney and Eric both start laughing.

Rebecca makes a stern face that's sheer rubbish. "What happened to respecting your elders? I should disown you both."

Watching these three tease each other reminds me of my family. And that makes me want to share something about them with Rebecca and her children. "My family is a lot like yours, you know. We like to harass each other with sarcasm, but we always end up laughing. Only families that really love each other behave that way."

Eric slides forward, resting his arms on his knees while he focuses on me. "Tell us more about your family. We should know everything since we'll be your stepkids pretty soon."

Rebecca smacks his arm. "Eric! For pity's sake."

He holds his hands up. "I'm just saying what we all know is true."

"The laddie might have a point," I interject. "So, I should tell you about my clan. I have a brother, Ramsay, as well as a sister, Iona. My parents are Keith and Elsa."

Eric's brows lift. "Elsa doesn't sound very Scottish."

"My mother was born and raised in Sweden, but she came to Scotland on holiday and fell in love with a braw, strong Scotsman. That would be my father, Keith."

Our conversation goes on for a while, with all of us exchanging stories about our families. My clan is much larger overall since I have many cousins, aunts, and uncles. But Rebecca's family includes only her parents and her two children. She has no cousins. Eric and Courtney have their father, but he's an only child and his parents passed away years ago.

As the conversation winds down, I tell them, "I could entertain you three with many stories you wouldn't believe, but they're all true. The story of how Domhnall Sterling and Fiona MacTaggart got together is quite a tale. It ends with a strongman competition, a raucous round of Highland games, and a kidnapping."

Eric crosses his arms over his chest, eying me with feigned suspicion. "Oh, come on. You can't expect us to believe that."

I lean forward and chuckle with a wee bit of menace. "Believe it, laddie. Of course, the most incredible tale involves your mother, and it happened last week."

"She wasn't kidnapped. Somebody would have told us."

"No, she wasn't taken. But she did set off a land mine just outside this house to save me from a villain."

I wink at Rebecca. She understands my signal and goes on to share the story of how a former double agent tried to assault us. They love hearing how Odin helped out. So, I promise to introduce them to my llama security system in the morning. Right now, we're all jeeked and need a good night's sleep.

Maybe I will never have children of my own, but I have discovered something just as good. Better, even. It's all because of the woman who has captured my heart.

And it's time I introduced Rebecca and her children to my family.

Chapter Thirty-Four

Rebecca

If I'd had any lingering reservations about my relationship with Thane before my kids showed up on our doorstep, they evaporated the moment I hugged Eric and Courtney. They weren't at all offended that I hadn't talked about him. They loved Thane right away. So no, I don't need to worry about anything these days.

Well, except for the marketing campaign.

On Tuesday, Thane and I both need to get back to work. Jack and Autumn offer to show my kids around as their sightseeing guides. Courtney loves hanging out with their baby. For the rest of the week, she and Eric are escorted to various touristy places by various members of the Buchanan, MacTaggart, and Sterling clans. Eric develops a friendship with Cormac Buchanan, Thane's burly cousin, while Courtney enjoys hanging out with Emery, Erica, and Calli, the American wives of the three MacTaggart brothers.

The first ads have started running on TV, radio, and social media. Within a matter of days, we start seeing an uptick in visits to the distillery's website. I had hired a web designer to overhaul the site, paying extra to get it done quickly. The home page of the new site features Thane—the man, the legend, the hottest Scot in the Highlands—and, oh yeah, his whiskies too. He hadn't balked at all when I showed him the home page.

I didn't actually put that legend stuff on the website. That's strictly my private opinion.

Over the next two weeks, the campaign keeps gaining momentum at an ever-increasing pace. And during those two weeks, Thane surprises me with sweet little gifts that he leaves for me when I'm not around. All are Valentine's related things. We ride to work every day in his truck. One day, he texts me to say that he forgot his knit hat in the truck and could I go get it for him.

"As a favor to me, *gràidh*," he says. "It's in the glove box."

I jog out to the truck and open the glove compartment. No hat. But there is a heart-shaped box of chocolates from Sommerleigh Sweets.

The next day, I walk into my office in the morning to find a bouquet of roses sitting on my desk. The bouquet also includes smaller flowers interspersed with the roses. No one has ever given me a bouquet before. I almost cry just looking at the flowers because Thane is the most romantic man in the world.

On Friday, he hides a gift in our house. I don't see it until after dinner when I walk into the bedroom while Thane is washing the dishes. On the bedspread lies a pair of sexy red see-through panties and a matching bra, along with a bottle of edible massage oil.

We'll have lots of fun with that tonight.

But on Saturday, I finally get to meet Thane's family. Courtney and Eric are as excited about that as they used to be on Christmas morning. Courtney's boyfriend, Phillip, was treated to a trip on MacTaggart Air, as Thane and his friends call it. Evan MacTaggart offered his jet, though Rory and Lachlan also have a jet they share.

We arrive at Keith and Elsa's homestead on the far side of Loch Fairbairn and get a surprise.

All of Thane's relatives, including cousins and the rest, have gathered to welcome me and my family. I start to cry when Elsa Buchanan hugs me and says how happy she is that her son finally found the right woman.

Keith Buchanan also pulls me into a bear hug, then grasps my shoulders to hold me just far enough away to see all of me. "Rebecca, you are the bonniest lass I've ever seen. Thane couldn't help but fall for you. And it's about bloody time he settled down."

Thane aims a tolerant smile at his father. "Da, I've lived in the same house for a decade. That's the definition of settling down."

"No, that definition applies only to finding a woman."

I also get to meet Thane's brother and sister, but it's all a bit of a whirlwind. His cousins and other relatives rush to swarm us too, and the most imposing member of the family, his cousin Cormac, pulls me into a hug so boisterous that I feel like I might need a shot of pure oxygen afterward.

While Thane and his brother chat with Domhnall, his sister invites me to take a walk with her. We head out across the pasture behind the house. Once we're out of earshot of everyone else, Iona stops us under a small tree.

"Are you going to marry my brother?" she asks.

"You don't beat around the bush, do you?" I won't sidestep her question. That would be rude since I'm dating her brother. "The answer is that I don't know yet. We've known each other for four weeks, and it's been a wild time. I think we need to have some time without danger and excitement before we can figure out what we want to do next."

"I understand that. Did Thane tell you that I'm a journalist?"

"Yes."

"Then you must realize that I ask a lot of questions no matter who I'm talking to. But when it comes to my family, I can become an inquisitor."

If she's trying to scare me, it isn't working. I think she's testing me. "You can put me on the rack if you like, but nothing will change my mind about Thane. I love him."

"And he loves you, I'm dead certain of that." She smiles. "The inquisition is over now."

"That's all? I expected more grilling."

She shrugs. "I trust Thane's opinion of you. My questions were strictly pro forma. Welcome to the family, Rebecca."

I have officially made it into the Buchanan clan.

Thane and I spend the rest of the weekend with my kids and his immediate family. Eric, Phillip, and Courtney go to my apartment in Fort William to ride out the rest of the weekend. I won't need it anymore, and Thane insisted that the youngsters take it. The company will continue paying the rent for the time being. Yeah, it's good to be the boss's girlfriend.

On Monday, it's back to work. Now that we're in the final stretch leading up to the big dual event on Saturday, I expect to feel the pressure. But I don't. Instead, my excitement grows day by day as I add the final touches—with help from Fiona, Domhnall, and a bevy of MacTaggarts and Buchanans. That includes Thane, who seems almost as excited about the big event as I am.

Based on the amount of buzz lately about this extravaganza, I know our advertisements outpaced even my wildest dreams. We've gotten write-ups in newspapers throughout Scotland as well as the rest of the UK. Social media influencers have climbed onto the Thane train too. It helped that our friends and our friends' friends took word of mouth to unbelievable heights.

Saturday has arrived.

After a quick breakfast, we get dressed and head to the distillery. The guided tours will begin at ten o'clock this morning, and though we have the whole staff on hand to help out, Thane and I both need to be on the premises. He will be out there talking to visitors during the entire four hours of the open house. We've both dressed business casual for this portion of the two-part event since we'll be standing and walking for most of the time. But tonight, we'll bring out the formal ceilidh wear.

Thane looks damn hot in slacks, a long-sleeve button-down shirt, and leather boots made by his father. He left the top button of his shirt undone, but I reach out to undo the second one too.

"Show a little skin, sweetie. You are the brand, remember?"

"What has that got to do with my shirt?"

I grasp his shirt and drag him toward me. "Sex appeal, Thane. Your whisky is erotic, so let that inner sensuality peek out for everyone to see."

He palms my ass with both hands. "Anything for you, *mo chridhe.*"

"You're my heart too." I step back. "Now, let's get out there and dazzle the public."

We walk out of my office and march down the corridor to the main doors. T-minus four minutes until liftoff. The other staff members have taken their positions at their assigned stations. We're as ready as we'll ever be.

Thane peers through the glass doors. "Rebecca, have you seen this?"

I move up beside him and follow his gaze toward the parking lot. "Holy shit. Five tour buses? I thought we were only renting two, but I left Fiona in charge of that."

"She saw all your data from the adverts. I reckon she realized we would need more buses."

While we wait, two more buses arrive. I check my watch one more time. T-minus eight seconds. Then I press the button on my walkie-talkie— we all have them—and I give the order. "Open the doors, everyone. We're a go."

I move to the side as Thane swings the doors open. "Come inside, lasses and gents! Welcome to the Thane Buchanan Distillery."

His voice echoes off the trees and the mountainside.

People begin to pour out of the buses as well as the cars that overflow the parking lot. They're lined up along the roadside too. Fortunately, I had been highly optimistic about the turnout, so I got permission from the county and the village of Loch Fairbairn to let visitors park along the road.

Thane and I stand at either side of the doors, holding them open. Dougal and several of his cohorts from the malting floor rush out of the building. They make a beeline for the ropes we'd set up, just like what a nightclub might have, and they take control of the crowd. No one is freaking out. This isn't a nightclub, after all, and no one came here to see their favorite rock star. Of course, I think Thane is a rock star of the whisky world.

Soon, Thane and I are greeting people as the first round of visitors enter the building.

We lock the doors open, and the festivities begin.

During the full four hours of the event, Thane and I both rush here, there, and everywhere to ensure our visitors have the best experience possible. Several times, I take a moment to just listen to Thane talking to people. I follow along when he takes a group down to the river so he can explain the myths of the *Daoine Sith* and the mysteriously unnamed river as well as the connection with the castle of Dùndubhan.

I could listen to Thane's voice nonstop for the rest of my life and still not get enough. He does a fantastic job of infusing the myths with excitement and mystery, but he's at his best when he leads groups into the dunnage warehouse and introduces everyone to his three styles of whisky. His innate sensuality shows in every word he speaks and in the way he moves.

"We have three varieties of single-malt Scotch whisky," he purrs to the crowd. "Each has its own flavor and will tease your senses in a uniquely sensual manner. Thane Black Label was our first single malt, and it remains the benchmark for all our Scotch varieties. This one is a rich, smoky whisky. Would ye like to try it?"

A dozen heads nod vigorously.

Thane scans the crowd, then points to one person. "Come here, lass, please. I want you to taste Thane Black Label single-malt Scotch whisky."

She hustles up to him, her eyes alight with excitement as he picks up a bottle of Thane Black Label and opens it up. Then he grabs a shot glass and pours a measure of whisky into it. Thane holds the glass up to the woman's face. "Inhale deeply, lass."

The woman closes her eyes and sucks in a breath through her nostrils. Her lips curl upward a touch. She exhales gradually and opens her eyes. "The scent is incredible. May I taste the whisky now?"

Her British accent proves what my data had suggested. People from all over have come to experience what Thane has to offer. I've heard even more accents too, everything from American to French and Welsh, even Japanese. The couple from Japan had been on vacation here in Scotland when they saw advertisements for this event.

"What is your name, lass?" Thane asks as he holds the glass between himself and the woman.

"Darcy Woodburn."

"Well, Darcy, are you ready to sample my signature whisky?"

"Yes, please. I'm chuffed to taste it."

"Excellent." He offers her the glass, holding onto the rim until she has it firmly in her grasp. "Take a sip and be prepared to feel the warmth and succulent flavor suffuse your senses."

He has gotten so damn good at pleasing customers.

Darcy lifts the glass to her lips, closes her eyes, and takes a sip. For a moment, she simply slides her tongue over her lips, back and forth, again and again. Then her eyes fly open, and she lays a hand on her chest. "My goodness, this is bloody fantastic."

She drinks the remainder of the glass until it's gone.

And the rest of the crowd clamors to be the next to experience Thane Black Label.

Just wait till they taste the other two single malts. Thane will be the rock star of the whisky world for sure.

Chapter Thirty-Five

Thane

Never could I have imagined that a dozen people would rush to taste my black label whisky, or that they would be this excited to try the other two varieties. Rebecca is a marketing genius. I need to give her a massive pay rise and fuck her as soon as possible.

The love of my life corrals the crowd to keep everything in order as we move down the aisle to the area where my newest whiskies reside. I discuss them in chronological order.

I rest my arm on the cask while holding a bottle of the second variety I had ever created. "This, lasses and gents, is a newer single malt that offers a lavish array of scents and flavors. You will love this, I guarantee it."

Rebecca had suggested I employ "the art of the lull." By that she meant that I should occasionally pause to give everyone a chance to digest what I've said.

Now that I've given this lot a wee lull, I continue with my speech. "This unique single-malt Scotch is known as Sensual Secret, a Highland whisky with kick and sweetness and spicy seasonings. Who would like to step up and be the first to taste this one?"

Aye, the idea to name it Sensual Secret had come from me. But Rebecca agreed it was appropriate. She had never objected to that phrase, only to using the Gaelic version—for the whisky. She loves my mother tongue.

Later, I'll show her precisely what my tongue can do.

An older gentleman approaches me. "I'll go first."

"Excellent. What is your name?"

"Roger Standish."

"All right, Roger, it's time for your tasting." I open the bottle and pour a dram, then hold the glass up near his nose. "Now, my American friend, close your eyes and allow all the sensuous flavors to rush through you."

The gent takes the glass and lifts it to his lips, unleashing the flavors into his mouth. He licks his lips. Sniffs. Takes another sip.

And then it hits him.

His lips curve into a satisfied smile, and he opens his eyes in a leisurely manner. "Damn, that's good stuff. I've never tasted anything like it."

"Can you describe the flavors?"

"Sure." He takes another sip. "Kind of sweet, but not too sweet, and a little smoky too. Do I taste fruit?" He closes his eyes and drinks the last bit of whisky in his glass. Then he looks at me. "Could that be nutmeg and vanilla? I want to say honey too, but there's another flavor in there that's got me stumped."

"Wild Highland heather."

"Really? I never would've guessed." He hands the glass back to me. "I assumed this was just hype, the stuff about how incredible the whisky is. But it's the honest-to-goodness truth." Roger spins round and tells the crowd, "This whisky is amazing!"

Cheers erupt.

I raise a hand to silence everyone. "We have one more whisky for you to taste. Who will be my final test subject?"

A young woman thrusts her arm up, waving it frantically. "Me! Me! Please, let it be me!"

Cannae help chuckling. "Aye, lass, you may come forward to taste the third and final single malt."

She sprints up to me, pushing her way through the crowd. And she grins at me. "I'm ready."

"How old are you, lass?"

"Twenty-eight." She rummages about in her purse until she finds her driving license. "Here, you can check for yourself."

I do that and return her license to her. "It's fitting that a Scottish lass should finish out our tasting event. What is—"

"My name is Niamh Dunbar," she blurts out before I can finish my question.

"A lovely name for a lovely lass. Are you ready to try Dùndubhan Masterpiece, our newest entry in the Thane brand of single-malt Scotch whiskies?"

"Aye, I cannae wait to try it."

I grab the bottle and open it, then offer the lass a dram of the newly christened Dùndubhan Masterpiece. That name had been Rebecca's idea. Since the water for my distillery comes from the river that begins near the castle, she suggested we should honor Dùndubhan in this way. Rory and Emery, who own the castle, had loved the idea.

Niamh delicately sips from the glass while I hold it for her. She keeps her eyes open, unlike the others, and simply contemplates the flavors for a moment. "It tastes like…everything. Hints of sweet and spicy, but also maybe some type of peppers. So many flavors hit my senses at the same time, and I can't describe everything. It feels as if the whisky has gone straight into my veins and awakened all my nerves."

Rebecca had described it that way when she first sampled the newest iteration of my whisky.

I offer Niamh the glass, and she accepts it, finishing off her tasting with two more swallows. Then she shivers. "Oh, my, that makes me feel so…" She casts her gaze downward, biting her lip and glancing about as if she's embarrassed. "I wish my fiancé could have come with me today. I will definitely make him visit this place very soon."

Oh, aye, she has definitely experienced a similar effect as Rebecca had felt.

Now that I've demonstrated the power of my whiskies, Rebecca and I hand out more shot glasses and let the rest of the crowd discover my single malts. None say anything negative. In fact, they all give my whiskies five stars while quite a few declare that they would give my distillery ten, fifteen, or even twenty stars if it were possible.

Bod an Donais. Rebecca has done it. I knew the lass was clever and creative, but she has outmatched all my expectations which were admittedly high, though only because I knew she could do amazing things. Aye, she deserves a twenty-star rating for her work. No, it should be one hundred stars for her.

As our group exits the dunnage warehouse, two of our employees take over the task of guiding them through the next phase of the tour. Fiona and Domhnall will handle the next round of visitors to the warehouse. That leaves Rebecca and me with free time for the next half hour. And I know precisely how to spend that time.

I claim Rebecca's hand, leading the lass outside and down the river trail. She moves closer, and I fold my arm round her shoulders. "The weather is unusually warm today, as if someone cast a spell over Beann Dealgach and everything and everyone on the mountain. The temperature is perfect for an outdoor interlude."

She settles her hand over mine, where it lies on her shoulder. "I know what 'interlude' means to you. Aren't you worried someone might catch us getting it on?"

"Not at all." I tug her more firmly to my body. "I've made some…arrangements. You might call it my master plan."

"Well, you are the master distiller and the master maltster. How could I refuse you anything?"

I smile and kiss her temple. "You like saying the words master maltster, don't you?"

"Oh, yes. It's a fun tongue twister, and I love being able to say the words without screwing up."

We stop at the end of the trail. The river rushes past us, burbling and whooshing, both words Rebecca likes to use.

I wave toward the other bank. "We're going over there."

"You want to swim in the ice-cold river? The air temperature might have gone up considerably, but the water doesn't care about that."

"No, *gràidh*, you misunderstand. I told you I've made arrangements." I walk behind a tree, the same one we had shagged against five weeks ago, and bring out a rather large item. I'd hidden it behind the trunk. "This will get us there without dunking ourselves in the river."

She sets her hands on her hips and shakes her head, smiling with appreciation. "I should've guessed you'd have a well-defined plan. When did you hide that canoe back there?"

"Early this morning. You were in your office fretting over the final details of today's events."

She clucks her tongue. "You sneaky, horny man."

"May I take that as confirmation that you want me to fuck you on the other side of the river?"

"Yes, you may."

I set the canoe in the water and hold on to it while Rebecca climbs in. Then I get in as well. The spot I'd chosen for our rendezvous lies a wee ways down the river. Once we reach the location, I help the lass out of the canoe—by sweeping her up in my arms and stepping onto the shore. We now stand on the side opposite where the distillery and all our guests currently are. The bank is lower here, more of a step than a cliff, and the nearest tree leans over the water, providing sanctuary.

Rebecca glances around and smiles. "You really did map this all out ahead of time. You've got a blanket spread out for us and…" Her smile mutates into a smirk. "You brought the edible massage oil."

"Of course I did. Undress, Rebecca."

"You first, Thane."

I undo the buttons on my shirt one by one, taking my time because I love the way Rebecca follows my every movement. Then I roll my shoulders to push the shirt off and toss it away.

Rebecca removes her blouse over her head and sends it flying.

My turn again. I unhook my belt, flinging it away.

She frees the button on her trousers and drags the zipper down so slowly that my cock twitches. I'm getting harder by the second, but she isn't done with me yet. "I'll take my pants off if you do it first."

"Anything for you, love." I push my trousers down and roll my hips as I do that, strictly because I can tell the lass loves it. But I keep hold of my trousers to ensure I'm lowering them as gradually as possible. Rebecca's chest is rising and falling more heavily. That means I've accomplished my goal. So, I kick my trousers away. "Your turn, *gràidh*."

"You're already naked. That's not fair. I should get the same amount of striptease that you'll get from me."

"Dinnae worry. I'll make it up to you." I know she was teasing me. The lass loves to do that because she knows I enjoy it. "I need you naked, Rebecca. Hurry up."

She reaches behind her to unhook her bra and toss it away.

I cannae wait any longer. My cock feels about to burst, and I can barely breathe from the intensity of my need for her. I might pass out from lack of oxygen if I don't take her right now. The lass has just removed her knickers, so at least I won't need to wait any longer. I pick her up and lie her down on the soft blanket.

She links her hands above her head, shimmying her hips.

I lie down beside her, on my side, and trail my fingertips up and down her body, making her shiver. "Ah, Rebecca, ye make me so *dàrail*. My *luirgean* is under your spell, ready to give you all the pleasure you deserve. My *slat* is hard as granite. Your cream tastes better than any *mac-na-bracha*, and even my best whisky can't compete."

She bites down on her bottom lip while I go on skimming my hand along her skin. My *slat* rests on her hip, and a bead of moisture hovers there.

When she reaches out to touch it, I cuff her wrists with my other hand. "Not yet, *mo chridhe*." I shift position, kneeling above her while still restraining her wrists. "Ahmno fucking ye until you're so wet and sensitized that ye cannae stand it."

"Please do that to me. I want it, I want you, so much that I never want the pleasure to end."

Still on all fours, I bend my arms just enough that the crown of my *slat* brushes her skin. The sensation feels so bloody good that I suck in a sharp breath. I need all my willpower to keep brushing my cock over her skin, everywhere from her tits to her belly and lower still, to her hips and inner thighs. But when I graze her mound, she jerks and cries out.

Time to increase her need. Bloody hell, I'll be increasing mine too, and I dinnae know if I can take it.

I push her legs apart with my knee. Now, I need to release her wrists so I can crawl backward until my face hovers above her mound. When I gently separate her folds, she moans deeply. For a moment, I gaze at her swollen, slick flesh and suck in a deep breath of her scent. The musky, sweet aroma makes my cock throb. Since I know I won't last much longer, I hoist her knees onto my shoulders and shove my face into her folds, licking and lapping and devouring the lass like I'll die without the taste of her on my tongue.

She plunges her fingers into my hair. "Yes, Thane, oh God, yes. Suck my clit, please."

I ignore her plea and lick everywhere around her hard nub without touching it. That makes Rebecca thrash her head. The silky smoothness of her cream drives me mad, and I finally lose my last shred of control. I scrape my tongue up and down her cleft swiftly until she cries out, then I thrust a finger inside her sheath and latch on to her clit at last, devouring it like this is my last meal before I die.

Her shouts echo off the trees.

I fuck her with my finger, and when her body freezes, I plunge two more fingers inside her.

Her body folds in on itself as her mouth falls open but no sound emerges. She clenches her fingers in the blanket. And at last, while her sheath milks my fingers, she comes. Her wild cries echo around us, and I keep fucking her until she goes limp.

I'm breathing hard as I rise to my knees and gaze down at her. "Need to fuck ye, *gràidh*, right now."

Chapter Thirty-Six

Rebecca

The second Thane voiced his need, my own lust ramped up to a level I've never experienced before. Only Thane can do this to me, because only he understands me so thoroughly, inside and out. "Do it, Thane. I need to feel you inside me. Take me as hard as you need to."

He shoves his arms under my body and lifts me into a sitting position. My pulse is racing so fast, and as he pulls me up onto his lap, I fling my arms around his neck. He hugs me to his body, lavishing wet kisses over my throat, while my head falls back and I moan deeply. God, I need him to take me right now. In this position, seated on his lap with my legs wrapped around him, I can't do anything but writhe and moan.

Thane is squatting on the ground, but his dick keeps rubbing against my cleft. The sensation is maddening and wonderful, and I lock my ankles behind his ass, unable to speak a coherent syllable, desperate for him to start moving. He hisses in a breath and begins to thrust. The position we're in proves too awkward, though, despite Thane's attempts to thrust up into me. We're both so turned on that we can't think straight. I cling to him as he hoists himself off the ground, then bends his knees, using them as leverage to thrust upward, pushing his length inside my body so forcefully that I bounce on his cock.

I love what he's doing, but this is taking too damn long. "The riverbank. Take me there. We can, unh, do it in the water."

Thane freezes and stares at me while struggling to regain his breath. "What? The river? It's bloody cold."

"I'm so hot, I'm on fire. Take me there, please."

He stalks over to the bank, turns around, and jumps into the river feet first.

The shock of the cold water stuns me briefly, but the river isn't as freezing cold as I'd expected. I could swim in this water without risking hypothermia. Thane backs me up to the bank, grasps my hips, and starts thrusting. I let my head fall back, reveling in the delicious friction of his firm dick gliding in and out, the feel of the cool, damp earth behind me, and the scraping of my nipples on his chest.

"*Tha mi a'bualadh do craigeann, neach-gaoil*," he growls. "*Tha thu bòidheach*."

No clue what he said, but the rough growl of his voice does me in. My head snaps forward while all my limbs clutch him, and my nails dig into his scalp. A tiny whimper bursts out of me just as the orgasm strikes. My inner muscles pulsate around his cock. I can't speak, can't move, can't even breathe. Just as my ears begin to ring, a breath explodes out of me. I keep holding on to him while he pummels me into the riverbank again and again, snarling like a beast, gritting his teeth, until I finally feel him blow apart inside me.

For several seconds, neither of us moves. Our gasping breaths mingle with the sounds of nature—the rushing river, the whispering of the breeze, the songs of birds. At last, Thane heaves himself up and onto the bank, still clutching me to his body. I haven't let go of him yet either.

He tenderly lays me down on the picnic blanket, then settles onto his back beside me. "*Bod an Donais.* Anyone who says middle-aged adults lose their sex drive doesn't have a fucking clue."

"Definitely." I roll onto my side to look at him. "Being with you is not only the best sex ever, but it's also the most fun I've ever had with any man."

"You inspire me, *m'eudail*."

"What did you just call me?"

"My dear. It's essentially the same sentiment as *gràidh*." He pushes his fingers into my damp hair. "No phrase on earth could accurately describe how I feel about you, *gràidheag*. That means 'darling.' By the way, what I said when we were shagging was that I'm fucking you and you are beautiful."

"I would love to learn Gaelic."

"Later." He pushes up onto his elbows. "We still have work to do before the open house is done."

"And then there's the ball. I can't wait to dance with you tonight."

"Likewise, *mo chridhe*." He sits up all the way and scans the vicinity. "Where did I leave my *aodach*?"

"Is this the start of my primer on Scottish Gaelic? I have no idea what you're asking."

"*Aodach* means clothing. Cannae recall where I left mine."

I sit up and wave toward an area behind him. "It's kind of strewn all over that vicinity."

Now that we've satisfied each other's needs, all that's left to do is get dressed and go back to work. By the end of the open house event, we know we've accomplished something amazing today. We don't have all the numbers yet, but it's clear we've sold at least four times more whisky today than the distillery would sell in an average month. Thane hopes to earn enough profits that he can buy out his investors, but I point out that those people are our friends. Why not let them stay a part of the business? They aren't likely to try a hostile takeover.

Thane agrees. But he insists we need to thank each and every investor in person, even if that means we'll have to travel to England and the US to do that.

I will go anywhere in the world as long as Thane is by my side.

Only after our employees have left do we walk out of the building. Naturally, everyone at the distillery has been invited to the big bash at Dùndubhan.

How do Thane and I prepare for tonight? We go home and take a nap. Yeah, we might have great stamina and vigor, but we're still not teenagers. I love sleeping with Thane, anytime, anywhere. We arrive at Dùndubhan half an hour before the ball is set to begin, just so I can make sure everything is going according to plan. Yes, I'm slightly anxious about organizing my first ball, but Thane stays with me while I double check the preparations. Holding his hand always soothes me.

Fifteen minutes before liftoff, I shoo Thane away. "Go, get dressed. You can't wear jeans and a T-shirt to a formal ball. Go, please, shoo."

He grins. "I love it when you're bossy and frantic at the same time. It's endearing."

"Do I have to kick you in the shin? Go, Thane."

Finally, he trots off to get ready. I already know pretty much what he's wearing tonight—his formal kilt ensemble—but he hasn't seen my outfit. Once I'm dressed, I hustle up the spiral staircase in the vestibule, holding my gown up a touch so I won't trip over it. I'm carrying my spiffy heels, otherwise I'd trip and break my ankle, possibly my neck too. I breeze past the great hall, then burst into the long gallery, aka the ballroom for tonight.

As I slip my shoes on, I survey the room—and for a moment, I can't move. Seeing the decorations in the daytime hadn't given me the full picture. Here, after dark in a medieval castle, I realize just how incredible this ball will be. Gauzy fabric streamers of red and pale pink festoon the periphery, with heart-shaped white clips holding them in place at strategic positions. The tables each feature red tablecloths, pink napkins, and white plates with a simple pink and yellow rose pattern. And of course, red, pink, and white balloons hover near the ceiling. As the final touch, a sparkly crystalline ball hangs from the center of the ballroom.

Soft music plays right now, but once this event really gets going, we'll crank up the volume.

"Feasgar math, mo chridhe."

I spin around—and my heart skips a beat. "Wow, Thane, you look even more incredible than I expected. Did you add more stuff to your outfit? I thought I'd seen the whole thing."

"How could I not save the best for tonight?" He eyes me up and down. "You are a vision of classical beauty and grace, Rebecca."

I can't focus on what he said. All my attention remains glued to his body and the formal kilt outfit he's wearing. Thane had told me that most Scotsmen don't wear the old-fashioned kind of kilt anymore, known as a great kilt, though he loves the tradition of wrapping a long piece of Buchanan plaid around himself and sometimes does that during family events. Tonight, he's wearing a knee-length kilt with a length of plaid slung over his shoulder, held in place with a fancy silver brooch. A black leather belt holds the kilt in position.

Thane went all in for this ball. Not content to simply wear a kilt, he also has a formal black jacket, waist length, with silver buttons and a crisp white shirt underneath as well as a black bow tie. Since he's a traditionalist in many ways, Thane also chose to wear a sporran, which looks like a small, furry pouch. It hangs over his groin, held up by a silver chain. He even has a pair of silver brooches holding the cuffs of his shirt together.

But damn, the sexiest part of all is the dagger in a leather scabbard that hangs from his hip. I've grown to love the *sgian dubh*, especially when Thane wears it. And I love that he wore fancy leather boots that his father made specially for him. His mother made the tartan socks he wears. They're in the Buchanan clan tartan, of course. His dirty blond hair matches the lighter colors in his kilt as well.

Thane strides up to me, and the sparkling ball above our heads makes his eyes shimmer with blue fire. "Rebecca, you are the queen of the ball and the owner of my heart and soul. No other woman could match you."

My throat tightens. How could I not get choked up when he tells me such sweet things? I will love him for the rest of my life and whatever comes after that.

Chapter Thirty-Seven

Thane

I have never seen anything as beautiful as Rebecca Taylor in a Valentine's Day gown. Aye, the dress is lovely. But she turns a posh frock into a masterpiece simply by wearing it. I am one hundred percent biased in this matter, but that doesn't change the facts. She is a vision, and no other woman could match her beauty.

Rebecca wears a strapless red gown fashioned from a silky material that might be genuine silk. The American Wives Club had helped the lass find the perfect dress, and I have no doubts they insisted she buy an expensive outfit for tonight. The fabric hugs her torso and hips, then gradually fans out into a flowing skirt that swishes around her calves.

Mhac na galla. I used a woman's word—"swish."

As I move even closer to Rebecca, I notice her sparkling red earrings and red painted fingernails. But none of that registers in my mind as more than a passing interest. It's the woman herself who captivates me. The way her long, coppery brown hair falls over her bare shoulders makes me want to push her against the wall and shag her in this empty ballroom. The guests haven't come upstairs yet, but I'd love for Rebecca to come here in the long gallery. Her ruby red lipstick makes my *slat* wake up.

Before I can say another word to the lass, the guests begin to pour into the long gallery, which for tonight has become a ballroom.

I claim Rebecca's hand, leading her to the periphery of the room. The guests, our mates and family, begin to gather in small groups. A lucky group of strangers had won a contest and now joins us for the ball. The contest had been Rebecca's idea, and she announced it on every advertising channel she could find. How better to introduce more people to the Thane Buchanan Distillery? Rebecca is a marketing genius.

As the volume of the music intensifies, couples begin to take the floor.

I draw Rebecca out into the center of the room, slide an arm round her waist, and clasp her hand in the usual ballroom posture, though I dinnae claim to be an expert on that. We gaze into each other's eyes while we glide across the floor. Other people greet us along the way, but we're too engrossed in each other to care about making small talk. The depths of her honey brown eyes draw me in and transfix me. For several minutes, or maybe it's hours, I guide Rebecca round and round the floor until I can tell she needs a wee rest.

We sit down on one of the plush velvet benches set up beneath the windows of the long gallery. I lay an arm across her shoulders. "How do you feel? It's been a whirlwind for the past five weeks, but now the excitement will wind down."

"I thought I might experience a bit of a letdown after everything that's happened, but I don't." She rests her head on my shoulder. "I've loved every minute of my life since the day I met you."

"The same for me." I kiss the top of her head. "You are *luaidh mo chèile*, Rebecca. That means you are the love of my life."

"Do you believe in soul mates?"

"If you'd asked me five weeks ago, I would have said categorically no. But now, I do believe you and I were meant to find each other."

"So do I." She lifts her head to aim those beautiful eyes at me. "Thank you for teaching me how to enjoy life again. I was bummed out and stressed out, but those feelings vanished when I met you."

My brother Ramsay saunters up to us. "Mind if I borrow your lass? I should get to know my future sister-in-law, and there's no better way to do that than on the dance floor."

"Ask Rebecca, not me."

The lass holds out her hand to Ramsay. "I would love to dance with another big, sexy, handsome Buchanan man."

Ramsay winks at me. "Better watch out, Thane. I might steal your lass."

"You have a better chance of convincing Ma to wear a clown suit." I tell Rebecca, "She hates clowns and circuses."

"Me too."

I watch as Ramsay leads Rebecca out onto the dance floor, and they begin to chat about who knows what. My brother makes her smile, probably by recounting a humorous tale about our family. I love seeing her this way, dancing like a fairy-tale queen, enchanting every man she meets. But I know she will leave tonight with me.

Aye, Rebecca Taylor is magnificent.

I notice my sister hovering at the periphery of the dance floor, alone, with her arms wrapped round herself. That won't do. Iona should be having a good time like the rest of us. Even Eric and Courtney Taylor are enjoying the evening. Evan MacTaggart holds out his hand to Iona, inviting her to dance with him, but she hunches her shoulders and shakes her head.

Evan walks away.

No, this won't do at all. I march around the edges of the dance floor until I reach my sister. "Iona, why aren't you dancing? You love a good ceilidh."

Her expression cinches up tight. "Dinnae feel like dancing, Thane. I'm the only one here who doesn't have a significant other."

"Eric Taylor is single too."

"Aye, but he's almost twenty years younger than I am."

I lean against the wall beside her. "What's really bothering you about this ceilidh?"

She turns her head toward me and sighs. "It's a ball, Thane, not a ceilidh."

"Well, it all sounds like the same thing to me." I slant my head down to meet her gaze head on. "You haven't answered my question. What's really fashing you?"

"I'm old, that's what fashes me. I'm well into my forties, and no man wants to date me because I have two children. The fact that they're adopted only turns men off even more." She rubs her neck as she glances out at the dance floor. "Besides, I'm a nosy journalist. Blokes like that even less. I might as well hang a shingle on my front door that says 'old maid lives here, run away now.' "

"Ramsay isn't married anymore. Dinnae see him standing in a corner having a self-pity party." No, I won't leave her here like this. So, I grab her hand and drag her away from the wall. "Come with me, Iona."

I keep hold of her hand as I start walking.

She refuses to move. "Leave me alone, Thane."

"Cannae do that." I sweep her up and throw the lass over my shoulder. "If you won't cooperate, I'll make the decision for you."

I march across the floor, forcing other people to scatter to get out of the way, and halt in front of one man. And I set my sister on her feet. "Iona needs a dance partner. Eric, would you care to escort my sister round the floor?"

He flicks his gaze between me and Iona, then holds out his hand to her. "Come on, let's have some fun. I bet you're a great dancer. I noticed you're very graceful when you're walking around."

Eric must have been watching my sister for a while. Oh, aye, I've made a good match with these two. I don't expect them to get married, but at least they'll have a good time tonight.

Since Rebecca is still making the rounds among the men, I take a spin round the floor with every member of the American Wives Club. Not all at once, obviously. They are all sweet lasses, and I enjoy chatting with them. The last member of the club who takes a spin with me is Rory MacTaggart's wife, Emery. And she has a few things to say.

"I'm so glad you and Rebecca hit it off," she says. "You're made for each other, and everyone can see that. We weren't sure our meddling would lead to a wedding, but I foresee one in the near future."

"Aye, so do I. But you lot didn't meddle. I kept waiting for that to start, but it never did."

"Oh, sure it did." She smiles, and the expression has a bit of mischief in it. "After all, we hired Rebecca to work at your distillery. That's why Fiona flew all the way to America to interview her. Her report proved there was a high probability you two would hit it off. Of course, we would've hired her even without your romantic chemistry. She had the marketing creds the distillery needed."

Though I continue dancing with Emery, my feet move by rote. I'm too stunned to think about anything except what she just told me.

Emery grins. "That's the look I expected to see when I dropped that bomb. The club also organized bringing Eric and Courtney here."

"That's far less of a shock than what you said about Rebecca."

"Are you okay with these revelations? We already told Rebecca a little while ago, and she was surprised but appreciative."

How do I feel about their meddling? Considering how much my outlook on romance has changed lately, I experience a shocking revelation of my own. "No, I don't mind at all what you lasses did."

Emery kisses my cheek. "I'm so glad to hear that. Happy Valentine's Day, Thane. I need to go tend to my hubby. He gets lonely without me."

The lass walks away.

I notice Eric and Iona are now enjoying a piece at the buffet, and they're laughing. Will a romance develop? Dinnae know. But at least my sister is enjoying herself now.

And I have a wee surprise for Rebecca.

I wave at Errol. When he sees me, he nods and jogs toward the console that holds all the music-related equipment. He turns dials or whatever, and the music stops. "Listen up, laddies and lasses! We have a special request to fulfill, and we need everyone to make room in the center of the dance floor."

Everyone obeys without hesitation, even the contest winners.

A new song begins, and I approach Rebecca, holding out my hand. "Dance with me, *mo chridhe*, please."

She takes my hand as we walk into the center of the floor.

Errol turns more dials. A song begins to play—"Hungry Like the Wolf."

Rebecca laughs. "Are we dancing to this?"

"Of course." I pull her closer and rest a hand on her hip to encourage her to move with the beat of the music. Once she's in the groove, we move round the floor together, our toes tapping. When I lift her hand above our heads, she spins round for me. We are no professional dancers, but no one gives a toss about that. As the song reaches its climax, I dip her backward and then pick her up with one hand lifting her erse and the other holding up her shoulders. I whirl round twice, then set the lass on her feet.

But I'm not done yet. I fall to one knee, pulling a velvet box out of my pocket. "Rebecca Jeannette Taylor, I love you with all my heart and soul. Until you came into my life, I'd given up on ever finding the right woman for me. But with a wee bit of help from the American Wives Club, that woman walked into my distillery five weeks ago and changed my world forever."

Her lips quiver slightly, and her eyes shimmer with gathering tears.

I open up the box and show her the glittering diamond ring. "Will you marry me, Rebecca?"

She covers her mouth, clearly overcome with emotion.

"Say yes, Mom!" Courtney shouts.

"Yeah, Mom, go for it!" Eric declares.

"How can I say no to that?" Rebecca plants a firm kiss on my lips. "Yes, Thane, of course I'll marry you."

The crowd erupts in cheers and whistles.

Valentine's Day used to be my least favorite holiday. But now, I can't wait for it to come again next year.

We make the rounds in the ballroom, accepting congratulations from everyone including the contest winners. The ball goes on for a while longer, but Rebecca and I are jeeked and ready for bed. Not to shag. No, we need sleep. After all, we have a wedding to plan now.

As we walk down the spiral staircase, we catch Iona and Eric standing in the vestibule. Her cheeks are pink, and he keeps touching her hand. Then the two of them walk out the door to the outside. They didn't seem to notice us.

Rebecca and I halt in the vestibule.

She whispers, "Do you think they're going to…"

"Have a poke? Dinnae know. I want Iona to have a good time tonight, that's all. Let's not engage in speculation."

"You're right. But I'd love to see her getting out there and dating again."

"So would I. Now, *mo chridhe*, let's go home."

Love the

Hot Scots

series?

Visit
AnnaDurand.com

to subscribe to her newsletter
for updates on forthcoming books in the series
&
to receive exclusive content!

Anna Durand is a bestselling, multi-award-winning author of contemporary and paranormal romance. Her books have earned bestseller status on every major retailer and wonderful reviews from readers around the world. But that's the boring spiel. Here are the really cool things you want to know about Anna!

Born on Lackland Air Force Base in Texas, Anna grew up moving here, there, and everywhere thanks to her dad's job as an instructor pilot. She's lived in Texas (twice), Mississippi, California (twice), Michigan (twice), and Alaska—and now Ohio.

As for her writing, Anna has always made up stories in her head, but she didn't write them down until her teen years. Those first awful books went into the trash can a few years later, though she learned a lot from those stories. Eventually, she would pen her first romance novel, the paranormal romance *Willpower*, and she's never looked back since.

Want even more details about Anna? Get access to her extended bio when you subscribe to her newsletter and download the free bonus ebook, *Hot Scots Confidential*. You'll also get hot deleted scenes, character interviews, fun facts, and more! Plus you'll receive audio bonus content.

Visit AnnaDurand.com to sign up.

www.ingramcontent.com/pod-product-compliance
Lightning Source LLC
Chambersburg PA
CBHW061252210726
48293CB00003B/939